Praise for

The Other Shulman

"Pleasantly diverting . . . [Zweibel has] a deft humorous touch."
—*The New York Times*

"You have to love Shulman."   —New Jersey *Star-Ledger*

"Mixes wise-guy humor with a little Jewish magic realism."
—*The Miami Herald*

"Comic, haimish and heartfelt."
—*The Jewish Journal of Greater Los Angeles*

"A hilarious and sweet look at middle age and one man's choice to fight against mediocrity and complacency . . . Shulman is a shlubby and likable everyman, and along with the marathon bystanders in each of the boroughs, we cheer for him to make it to the finish line in one proverbial piece. . . . Zweibel's novel is funny and charming."
—*Bookreporter.com*

"Alan Zweibel is a very funny guy. And he has written a very funny book. If this does not make you want to buy it immediately, perhaps you should sit down and take a long, hard look at what your problem really is."
—Merrill Markoe, author of *It's My F---ing Birthday* and *What the Dogs Have Taught Me*

The Other Shulman

VILLARD New York

The Other Shulman

A NOVEL

Alan Zweibel

September 2005

To Jonathan -

This book is really good!

Your pal,

2006 Villard Books Trade Paperback Edition

Copyright © 2005 by Alan Zweibel
Map copyright © 2005 by David Lindroth

Published in the United States by Villard Books, an imprint of The Random House Publishing Group, a division of Random House, Inc., New York.

VILLARD and "V" CIRCLED Design are registered trademarks of Random House, Inc.

Originally published in hardcover in the United States by Villard Books, an imprint of The Random House Publishing Group, a division of Random House, Inc., in 2005.

Grateful acknowledgment is made to the following for permission to reprint previously published material:

Paul Simon Music: Excerpt from "The Boxer" by Paul Simon, copyright © 1968 by Paul Simon. Reprinted by permission of Paul Simon Music.

Williamson Music: Excerpts from "The Lonely Goatherd" by Richard Rodgers and Oscar Hammerstein II, copyright © 1959 by Richard Rodgers and Oscar Hammerstein II. Copyright renewed. Williamson Music owner of publication and allied rights throughout the world. International copyright secured. All rights reserved. Reprinted by permission of Williamson Music.

ISBN 0-8129-7283-X

Printed in the United States of America

www.villard.com

2 4 6 8 9 7 5 3

Book design by Dana Leigh Blanchette

For Robin ... forever

The Other Shulman

Mile 1

By the time Shulman reached the starting line, the race was already seven minutes old. Not that it mattered. All the runners wore a microchip laced onto their shoes that wasn't activated until they stepped on the red mat. So, theoretically, it was possible for someone to not finish first but still win if he covered the distance in less time than everyone else. But that didn't matter either. Shulman's decision to line up toward the back of the 32,000 participants in the New York City Marathon was less strategic than it was logical. Similar to the reason why cowboys, if given the choice, preferred to be behind the horses during a stampede. It just seemed less likely that he'd fall, be trampled by 64,000 muscular legs, and have his body pounded into domino-size cubes on the roadway's steel grating if he hung back a little.

"Look where we are!" Maria shouted as they took their first running steps onto the Verrazano Bridge, which, as far as most New Yorkers knew, was named after the Italian explorer best known for having this bridge named after him.

"Can you believe it?" she added.

In fact, he couldn't. Despite all the training and anticipation, there was no way he had truly ever envisioned himself doing something like this. But here he was. Shulman. A middle-aged stationery-store owner who until a few months ago used gym shorts only as pajama bottoms was now running across a toll bridge, with a number pinned to his shirt, being swept along by the adrenaline flow of the moving throng around him.

"Remember what Coach Jeffrey said!" Maria shouted again.

Boy, is she beautiful, he said to himself. Even in this setting. Among the thousands of runners from hundreds of countries participating in this event, she still stood out.

"Remember? Don't start too quickly!"

Boy, is she loud, he said to himself. Even in this setting. Among the thousands of runners from hundreds of countries also calling out to friends, hers was the voice that rang out above the rest.

But she was right. Coach Jeffrey always stressed the importance of having respect for the distance they were about to run. Twenty-six miles. Actually, 26.2 miles. So it was advisable to stick to the prescribed pace and resist all urges to speed things up. The key was to conserve for the long haul. All of which suited Shulman just fine. He was in no rush. His goal was simple. All he wanted to do was finish. Try to soak up all that he could along the way. And then, when the race was over, figure out how to completely change his life and decide what he was going to do for the next thirty or forty years. That's all. Simple.

Last Memorial Day. At a family barbecue. Shulman was about to make his announcement.

Not that his plan would be of particular interest to anyone at *this* picnic table. Even at this advanced age, his older siblings did not take him seriously. At best, he was tolerated. Humored. They were doctors. Medical and PhDs. They called each other "Doc." Shulman owned a stationery store. They hardly called him at all.

Still, it was imperative that he have his say. The deadline was tomorrow and Shulman knew from experience that only when an idea was actually translated into spoken words would it begin to exist in the world outside his head. That's how it would be liberated. Given the freedom to live or die on its own accord in lieu of banishment to that sad limbo where stillborn ideas reside.

So it was in this setting, at this holiday outing, that Shulman, who had recently billowed out to a record-high 248 pounds, revealed that he was thinking of running a marathon. That it would be for charity. And that he'd have people sponsor him.

"The money will benefit AIDS research, with a portion of it going toward a training program that starts next Sunday, so I'll be prepared for the big race in November," he explained.

Reaction was swift and hailed from all schools ranging from the psychiatric ("You're out of your fucking mind"), to the religious ("God, you're out of your fucking mind"), to the scientific ("A mass that large, unless dropped from a tower 26.2 miles high or strapped to the top of one of those mercury boosters they send up at Canaveral, could never generate enough energy on its own to cover a distance like that"). However, the most dramatic take on Shulman's declaration was turned in by his impossibly tan parents, who made the trip from Boca to his New Jersey doorstep in what had to be record time.

"Mom, Dad, what are you doing here?"

"What are we doing here? *You* have children. If one of them was dying, wouldn't you get on a plane?"

"Dying? Who's dying?"

"You are."

"I'm dying?"

"Stop with the jokes. You have AIDS. Now help your father with the bags."

An hour later. With his wife, Paula, who knew better than to interfere, at his side, this discussion was still raging over coffee.

"So you were lying."

"No, Mom, I wasn't lying. I said it was a charity run to raise money for AIDS."

"No you didn't."

"You weren't even there when I told everyone."

"What does that have to do with anything?"

"Look, why would I say I have a terrible disease if I didn't?"

"And why would your father and I drop everything and fly our asses up to Jersey unless you said that you did? We have very busy lives. I'm learning Spanish so I can understand the gardener, and your father's going to take up golf after he gets his new hip. This cake is delicious. Henry, try the cake."

"I'm too aggravated to eat."

"Henry, the beauty just said he's not dying."

"Okay, maybe a small piece."

"Why *are* you doing this?" Paula asked several hours later.

It was evening. Shulman and Paula were in bed. She was leafing through catalogues while Shulman was pretending not to mind that she was leafing through catalogues instead of noticing that he was very interested in having sexual relations with her. Her question was a fair one, however, because Shulman hated running. Always did. To him, the act of alternately placing one foot in front of the other as quickly as possible was never regarded as anything more than a slower form of transportation employed solely as a means to get to a faster form of transportation. You run to catch a bus. You run to make a plane. Mission accomplished, you take a seat. No more running.

But as much as he hated running, Shulman had even more disdain for runners because it seemed that all runners ever talked about (with the possible exception of mute runners) was running. How today's run felt. How today's run felt compared with yesterday's run. How they felt a cramp around the seventh mile of their run but it started to loosen up around the fortieth mile of their run. In addition to their smug implications that because they wore shorts and owned watches that beeped intermittently they were now members of an elite segment of middle-class white people whose metabolism had magically turned Kenyan. That their hearts now beat only once or twice a year, that pasta now just slid through their bodies and out their asses looking exactly the way it did when it went in, and that someday they were all going to get together and have a huge electrolyte festival that the rest of us wouldn't be attending because we'd all be dead because we weren't runners.

These were rather strong feelings, so even Shulman was surprised how his curiosity was mysteriously aroused when he saw that poster in Ben & Jerry's (of all places) claiming that in six months a person could be trained to complete a marathon.

"Well, it's for a very good cause," he offered up to Paula.

Her stare let him know he should keep talking. That there had to be more. Primarily because none of his previous charitable gestures had involved jogging around five metropolitan boroughs. "There's also a part of me that's intrigued by the challenge," he continued.

"The challenge?"

"Yes," he said, "the challenge."

"I can't remember you ever being intrigued by a challenge before."

"Are you kidding? I've always been intrigued by a good challenge. I've just never done anything about it before."

"So that's the reason? The challenge?"

"That, plus I read somewhere that the greatest gift a man can give his family is to get in shape. You know, try to make the odds work in my favor so I won't end up being one of those old men who watch their grandchildren's Little League games hooked up to a generator in foul territory. So far, those are my reasons. Then again, maybe if you and I had some sexual intercourse about now, it could provide further clarity to this whole thing."

"But aren't you in training?" she asked while simultaneously picking up the phone and dialing an 800 number. "I thought that athletes in training were supposed to abstain because it sapped their strength."

"No-o-o-o-o," Shulman responded with what he hoped were enough *o*'s to imply that she shouldn't be silly. "That's just an old wives' tale that's been scientifically dispelled. In fact, all the current medical literature indicates that the *more* conjugal activity a man has prior to an athletic event, especially one that requires incredible endurance for, oh, let's say a race through the streets of an East Coast city that never sleeps, the more it will actually enhance his performance. You see, sweetie, when seminal fluid accumulates, it tends to weigh a guy down. So it stands to reason—"

"Yes," Paula said into the phone. "I'm interested in these hassocks you have on page ninety-seven of your catalogue."

Her smile helped. Somewhat. Though slight and with a meaning vague enough to inspire lively debate, Shulman opted for an interpretation that said, *Hey, I love you and isn't it a kick that we can still make these little connections after all we've been through and, if not for the uncanny timing of this salesperson, I'd be all over your still remarkably attractive bones at this very moment.* And while this take may indeed have borne little or no resemblance to her actual message, it was yet another shining example of the spin that had helped Shulman weather the pounding the human spirit took during its trek from one end of life to the other. It was a useful piece of artillery, serving as both weapon and shield in a line of defense that had helped him survive four childhoods (his own and those of his three children), the uneven terrain of a twenty-six-year marriage, and the slow deterioration of a business that he'd built from scratch.

His this-glass-is-not-only-full-it's-full-of-champagne perspective came into existence early on when attempting to satisfy parents with stratospheric expectations. Was refined along the way to bridge any gaps between where he actually was and where he felt he should be at that point. And was honed to a near art form when it came to using his overinvolvement in his kids' lives as noble justification for the underachievement of his own. But now, as their youngest child was college-bound and would soon have an address that was different from theirs, Shulman was left with few distractions. And even fewer places to hide. No high school baseball games to fill those weekday-afternoon voids. No all-nighters paraphrasing CliffsNotes in an attempt to camouflage the fact that someone hadn't read *Silas Marner*. Conversely, there was no longer the need on the part of his children to heed the wisdom of a man desperate to get things right his second time around.

And this is where Shulman was stuck. Unprepared for the sudden absence of all of the activity that had made life so easy to deflect. Or to deny. With no choice but to return to himself and take a long look at the sum of all that had happened. Examine the residue of the choices made. Then devise his own redefinition now that "dad" would no longer be the verb he'd made it into.

Uncomfortable as he was with the expanding emptiness around him, Shulman, true to form, had recently started doing some serious expanding of his own. To his great dismay, the weight was back. Once again. The downbeat of a cycle that had begun at the conclusion of Shulman's tenure as a skinny kid and continued to this very day, when people who saw old photos were prone to remark, "My God, it's hard to believe you were such a skinny kid."

The numbers were unofficial, but according to his calculations, Shulman had been losing and gaining the same thirty pounds since his bar mitzvah. And if you added up all that weight, it more or less equaled a whole person. Another Shulman. Whom he hated. And pinched. And tried to conceal by wearing oversize shirts while he dieted and did crunches in health clubs in an attempt to rid himself of the Shulman he didn't want to be.

There were times when he just couldn't shake the specter of that Other Shulman. Times when he would close his eyes and try to conjure up an image of this discarded person, the Shulman he chose to rid himself of in favor of the husband of this woman who was ordering furniture at one o'clock in the morning. In favor of the proprietor of a store that no one came into anymore. *What would* that *guy's life be like?* he'd wonder. Were there parts of him that Shulman should have kept for himself? Should he, dear God, have kept *all* of him? Was it possible that Shulman, after all this time and effort, had indeed opted to be the wrong Shulman?

Such thoughts used to appear only occasionally. Haunt him for a while. And then move on. But lately they were occurring with enough overlapping regularity to constitute a general condition. A condition that now refused to pass. So, as an extremely uncomfortable Shulman resigned himself to still another night of pay-cable titillation and worries about a livelihood that was barely alive, he couldn't help but wonder what the Other Shulman was doing at that very moment.

Mile 2

Brooklyn

Shulman, who was born in Brooklyn, ran off the bridge and entered the city's most populous borough the same way he came into the world, headfirst. And, very much like his birth, it was instigated by a push. But this time it was from a pregnant woman aiming a camcorder at her husband, who was running next to him. But what she ended up videotaping when she turned in the direction of his cry of "Jesus, lady!" was the image of Shulman lurching forward with his arms flailing in circular, butterfly-stroke motions before falling into the arms of a fireman who'd been watching from the curb.

"You okay?" he asked.

"Yes. Thank you . . ." Shulman answered while consulting the badge above the man's breast pocket, "Chief Perrotta."

"Well, good luck with the rest of the race," Perrotta said while setting Shulman upright.

After a quick moment devoted to reorientation, Shulman nodded, gave what he just assumed was a fire officer's salute, and continued on.

Brooklyn was going to be a twelve-mile leg of the race. Starting out flat. But Shulman knew from his talks with Coach Jeffrey that there would eventually be a slight incline upward that would barely be discernible. What was immediately obvious, however, was that once they left the bridge, Shulman was running only with men. It was the marathon organizers' way of thinning the field until the runners reached the wider boulevards that could accommodate everyone. So Shulman would be going at it alone for a while. Without Maria's company. But to his great delight (his little swan dive into the fire chief's surprisingly bony arms notwithstanding) he was doing well. No cramps. No aches. And his pace was about what he wanted it to be. At the mile marker, his time was exactly thirteen minutes. Remarkably slow for the overwhelming majority of two-legged Earth-dwelling creatures. But just fine if your name happened to be Shulman.

So he kept running. Along this street lined on both sides with spectators who were cheering. Applauding. Offering drinks and words of encouragement. Residents who came downstairs from their apartments. Others who leaned out their bedroom windows. Homeowners who walked the few blocks to the sidewalks of Fourth Avenue. Some who sat in beach chairs. Wooden folding chairs. On top of corner mailboxes. Some who stood with young children perched on their shoulders so they could get a better look. And shopkeepers whose doors were open this Sunday morning with the hope that even just a fraction of the crowd would find its way into their small hardware stores and bakeries. Some of them brought their goods out to the sidewalk and set up shop on

tables and from racks. Sandwiches. Toys. T-shirts. Blouses. CDs.
Bins filled with shapeless underwear. Another one filled with
beach balls. Real plants. Fake plants. Shelves filled with books.
Desk lamps. Floor lamps. One of every kind of shoe. Picture
frames. Eyeglass frames. Cellular phones. Rugs. Some guys from
Petco were carrying out aquariums and birdcages.

And when Shulman passed a stationery store, he waved to its
owner. A small, older man arranging calendars and office supplies
in a quest to lure pedestrian traffic. But this wave wasn't clumsy
like the one he gave Chief Perrotta. This one had a conveyance of
fraternity. That unspoken language between strangers connected
only by a shared situation. The way bus drivers honk to each
other on the road. Or the way shoppers roll their eyes when the
cashier is taking forever to ring everyone up. So when the small,
older man returned the gesture, as far as Shulman was concerned,
a connection was made.

Shulman loved stationery. And stationery stores. Always did.
Not the big Staples or Office Depot stores that sold twenty-five
ballpoint pens anonymously packaged in clear plastic bags piled
on top of one another in huge bins and costing $1.99. But the
kind of store that respected the unique personalities of its pens,
composition books, erasers, and loose-leaf binders. That appreciated the relationship that forms between such items and their
young owners during the course of a school year. And understood
those burgeoning sense memories capable of accessing the smell
of sharpened pencils years later when those kids became adults.
The kind of store that Shulman owned.

Today it was located exactly in the middle of the nine establishments that collectively called themselves the Rolling Fields
Shopping Plaza. But when Shulman's first opened its doors
twenty-three years ago to the stationery-buying public, it stood
alone on what was a small turf of land a short distance from the

Jersey side of the George Washington Bridge. And though it would be an exaggeration to say that cries of "Let's go to Shulman's" or "I don't want to go skiing this Christmas, I'd rather go to Shulman's" rang throughout the Garden State, the store did quickly become that part of everyone's lives they just naturally gravitated to for all of their stationery, newspaper, greeting-card, sweet-tooth, last-minute-gift, or lottery-ticket needs. Newspapers? Bottom shelf on the right. Maps? Against the back wall under the clock. Forgot your wallet at the house? So you'll pay me next time you're in. In a life filled with twists and hairpin turns, the comfort people derived from having something they could count on was regarded as precious. At the end of a trip with the kids asleep in the backseat, Shulman's was the signpost that told them they were home.

Everyone came to Shulman's. Kids on bikes came to sneak peeks at the magazines their fathers hid from them at home. It was at Shulman's that housewives found out whose marriages were in trouble. And where unshaved men in sweats would linger on Sunday mornings long after the *Times* was paid for to update other grungy men about their week or make a friendly bet on the Jets game that afternoon.

Shulman's was more than a store. It was a landmark. A haven whose proprietor was as popular as the store he owned. In those heady days, Shulman's was "Shulman's" and, consequently, Shulman was "Shulman." A young man with a young family who filled a special role for his neighbors in a young growing town. He was greeted on the street. Seated quickly in crowded local restaurants. He was appreciated. He felt love.

Of course, this was all before the creation of the Rolling Fields Shopping Plaza twelve years ago. A group of old friends bought the undeveloped acreage surrounding Shulman's and built a strip mall that they named Rolling Fields by taking letters from their first names (*R*oger, *Ll*oyd, *I*ra, Ned, *G*reg, *F*rank, and Art), with the exception of Art Fields, who gave his last name to the venture so it wouldn't be called Rolling Fart Shopping Plaza.

At first, Shulman welcomed the company. Very much so. There was plenty of room for more stores that could bring more business into his place. And they did. Even during construction, his makeshift sign that read WE'RE STILL OPEN attracted both the faithful and the curious. And when the transformation to Rolling Fields was complete, everyone referred to the new plaza as Shulman's. Even after all the new conjoined establishments were up and running. After the new parking lot was rolled, paved, and painted. And after the freestanding marquee boasting the name of this new united entity was anchored into the ground. Whether out of habit or unwitting respect for seniority, Shulman's succeeded in making the jump to the generic. These newcomers, despite individual signs proclaiming identities of their own, were merely the supporting cast to a star attraction. Shulman's was Gladys Knight. The rest of them were the Pips.

Unfortunately, the act was short-lived. These Pips very quickly became stars on their own, as discount warehouses and logo-driven outlets were more in step with the revved-up pace that life was starting to be lived at. A newer world where convenience replaced charm. Where quaint took a backseat to bulk. And where people, by pressing just a few keys on a desktop, were able to save even more time by converting shopping into an at-home activity.

Initially, these developments were the topics of conversations among the regulars who came into Shulman's store. Men spoke about the new LensWorld that was driving the optician out of business. An amazed woman told of her trip to Costco, where she bought a box of cornflakes too big for the trunk of her car that now had its own room off their den. And still another said that she stopped using her travel agent after her seven-year-old retarded nephew went online and booked a vacation that was cheaper and more exciting.

Shulman partook in many of these discussions. Lamenting the troubles of neighboring merchants. Marveling at the cost-saving options now available to the average consumer. And not even realizing his customers were becoming so infatuated by these new time-saving options until they began to have trouble finding the time to come to places like Shulman's.

Today? The brittle photographs of Little League teams he once sponsored? Most of those boys were out of college by now. Packages of twenty-five ballpoint pens for $1.99? "Sorry, we don't carry them." The smile was still there. Maybe out of habit, but more likely from the need for Shulman to still, somehow, be "Shulman." The guy who still loved stationery and stationery stores. And not succumb to that bitterness suffered by those the world has set aside. Or outgrown. Or merely needed a break from. They'll be back, he kept telling himself. Once they tire of the fad and seek the thrill of rediscovering.

So Shulman waited. Like a parent trying to endure the uncharted behavior of a renegade child. Coping. Quietly praying this was but a passing phase. All the while staring at newspapers on the bottom shelf on the right, knowing that the stacks of returns he placed outside every night were getting bigger and bigger.

The First Day of Training

The intersection of Fourth Avenue and 81st Street in Brooklyn is the beginning of a five-mile straightaway of ethnically diverse neighborhoods. As Shulman eased into the turn that lazily branched off at what his old geometry teacher would've called an obtuse angle, he looked ahead and saw that the better runners were starting to put a little distance between themselves and the rest of the pack. Not the leaders. Hell no. In fact, Shulman just assumed that by now the winner of this thing had already crossed the finish line, gotten his picture taken with the mayor, and was already on a plane back to his native country. But the better runners, the ones whose strides looked like they knew how to run, were already leaving the communities Shulman was about to enter. Small enclaves quietly segueing into one another. A few blocks of cheering people, with Latin music coming through large speakers, filling the sidewalks in front of stores that had Hispanic names. Then cross a street and the people, their music, and restaurants magically turned Korean. A few more blocks and they were suddenly Chinese. A few more blocks and Shulman couldn't get the song "It's a Small World After All" out of his head. Over and over again. It would play through, Shulman would think it was mercifully done with, and then, as if some dork at a party had his finger on the REPEAT button, it started again. And any attempts to drown it out proved to be equally annoying. Songs he began to sing out loud were soon overtaken by the tune. So he sang louder. But the louder he sang, to the great bewilderment of runners within earshot, the louder those infernal Disney characters got— to the point where Shulman was now running through the streets of the Bay Ridge section of Brooklyn muttering some very uncomplimentary things about Walt Disney, the Bay Ridge section of Brooklyn, music in general, and marathons in particular. About what a ridiculous race this was. About how it started. And about who started it.

His name was Phidippides, and in 490 B.C. he was dispatched from the ancient city of Marathon to deliver the news of their miraculous defeat of the Persian army. So he ran as fast as he could. Twenty-six miles. Uphill. Along flat plains. Then downhill into Athens, where he proclaimed, "Victory!" and fell dead.

"What was his rush?" Roy Toy had asked Shulman the night before. "I mean, I can understand the guy being excited about beating Persia and everything. But isn't it *bad* news that's supposed to travel fast?"

Roy Toy was an idiot. Always was. Shulman met him when he was an idiot in college and took a lot of Roy Toy's exams for him so he wouldn't flunk out and wind up being an idiot in Vietnam.

Then a few years after graduation, when the war and its draft were no longer factors in anyone's life, Roy Toy managed to make his acute shortage of gray matter work for him when he wrote down hundreds of the questions that confounded him, placed them into categories, and sold this frightening package as a television quiz show that netted him the kind of fortune only someone who has no idea what he's doing can make. Still, Roy Toy never forgot what he believed were his roots, which is why he showed up at Shulman's house, the night before his marathon-training program began, with two dozen shoe boxes.

"You saved my life in Vietnam," he told Shulman.

"You were never *in* Vietnam."

"And I have you to thank for that."

"Roy Toy, we've been through this a thousand—"

"So that's why I want you to have these." He pointed to the small city of rectangular boxes stacked behind him. "This company's a sponsor on my show. They're supposed to be very good running shoes."

"Roy Toy, I already have a pair of running shoes."

"Who knows? Maybe if that first marathon guy was wearing these—"

"He'd still be alive today?" Shulman asked with a rhetorical smile, sparing both of them potential embarrassment in the event that the end of Roy Toy's sentence was really going to be the claim that if Phidippides had worn New Balance running shoes with air cushions and built-in orthodics, he'd be celebrating his fifteen-hundredth birthday about now.

Shulman loved Roy Toy. In him he found a purity that was always above guile despite how maddening it could become. Nothing seemed to bother him. Not then, not now, not ever. None of the philosophical questions posed by adolescents. None of those disturbing conclusions that now plagued them as adults. Call him at work and they'd answer, "Mr. Blankman's office." Get a message from him and it would say, "Roy Toy called." Roy Toy. The nickname a mother gave her chubby, baby-faced boy, who was now a chubby, baby-faced man holding a pair of running shoes, who was telling Shulman, "I think these blue and white ones are really cool."

Sunday. Six o'clock the next morning. Though not a stranger to this time of day, Shulman still marveled at the difference between Sundays and all of the other mornings at this exact hour. When even the sun and its attendant shadows, without the accompaniment of alarms, shock jocks, or oldies blasting from bedside radios, seemed to quietly rise so as not to jolt those who wanted to awaken on their own terms. A small yet thoughtful gesture in deference to the respite they'd earned by week's end.

The drive was a short one. Not ten minutes from the house, where Paula wished him luck, offered to make him breakfast, and told him to be careful all in the same yawn before turning over, staking claim to his side of the bed a millisecond after he'd vacated it, and falling back to sleep. He looked at her. My God, she was still beautiful, Shulman thought. The years had not only been kind to her but, in most ways, appeared to have forgotten about her altogether. Perhaps a line here. A half-inch there. But certainly nothing that compared with the utter devastation he had allowed his own body to undergo. Far beyond the curve one normally marks on when allowing for the wear and tear withstood over the course of time. To the point where more than one person, and perhaps not so coincidentally, had described Shulman as looking like Woody Allen with a glandular condition. He wondered if he'd been unfair to Paula. If all of the compliments she'd been getting about looking like his trophy wife were satisfying. Or if his jokes about him busting his ass so she could live the good life were beginning to wear a little thin. Mostly, he wondered if she was disappointed.

When they met, things were different. They were in jail. An on-campus protest had gotten out of hand so the local police rounded up everyone and took them downtown until things got sorted out. Shulman hadn't been protesting. He went to the rally because he knew there'd be a lot of girls who wouldn't be wearing bras. Paula had gone with a few friends who *were* protesting so she pretended that she was as angry as they were. But when they were all arrested she was the only one in the entire holding cell who was crying. Shulman found this attractive. He told her a few jokes, she laughed, and this made her more attractive. And when he noticed that she was also the only one in the holding cell who was wearing a bra, he fell in love.

"Would you like to go out?" he asked.

"You mean when we get out?"

"Yes. Would you like to go out when we get out?"

"Sure," she answered, smiling.

She was in the school of interior design. He was a premed student but not comfortable with it.

"What do you really want to do?" Paula asked him.

"I'm not sure yet. I just know that I don't love medicine," he told her.

"Well, is there something that you do love?"

"Yes," he answered shyly. Extremely shyly.

"What?"

"Stationery."

She laughed. Another one of his jokes, she thought. Then she realized that he was serious.

"Well, then that's what you should do," she told him.

This time *he* laughed. He thought that she was joking. Then he realized she was serious.

"Really?" he asked.

"Of course. What good is anything unless you're happy doing it?"

Six weeks later they got married.

Shulman pulled into the lot, removed the key from the ignition, opened the car door, placed a foot covered with Roy Toy's running shoe onto the pavement, and took his first step toward his marathon-training group. Everyone in various states of consciousness and attire; they too were responding to the e-mail that said they should come to this park at this hour. Shulman looked at them the same way he looked at all groups when he was in a new situation—with the assumption that everyone already knew one another and that he was the only stranger among them. He acted accordingly and took a place at the outskirts.

"Good morning, volunteers!" shouted a guy with an amazing number of visible muscles, and all of the marathoners-to-be suddenly fell silent. "I'm Coach Jeffrey," the muscle guy continued, "and I want to welcome all of you to the first of twenty-six Sunday mornings we'll be spending together in preparation for that big day in November when we go to New York City!" The way his voice arched upward as he neared the end of that sentence, in particular the two syllables in "Ci-ty," somehow managed to elicit the kind of applause and scattered shouts of "Yeah!" that, on the surface, seemed disproportionate to the fact that he was referring to a place only the span of the George Washington Bridge away (and whose skyline was eminently visible) from where they stood at that very moment. So while Shulman personally found it difficult to muster any enthusiasm about going to a city where he'd just seen a movie the night before, the collective energy of those around him did manage to draw him in from the fringe.

"Have you ever run a marathon before?" asked the heavy woman now standing next to him.

"No," Shulman answered. "How about you?"

"No way," she said, shaking her head and smiling. Shulman figured her to be about thirty, maybe thirty-five years old. She was pretty. Heavy, but pretty. On closer inspection, the kind of pretty that could very easily be considered beautiful if she weren't so heavy.

"What made you decide to do this?" Shulman asked.

"Last January my brother died of AIDS."

"Oh, I'm so sorry . . ."

"He hung on until it was ten minutes past midnight on my birthday. We sipped champagne, he told me not to marry a lawyer, that it's okay to order desserts, and then he closed his eyes. . . . I don't know, doing this is the closest I can get to him right now."

Although she paused, Shulman had the feeling that it still wasn't his turn to speak. Whether her words were an often repeated mantra or an untested outpouring to a complete stranger, he couldn't figure out. But as he looked into the face of a grieving sister who was not even close to making sense of what had occurred, he was certain that she still had things to say.

"My name is Maria. Truth is, I used to run track in high school but that feels like such a long time ago. I can only imagine what it must feel like for *you*."

Shulman sensed it was okay to laugh and did. She was right, though. As he looked around at his fellow trainees, who were now, per Coach Jeffrey's directions, slowly starting to inch toward a starting line, he couldn't help but notice that he did indeed have a few decades on most of them. Were they like Maria? Here at dawn thanks to different versions of the same story? Attempting to reconnect? To say good-bye before moving on?

Shulman, now enveloped by sounds of the herd, managed to catch fragmented bytes as they filtered through the din. From a black guy who had lost a boyfriend: "Thursday was two years." A woman lamented a son's bad luck: "It was the first and only time he ever used a needle." A young husband's wife had survived an operation, but not the transfusion: "Robin would really be laughing her ass off if she knew I was doing this."

Shulman suddenly understood the special brand of guilt he imagined people felt after they walked away from a plane crash. And the tacit bond that united them only by a tragic link. It was a club with no rules. Talk if you want to. Cry if you need to. The only dues are the look in your eyes, the one that says that things will never be quite the same.

Shulman started to wonder what he would say if Maria asked why *he* was here. If he had someone to reconnect with. Or say good-bye to. He had no idea how he would he even begin to explain that he was doing this because he wanted to rid himself of another chunk of that Other Shulman.

Thus far, Shulman had been lucky. A few bumps and psychological bruises were merely the badges gathered by life's travelers along the way. But nothing that anyone would even dare think of labeling as tragic. Paula and the kids were alive and relatively well. Somehow, he had managed to elude those late-night knocks at the door from police sergeants and calls from doctors with positive lab results. Still, he was under no illusions about exemption. He knew that in the long run no one leaves with the casino's money and that eventually it would be his turn.

Years ago, he and the kids booed Paula roundly upon her suggestion that they say "I love you" at the end of all phone conversations, since they never knew if any call would be the last time they ever spoke. The opposition stated that the suggestion fell somewhere between corny and morbid. So, in her customary manner, she yielded to the majority, took the ribbing in stride, stopped saying "I love you" anytime, not just at the end of conversations, and now ordered hassocks from their bed.

"Would you like to run together?" Maria asked at that very first training session.

"Sure," he said.

And then Shulman had to restrain himself from telling this total stranger that he loved her.

That same Sunday. It was now ten in the morning and Paula was still in her robe but no longer sleeping on Shulman's side of the bed. Instead, she sat on the edge of the bathtub, which her aching husband was submerged in with no plans of ever leaving.

"You really ran three miles?"

"Well, that depends on what your definition of 'ran' is," Shulman answered with a breath that, when expelled, somehow hurt three of his eyelashes. "If you're going to be a strict traditionalist about it and say that 'ran' is the past tense of 'run,' then no, I didn't run three miles. But if you're going to cut me some slack and allow it to include walking and stopping a few times to bend at the waist so I could bone up on my dry-heaving skills, then yes, I ran like a gazelle."

Coach Jeffrey's instructions to the more than three hundred volunteers were to cover the distance any way they could. Their individual times were then inserted into a formula, the result of which was the pace that they would then be training at. Consequently, it was determined that he and Maria, upon completing the session in a prearranged dead heat, were to be in a group that would be training at a ratio of three to one. Three minutes of running, then one minute of walking. A cycle to be followed during all prescribed runs.

"Next Sunday we'll do four miles. The Sunday after that, five. It keeps increasing by a mile every week. Unless my math is wrong, in two years I'll be able to run to Portugal."

He could sense Paula's reaction without looking. Their almost three decades of history told him that she was smiling. And he was more than willing to glance up to verify that hunch but, at the moment, his neck was being less than cooperative, if not totally remiss, in its duties of keeping his head aloft. It had taken an unscheduled sabbatical, leaving his chin, now in triplicate, resting against the northern province of his chest as his slumping body made him look more and more like the victim of a gangland slaying.

"Are you sure you want to go through with this?" Paula asked. "I mean, if you're not up to it, there's certainly no shame in—"

"Who says I'm not up to it?" he asked into his left nipple. And then fell asleep in the bathtub.

Shulman Gets Mad at His Doctor

"I *gained* weight? How's that possible?"

"Three pounds since your last visit," said the nurse with the mole smack in the middle of her left eyebrow.

"But I've been running."

"Since when?"

"Sunday."

"Well, today's Thursday. What did you expect to happen in four days? That you'd look wispy?"

Last June. In Dr. Martin Gordon's office. Shulman, all 251 pounds of him, stepped down from the scale, sending its metal balancing bar crashing upward with a vengeance.

"That number can't be right," he said, reaching behind his neck and starting to undo the knot on the flimsy gown that covered the part that would render him inappropriately exposed if this were, say, a public library. "Maybe if I took this off we could get a truer read."

"That gown weighs twelve grams."

"Yeah, but it billows."

"Well, if we're going to be this exact about it, maybe I should shave your head and weigh you on one of those little scales drug dealers use."

Marty Gordon had been Shulman's doctor for years, and this nurse with the mole smack in the middle of her left eyebrow had been working there forever. Jill, he thought her name was. But he wasn't positive. And the statute of limitations had long passed for him to ask without it being an unadulterated insult to her. So now, at this stage of his existence, he was stark naked and stepping back onto a scale in front of a woman whose name he didn't know. No doubt a very common, just-another-day-at-the-office occurrence for any nurse with or without a mole smack in the middle of her left eyebrow. Still, the guy part of him wondered if the girl part of her ever overpowered her nurse part. And allowed that girl, even for a moment, to take notice of someone as a man, not as a patient. And, if so, could this possibly be one of those moments?

"If you stand still I'll be able to get that true read I know you live for," she said while sliding the scale's shiny metal weights to the right.

And if this was one of those moments? No, it really wouldn't change anything. He was just wondering.

"Sorry," she said, shaking her head. "No matter how I coax it, you still tip this thing at just over an eighth of a ton."

Shulman liked this nurse. Dry. Understated in attitude and approach. He even appreciated her wit when it came to her choice of words. The way she offhandedly compared Shulman's current poundage with that of cargo. But the moment she turned around and just matter-of-factly wrote the weight down on his chart, as if it were just *any* overweight patient's weight, he suddenly felt naked. So he quickly slipped back into the flimsy gown, took a seat on the edge of the examination table and waited for the doctor to see him.

Marty Gordon looked old. Older than he did in the pictures of him with his family that were sitting in frames on the shelves. More than six months older than when Shulman last saw him six months ago.

They were in Marty's office now. The small talk, the questions, the blood taking, head turning, mouth opening, coughing, touching, probing, X-raying, bending, greasing, and gloved finger inserting had already taken place in other rooms. So here he was, fully clothed once again, sitting across a desk from a man who, according to the dozen or so plaques on the wall, was certified by a number of boards and institutions to make sense of the chart he was looking at. Shulman's chart. In Shulman's folder. Literally. For years he'd been ordering all kinds of stationery for Marty and some of his other professional customers, letting them have it at cost. Paula said he was insane for doing so. "They charge *you*, don't they?" she kept repeating. Yes, they did. But what did one thing have to do with the other? This wasn't a business move with a calculable return. Stationery for medical services quid pro quo. My God, Shulman couldn't even imagine how many manila folders and notepads sold at cost would ultimately entitle him to one free colonoscopy. Nor did he care. Goodwill was contagious. With a value transcending measurement. Priceless. Like a memory. Shulman loved providing fond memories. And in the case of Marty Gordon, well, he was certainly provided with a fonder memory than most. For every time he even touched a folder or used a three-hole punch, Marty was able to think of Shulman's stationery store and remember it as the location where his child was conceived.

It was on an August night, sixteen years earlier, when a chipmunk that was either too curious or too suicidal for its own well-being found its way into a Con Ed generator, causing a total blackout in the greater parts of northern New Jersey. At first Shulman, like everyone else, assumed that the sudden departure of electricity was due to the torrential rain that had broken from the sky about an hour earlier. One of those late-summer cloudbursts where, within seconds, noon becomes midnight and parks become rice paddies. Where those indoors race to close windows, and those in cars pull off to the side.

Shulman had just gotten off the phone with Paula after an exchange of assurances that each was safe and dry. From there he moved out from behind the register and over to the window, where he sat on its sill and stared at the eerie sight of a traffic light that was changing colors for no one. Green. Yellow. Red. Green. Yellow. Red. Dutifully performing to program. Oblivious to the fact that it was, at least for that particular point in time, unnecessary. Irrelevant. Still, it was the yellow light that actually made him feel the most sorry for it. The color that actually belied its sorry state. In the off chance a motorist did come along, foolhardy, desperate or otherwise, both the red and the green would inform him what to do in no uncertain terms. Stop. Go. Definite, firm commands issued during a time of confusion. Yielding a much needed, even if momentary, semblance of order. But the yellow light exposed its own vulnerability under these conditions with an overzealous presumption that vehicles were *indeed* approaching and that they should slow down. It was a frantic display so far removed from reality that it undermined any credibility the traffic light, as a whole, might have otherwise had. So, on a symbolic level, it sort of made sense that it was during one of those misguided amber phases that all power in the entire area went out.

Word spread quickly that Shulman's had flashlights. And candles. Products not traditionally associated with a stationery store unless its owner also served as gatekeeper to a community. But the truth was, it galled Shulman to no end that in the aftermath of similar states of emergency, one always heard horror stories about greedy convenience store owners who had a supply and took shameless advantage of the demand by gouging ten dollars for a battery. Or twenty for bottled water. So to safeguard against such a thing from happening in *his* town, Shulman stocked his back room accordingly. And when the storm subsided, it wasn't too long before those very same cars that had gone into hiding ventured out, pulled up to his curb, sat idling while their owners ran into his place empty-handed, ran out clutching bags of supplies, then carefully returned them to the safety of their homes.

This went on for hours. A steady procession of suburban night travelers drawn to a little store whose glow could be seen for miles. A beacon illuminated by strategically deployed flashlights on the inside and approaching headlights from the outside.

And then the rains returned with a vengeance, as if resuscitated during the lull by an angry wind that caused flash floods. Knocked over trees. Toppled already impotent power lines. And sent about twenty idling motorists dashing from their cars to seek shelter inside Shulman's. At first they huddled, swapping storm stories and keeping warm with the cocoa he served them. Then they sat on cartons, stools, and the few folding chairs he put out for them. Then they slept on carpeted floors under blankets he found to cover them. And among the slumbering was a young couple named Marty and Debby Gordon, off by themselves near the greeting cards. They were new to the neighborhood and frustrated by their many unsuccessful attempts at conception. But nine months later they had a child they named Tommy. And though they denied it at first, they later confessed where it had happened and, for the next decade, sent Shulman a thank-you card every year on their only child's birthday.

"So how's everything doing down at the store?" Marty Gordon inquired with his face still buried in Shulman's chart.

"Not bad," Shulman fibbed. "Haven't seen you in a while, though. Is everything okay with you?"

There has to be a reason that he looks so bad, Shulman thought sympathetically.

"Yeah, I've been good," Marty Gordon answered.

He has?

"I've been good," he repeated with affirming nods.

Then is it possible that he's been good, but looks so lousy because someone close to him is in bad shape and he's so deeply concerned about him or her?

"And the family? Debby? Tommy? They're good too?"

"Couldn't be better."

They couldn't?

"Your parents?"

"Alive and well and loving the Miami sunshine."

Who else does he know?

"Herb Hogel?"

"Who?"

"That mechanic over in Englewood. The one who takes care of your car."

"I think he's okay." Marty Gordon laughed. "Then again, my car's been running beautifully so I haven't seen old Herbie in a while. Now, as far as you're concerned . . ."

As far as I'm concerned, if everything is so fine and dandy, why the hell haven't you been to my store?

"I wouldn't worry about the slight weight gain," Marty Gordon continued. "Your body may take a week or so to adjust to your new regimen and then you'll start to see a difference."

Or are you so fine and so dandy that newspapers and stationery would just get in the way of all your merriment?

"Your system's probably just a little confused right now," Marty Gordon added as he reached for a notepad that Shulman had given him two boxes of for free.

"Yeah, it does feel a little confused," Shulman said through a forced smile.

And how confused would you be if I walked over and ripped the arms off of that skeleton you've got hanging in the corner and then came back and sat down like nothing happened, you ungrateful turd?

"I'm giving you a list of vitamins and a few supplements that will help your body deal with some of the pounding it's going to take." Marty Gordon finished writing with a rather fine-looking Papermate pen that Shulman was positive was the same fine-looking Papermate pen he'd thrown in with those free notepads.

Your wife is fat.

"But as far as your vital signs go, everything looks good and strong and I see no reason why you can't give this marathon thing a shot."

Is Tommy gay?

"Although I've got to tell you that I think you're a little crazy to be doing this," Marty Gordon added. "I was just reading in the newspaper about how the incidence of joggers getting hit by cars is on the rise."

Newspaper!!!! Where the hell did you buy that newspaper!!!!

Marty Gordon smiled and extended his hand. Shulman's cue to do the same. His doctor's appointment was over.

"Nice seeing you, Marty."

"Yeah, you too."

"My love to Debby and Tommy."

"Take care of yourself."

I hope your ass locks.

"You know, you're allowed to be angry," Paula said after he told her about his infuriating trip to the doctor. They were in the car. Driving home from a movie she had already seen without him and thought he would enjoy. He didn't. But said he did. Two weeks before, he had taken her to a movie he'd already seen that he thought she might enjoy. She didn't. But said she did. They did this a lot. It kept them from growing apart.

"I *am* angry," Shulman answered.

"No you're not. Your feelings are hurt. That's different because hurt is directed inward. If you were really angry you would come right out and say it to whoever's let you down."

"Like Marty Gordon."

"Not just him. Anyone who has acted like a jerk. The role of victim only plays for so long. After that, if you don't let people know you're pissed off, then you're basically telling them that *you* don't think you're worth defending."

Shulman looked over at his wife. It didn't surprise him that her eyes were staring straight ahead, trained on nothing in particular through the windshield of their car. Nor that her words were devoid of emphasis or passion. She had made that speech many times before. The same thoughts rephrased a thousand different ways, in an attempt to make them sound like new thoughts. New revelations. Each with the hope that *this* would be the configuration that would finally jump-start her husband into taking a stand.

"I'm not asking you to do anything other than acknowledge your anger and then act accordingly," she would tell him. "People are bound to squeeze you," she'd say. "There's no law that says you can't squeeze back."

But paralysis comes in many forms. And when it came to squeezing back, Shulman was indeed paralyzed because anger was an emotion he had never been programmed to access. Perhaps the result of a wiring snafu that occurred during a developmentally appropriate phase. Or more likely because his parents, during the wee hours of infancy, willfully broke into his consciousness and sabotaged all mechanisms that would've allowed him to place blame on anyone other than himself. Which left him hungry, in fact starving, for acceptance and landed him in his lifelong audition for the role of great guy. And kept him reshaping himself in accordance to what others needed him to be. Leaving him unable to understand that patience, after a reasonable amount of time, ceases to be a virtue and instead becomes a euphemism for cowardice. And finally, it left him holding on to the potentially fatal belief that great guys never get angry.

And the Other Shulman? That mythical counterpart he had shed along the way. Did *he* manage to escape? Did he somehow figure out how to bridge those bombed-out synapses and leap to the safety of the other side? Where healthier people already knew how to act, react, and, if the situation called for it, squeeze back. Shulman then started to wonder what would happen if he actually encountered that Other Shulman. Would the Other Shulman be angry that he was deemed unworthy?

Would he be angry that someone who couldn't get angry had deemed *him* unworthy?

Mile 5

Chasing Butterflies

The first thought that crossed Shulman's mind as he passed the marker for Mile 5 was that he didn't remember passing the marker for Mile 4. But he must have. For at no point had he strayed off course to suddenly find himself the only one running down a deserted street, then having to backtrack and go looking for the thousands of marathoners and spectators that he had somehow misplaced.

It was a startling moment, though. Being so engrossed in what he was thinking that it took his mind off the run itself. Similar to what a motorist experiences when he snaps back into awareness after his mind has drifted on the open road. Awakening to find that everything was still where it was supposed to be and happy that he hadn't veered off, run onto the sidewalk, and caused a minor scandal by plowing into Cub Scout Troop #185, who were standing at attention and dutifully offering their two-fingered salutes to all runners as they passed.

He knew it was far too early for the endorphins to have kicked in. Those magical neurotransmitters that, when released during the prolonged periods of movement, are responsible for what is commonly referred to as a "runner's high." No, it wasn't that. His brief hiatus bore no resemblance to the blissful state where the mind separates from the body, as described by those who'd experienced it. A condition that, were he aware of its existence some thirty years earlier, would have saved him the small fortune he spent on drugs when he was in college.

So he continued onward. Fully cognizant of his whereabouts. This stretch of Brooklyn was more residential. While the street was just as populated with spectators, against a backdrop of trees and garden apartments they looked more like neighbors. Folks with coffee mugs who stepped outside to watch the tens of thousands of people who happened to be running past their homes this particular Sunday morning. Women had baked cookies. Kids were handing out free lemonade. Some were running on the sidewalk pretending that they were in the race. One, on a bicycle, approached Shulman and asked, "Hey, mister, want a ride?"

Shulman, who was taking a walk break at the time, smiled and said, "Do I look like I need one?"

"Yeah, you really do."

Shulman smiled again and shook his head. "Thanks, anyway," he told him.

As the kid rode away, Shulman looked to see if he was making similar offers to other runners. Other marathoners whom the kid also perceived to be in need of some sort of vehicular assistance less than a fifth of the way through this race. He was not.

About a half block later, Shulman crossed another red mat deployed at the 10K mark. And while the microchip sitting atop Roy Toy's left running shoe was no doubt programmed to record the timing at this point in the race, the mat was also there to take attendance and act as a checkpoint. It was to help assure that no one did what a woman named Rosie Ruiz did back on April 21, 1980. When she was the first woman to cross the finish line in the Boston Marathon with the third-fastest time ever recorded by a female runner. Made all the more remarkable by the fact that she was curiously sweat-free and not even breathing hard as she climbed the podium to accept her wreath. Looking as if she had simply sat on a subway for the first twenty-five miles, then emerged onto the street and sprinted the rest of the way. Which was exactly what an investigation determined she indeed had done. She was disqualified and stripped of the medal she won for having done what instantly became known as "pulling a Rosie Ruiz."

What had always impressed Shulman about this story, aside from the woman's audacity, was the fact that she "sprinted the rest of the way," which was, by all accounts, at least a mile. She sprinted a mile. And she wasn't sweaty. And she wasn't breathing hard. And he thought anyone who could do that deserved a medal of some kind, considering the sorry state *he* was in after Shulman pulled what instantly became known as "pulling a Shulman."

It happened on the second Sunday morning of training. The practice run was scheduled for four miles. From the starting line in the park, along the bike lane of a wide boulevard, and back. Shulman arrived on time, and found Maria and a handful of others standing behind a sign that had FREDA MERTZ written on it.

"Who's Freda Mertz?" he asked.

"She's a famous marathoner," Maria told him. "Apparently they all are," she added while indicating the dozen or so signs deployed in the immediate area. All with names like Bill Rodgers, Frank Shorter, Alberto Salazar, and Beth Bonner written on them. And all with a number of marathoners-in-training standing behind them. Starting this week everyone would be running with their pace groups, which were named after Olympic or world-class long-distance runners.

"Oh . . ." Shulman said with mock disappointment just as Coach Jeffrey happened to be walking by.

"Are you unhappy with the name of your pace group?" asked Coach Jeffrey. "Is there someone you feel is more appropriate for you than Freda Mertz?"

"Yes," Shulman answered.

"Who?"

"Fred Mertz."

"As in Fred and Ethel Mertz? *That* Fred Mertz?" he asked.

"Yes," Shulman answered. "Lucy and Ricky Ricardo's friend."

Coach Jeffrey's glare informed Shulman that this had the makings of a defining moment. That it could very well set the tone for whatever relationship he was going to have with this coach, who could make Shulman's life difficult the way other coaches had done in the past. Like Mr. Gagliardi. The junior-varsity baseball coach who once made Shulman wash his car for striking out with the bases loaded. Perhaps this guy would be different. Yet, as much as Shulman hoped so, all early indications were less than promising. Because they were now standing face-to-face, and it was easy for Shulman to see that Coach Jeffrey wasn't even smiling. And because Shulman's left eye had a tendency to wander when he was nervous, it was easy for him to look past Coach Jeffrey and see Maria doing her best to keep a straight face before the eye found its way back to this man who seemed to have no trouble whatsoever remaining absolutely ex-pressionless.

"I think he hates me," Shulman told Maria after Coach Jeffrey moved away to welcome all the volunteers to this morning's training session.

"I wouldn't worry about it," Maria answered, smiling. "For some reason, I think your relationship will survive this little misunderstanding. Maybe even make it stronger. By the way, did you do your practice runs this week?"

In addition to the Sunday-morning sessions, the volunteers were given a schedule they were urged to follow. Practice runs on Tuesdays and Thursdays that lasted anywhere from thirty to forty-five minutes. Mondays, Wednesdays, and Fridays were to be devoted to an hour of cross-training—weight lifting, swimming, or anything else that didn't tax the same muscles running did. And on Saturdays, they were to rest. This last directive was the only one that Shulman had followed.

"No, I didn't train at all."

"Neither did I," she admitted and then laughed. A nervous giggle. Like a child who knew she'd been naughty.

After a few announcements, mostly about the fund-raising, Coach Jeffrey asked each group to choose a leader. Someone with a watch that could be programmed to beep at that group's prescribed run/walk intervals. So a heavyset (not as heavyset as Shulman) guy (much more of a guy than Shulman) named Carl immediately moved to the front of Shulman's group, and set his Timex Ironman to their training pace of three minutes and one minute. Then the moment the group before theirs was sent on their way, Shulman, Maria, and the others moved to the starting point, where Coach Jeffrey was standing.

"Are all of my Freda Mertzes ready for a good run this morning?"

Everyone except Shulman answered in different forms of yes. But apparently their response wasn't enthusiastic enough for Coach Jeffrey, who took a step toward Shulman, thrust his sharp coach's chin into Shulman's round stationery store owner's chest, looked upward and repeated, "Are *all* of my Freda Mertzes ready for a good run this morning?"

"Yes, Coach Jeffrey!" Shulman said as loud as he could muster, and the others joined in.

"Thank you," Coach Jeffrey whispered. He then reminded everyone to stay within the interval pace, wished them well, and they started running. Carl with the Timex was in the lead. Then seven or eight others. Maria and Shulman were at the rear. Around the park, out the gate, and onto the wide boulevard. They were supposed to run in a pack. At the very least, in twos. A buddy system assuring that no one who got sick or injured would ever find himself alone.

"Walk!" Carl shouted after three minutes that seemed like three hours. And then "Run!" after what seemed like three seconds.

"What the hell was that?" Shulman asked, trying his darndest to rev up enough energy to get his thick legs moving again. "Hey, Carl, a minute has *sixty* seconds, remember?"

It was not Shulman's intention to make the rest of the group laugh. To him, the walk break was but a tease. Like the momentary relief a very small fish must feel right after it's thrown back into the water right before it's devoured by a very big fish. But they did laugh and that perked him up somewhat. It was a collective laugh of recognition. The kind a comedian gets when mentioning a situation that audiences can relate to. But at the end of the next few walk breaks, his comments received the same diminishing returns any joke gets every succeeding time it's told, while a pain in his stomach was starting to increase at a similar rate.

"What did you eat for breakfast?" Maria asked during their walk break.

"Nothing," was Shulman's honest answer. "I wasn't very hungry."

"You should always eat before a run. Otherwise you get cramps. What did you eat for dinner last night?"

"Everything," was Shulman's understatement. "I was kind of hungry."

Paula had warned him. They were at the Old Homestead, New York's oldest steak house, with the statue of a cow on top of the awning. And, as it worked out, that statue was just about the only thing that Shulman didn't consume that evening. Another couple, Joy and David Simon, had made their way downtown with them after the show (a musical about the making of a musical, which included three songs about three songs they were going to sing) to put a little distance between themselves and the crowds that were due to descend upon the restaurants in the Theater District.

"Aren't you running in the morning?" she whispered after Shulman gave his order to a waiter who had trouble keeping up with him.

"Yes. That's why I'm not having any red meat. It has a tendency to lay around my stomach and loiter for a while," he mumbled through an exceptionally long breadstick.

"And a dozen cherrystone clams, a salad with blue cheese dressing, and a three-and-a-half-pound lobster stuffed with crabmeat is going to make a quicker exit?"

"The blue cheese is on the side," Shulman pointed out.

"What difference does that make?" she asked in a tone traditionally reserved for imbeciles.

At that moment, it dawned on both of them that it had been quite a while since they'd paid any attention to the Simons, who were doing a dreadful job of disguising their discomfort. So they curtailed the discussion, Shulman ate what he wanted, washed it all down with two iced coffees, went home, and slept without incident.

But now, as he and Maria were putting more and more distance between themselves and everyone in front of them by going slower and slower, the battle that was raging inside Shulman's substantial belly made him try to remember whether he'd removed the clams from their shells before eating them or if that's what the little guys were hurling at the three-and-a-half-pound lobster that Shulman was now certain was still alive.

"I really haven't known you for that long," Maria said. "But why do I get the feeling that you usually look a lot better than this?"

Shulman saw Maria's face and became concerned since it bore the same expression presidents usually have when they announce they're sending relief to a Central American country that just had an earthquake.

"Why don't you sit down for a few minutes?" Maria more than suggested.

They were approaching the turnaround. The midpoint in the run where everyone did just that. Turned around and started heading back toward the park. Volunteers were stationed there dispensing water, oranges, and words of encouragement. There was also a curbside bench that Maria was gesturing toward that Shulman, whose bent-over posture suddenly made him a dead ringer for the number 7, dismissed as unnecessary.

It was his sincere feeling that, despite all evidence to the contrary, he'd be able to walk this off until the pain subsided, and then resume his run.

"But I . . . don't want . . . to slow you . . . down," he told her between attempts to introduce oxygen into his lungs. "So if . . . you want to . . . feel free to . . . and I'll just . . ."

"Hey, I'm your buddy," she reminded him and stayed by his side. And together the buddies walked. Slowly. "That's it, small steps," she said. To the turnaround. Slowly. "Feeling any better?" Around the loop. The pain was not as severe. Slowly. He grabbed a cup of water. "Sip it slowly. You'll cramp up." He sipped it. Slowly. Took a slightly longer stride. "There you go." Feeling better. Starting to straighten up. The 7 was slowly becoming a 1. "Not too fast. You don't want to rush this thing. Got to ease back into it."

Enter the girl with the tattoo.

Blond. Medium height. Heading in the same direction Shulman was now going since the turnaround. She passed him. He looked up. Saw the butterfly peeking out above the band of her pink running shorts. And took off.

According to Shulman's upbringing, tattoos were indelible pictures worn only by sailors and men on death row. So the fact that vogue now had them adorning body parts, in plain view, of athletes, supermodels, and bank presidents was a fashion statement as unfathomable to him as if the current trend were to hang curtains from one's lips. But this image of a monarch butterfly that was intended to live below the pants line and only saw the light of day thanks to the movement of those very cheeks from whence it came fascinated Shulman to the point where it involuntarily drew his entire being in her direction. At her speed. Leaving the faithful Maria in the dust. Passing the faster members of his pace group. Passing the faster members of faster-pace groups. Almost bowling over an elderly man walking his dog. Separating a nurse from the wheelchair she was pushing. And somehow causing a pileup that involved bicycles, a scooter, and passengers getting off a bus.

There appeared to be no stopping him. His desire to see if below the tattoo of the butterfly there were also tattoos of the egg, larvae, and caterpillar that it evolved from took on a life of its own. The blood had rushed to his head and, not unlike a race-horse that will keep running until it drops dead, Shulman kept running until he threw up. Until the landfill he'd consumed the night before could no longer withstand the spin cycle and wanted out. Which brought Shulman's newfound hobby as a lepidopterist to a grinding halt. Whereupon he bent over. The 1 bypassing the 7 and going directly to a 9.

And the forsaken Maria happening to catch up to him just in time for her to hold his oversize head while whatever was left of the delicious sea and plant life he'd had at the Old Homestead came splashing out onto a row of unsuspecting azalea bushes.

"So?" Paula asked later. "Was the blue cheese still on the side?"

"Okay. You were right. I ate too much. There, I said it. Happy?"

Back at home. About an hour after Paula had picked him up because he was too weak to drive. An entry in her journal would reveal this to be Shulman's second Sunday of training as well as the second Sunday she spent looking down at her husband from the edge of a bathtub.

"Well, if it makes you feel any better, you do look like you've lost some weight," she said while ringing out still another wash-cloth awaiting its turn to do a stint on Shulman's forehead.

"I'd be surprised if I didn't, considering what I deposited onto those poor azalea bushes. I think I saw some of our wedding cake."

The spewed volume was, for the record, the talk of all the run-ners upon their return to the park. Some of them spoke of revisit-ing those defiled azaleas with cameras for fear that future audiences would question their credibility without visual corrob-oration. But if there was a silver lining to this episode (if, in fact, the terms "silver lining" and "vomit" could conceivably coexist in the same episode) it was that Shulman now realized the full extent that this marathon commitment was going to imply. His diet would have to undergo a dramatic rethinking and those weekday practice runs would definitely have to be incorporated into his life. This was a certainty. The only question remaining was whether he would actually make that commitment.

"I'll do whatever I can to make it easier for you," Paula assured him later, after the bath and his rather difficult extraction from the tub. She even gave him a cup of hot tea, along with a promise that it would serve as a preemptive peace offering in the event his embattled digestive system found anything left that it could possibly expel.

"If you want, I can stock the refrigerator with fruits and cut vegetables," she continued. "And I'll get rid of all of that ice cream and candy we've got so you won't have to live with the temptation."

"Okay . . ." he responded with nothing that even resembled enthusiasm. "But what about you? You love those things."

She did. And since she was blessed with one of those bodies exempt from weight gain, this would indeed be a sacrifice on her part.

"What will *you* do?" he asked.

"Move out."

He laughed. She could still catch him off guard and make him laugh a lot.

"Any idea where you'll be moving to?" he continued.

"Coach Jeffrey's house."

She'd always had that ability. It's what attracted him to begin with. And when times were tough between them, it's what he missed the most. Even more than the sex.

Before Paula there were several others, so he knew the difference. And if things between them ever did end, as much as it would hurt, he knew that the physical chemistry could probably be found elsewhere. But that night when he got into bed, when she was already lying there, facing away from him, reading a catalogue, with the back of her nightgown pulled slightly up and her panties pulled slightly down so he could get a clear view of the temporary tattoo of a butterfly she'd gotten at Paramus Mall that afternoon, Shulman was convinced that he would have an incredibly hard time finding someone who could make him laugh as much as she did.

Mile 6

Shulman Gets Mad at God

June 20

Dear

As incredible as this may sound, I am training to run the New York Marathon November 7th. I joined a group that calls for us to run a little further each week with the expectation of being able to run 26 miles five months from now.

I'm doing this because the money raised through sponsorship goes to AIDS Project New Jersey — a leading provider of AIDS services in the tri-state area. That's why any donation you feel comfortable making would be most appreciated. I have enclosed my pledge form and a return envelope for you to make a donation on my behalf.

Thanks for supporting me in this monstrous undertaking. As I chug along the streets of Staten Island, Brooklyn, Queens, the Bronx, and Manhattan on November 7th, I'll know that your compassion and generosity helped me along the way.

> *Sincerely,*
> *Shulman*

The letter took ten minutes to write but more than two weeks for Shulman to decide to whom he should mail copies. Asking people for money, even for a charitable cause, was something he never felt comfortable doing. A hesitance dating back many Halloweens ago when, instead of actually collecting money for UNICEF, young Shulman found it so much easier to avail himself of any stray currency he found at the bottom of his mother's pocketbook and donate it in the names of those very neighbors he *would* have collected from. This way everyone was a winner. Those famished Biafran kids got money his mom would never miss, his neighbors got credit for contributions they never made, and he got to appreciate how fortunate he was to live in a country where people gave out so much more candy to trick-or-treaters who also didn't hit them up for UNICEF money.

"Should I send a letter to the Hoppers?" he asked Paula.

"I thought you didn't like the Hoppers," she reminded him. "I thought you said he was a big blowhard and that if you were married to her you'd purposely commit a felony so you could hang yourself in your jail cell."

"That's true." He had said that about the Hoppers. He said it less than an hour after the Hoppers had come to Shulman's house, eaten Shulman's food, then proceeded to bore the shit out of the rest of Shulman's guests when they passed out Xeroxed copies of their daughter Rachel's report card and spoke as if the founding fathers themselves would sit up and applaud if they heard about the uncanny method that Rachel invented to memorize the thirteen original colonies. "But one thing has nothing to do with the other," Shulman concluded. "This money's for charity. It's not like we're asking the Hoppers to give us money so we can build a pool."

"Fine. Then how about the Gordons?"

"No," Shulman answered with no particular emphasis.

"Why not?"

"Because the Gordons are horrible people. Much worse than the Hoppers. They may even be worse than the Hitlers."

"But you just said—" was all she was able to get out.

"I mean, say what you will about the Hitlers. Sure, they had their faults. But at least they had the decency not to come into our store, fuck their brains out in one of the aisles during a storm, and then take their business elsewhere."

Twenty-two letters went out the next day. Shulman considered it to be a first wave. More names could be added later, of course. The minimum amount he had to raise to qualify for the trip to New York City was $2,600 so he decided that he'd keep an eye on his pledge total and make adjustments if necessary.

"Twenty-six hundred dollars to go to Manhattan? What'd they do? Raise the toll on the George Washington Bridge?" Paula asked him.

"No. Every year the charity attaches itself to a race in a different city. Like last year, they ran in the Chicago Marathon. And a portion of that money always goes toward an airplane ticket and a hotel. But this year, even though it's in New York, they'd like everyone to raise the same amount so they can reach an overall goal they're shooting for," he explained.

But perhaps the most surprising issue was whether he should

request donations from his family. Paula opposed the suggestion with a vehemence that startled him.

"Why set yourself up for disappointment?" she asked. "You already know they won't acknowledge it."

"I do?" This happened a lot. Her assuming that he already knew the answer to a question he never even knew to ask.

"Oh, come on . . ."

"It's not like they can't afford it," Shulman argued. "They're all doctors, for God's sake. They can check the box that says twenty-five dollars for all I care. It's the thought that counts."

The look on Paula's face, the one where the eyes rolled and eventually took the rest of her head with them, told him that this conversation was not worth continuing. That the subject matter was too obvious, and that this was one of those discussions she had no desire to reprise.

Shulman knew she was trying to protect him. And he loved her for it—at the same time hating that he still needed such protection. He thought he would've been immune to all old hurts by now; the same way you can't catch certain diseases after you've already had them. He'd guessed wrong.

Paula's role had always been tricky when it came to his family. From the day they met her. (It was Thanksgiving. And a nervous Paula, in an attempt to ingratiate herself to her new boyfriend's family, stayed up late the night before and baked a pumpkin pie. A fresh, homemade pumpkin pie that Shulman's mother took one look at, eloquently dismissed as "a plate of cat puke," and then stared down anyone at the dinner table who even thought about choosing it over the apple pie that she had bought at a local supermarket.) But, much to her congenital good fortune, Paula was born to different parents. So while she had the luxury of having only intermittent contact with her in-laws and enough time between visits to work on growing a thicker skin, the damage done to Shulman was deep-rooted and harder to shake.

To a person who sells greeting cards, the shelf life of any holiday is about three weeks. That's how much time he spends surrounded by pictured themes and inscribed good wishes before the actual day arrives, passes, and is then remanded to storage in favor of an occasion that will supplant it a few weeks hence. So while an average customer may not give Thanksgiving much thought until a few days before that Thursday, the holiday-card seller has been living with it since the day after Halloween. And that selection still available to the panicked, last-minute Valentine's shopper exists only because some proprietor started living with different-size hearts and cupids and sonnets once the Christmas stuff got put away in January.

So there's always a holiday presence in a stationery store. One celebration politely segueing into the next. Most of which are universally acknowledged. And some that time has repeatedly proven to be absurd (in over a quarter century of business, Shulman had yet to sell one "Happy Flag Day to You and Yours" card). But on a level specific to each store owner, these Hallmarked occasions also resurrect personal remembrances. Some cherished, others long forgotten. Still others are painful and buried. For these retailers, immersed in celebrations of mothers and goblins and Jesus and dead presidents, holiday cards have the mysterious power to undermine all their efforts to protect themselves from recalling and revisiting the unpleasant past.

For Shulman, the worst of such memories were sparked by Jewish New Year cards. It started every August, during the summer lull between Fourth of July and Labor Day cards (a blessed two months marked only by birthday and anniversary cards). Because the Hebrew calendar is beholden to a lunar cycle that renders it out of step with its January-to-December counterpart, there is always a variance as to when the new year will fall. When merciful, it comes as early as the first week of September. But when the moon's orbit takes a particularly lazy route it can occur a full month later—in total defiance of the three-week rule and taunting Shulman that much longer with the memory of an incident that occurred when he was ten. It was here in Brooklyn. It was the day that Shulman got punched in the head by an Orthodox rabbi.

When he was a little boy, Shulman's parents made him go to Hebrew school. Five afternoons a week. Most probably to satisfy *their* parents, who, having emigrated from prewar Eastern Europe, found salvation but now feared assimilation. So Shulman went. Sunday through Thursday. Where elderly men who knew nothing about growing up in America tried to impart ancient wisdom to young children who wished they were outside playing. Or dead. It was during this time of the year, just after the High Holidays, that that week's Bible portion featured Abraham. And his son Isaac. And God's (shall we say eccentric?) request that Abraham escort Isaac to the base of a mountain, take out a knife, and kill him. And Abraham (shall we say shockingly?) agreeing to this until God stepped in at the last second and stopped him.

Rabbi Rosenbaum's question was, "What does this story tell us about Abraham?"

The answer the rabbi was looking for was, "That he had faith in God."

But the answer Shulman said aloud was, "That he was a real lousy father."

Despite his full beard, Shulman could see the rabbi's face turning red. And that it and the body it sat on top of were now approaching.

"Excuse me, Eliyahu Shulman?"

"The guy was going to kill his son, Rabbi. That's not good parenting."

"But God stopped Abraham once he showed his faith."

"Yeah, but Abraham didn't know that God was going to stop him. So how's that supposed to make Isaac feel? That his own father was willing to slice him to shreds at the drop of a hat?"

"Special," the rabbi answered. "The Torah tells us that Isaac appreciated his father's actions and that he felt special."

"Well, then it sounds to me like Isaac was one big idiot."

In the aftermath, what bothered Shulman most was not the corporal punishment. Or that not one of his classmates came to his aid as the rabbi kept chanting, "Isaac was not an idiot! Isaac was not an idiot!" with each landing blow. Back then, the leeway given to elders in the name of discipline was far greater than it is today. If anything, it was not uncommon for the outrage in such a situation to be directed toward the kid. As in, "Can you imagine how disobedient he must've been to get a *rabbi* that angry?" Those were the rules. That's how the game was played. So young Shulman, like everyone else, went along with it.

However, the part that *did* upset him, the part of this story where betrayal made an appearance, was when his *mother* sided with Abraham. When she declared that given the same set of circumstances, she would have done as Abraham did.

"You would've plunged a knife into me at the base of a mountain?"

"Absolutely," his mother answered without hesitation.

"But I'm your son."

"Yes, but he's my God."

In that moment it was hard for Shulman to determine which hurt more, his mother's words or the unwavering conviction with which she pronounced allegiance to a deity who would have the need to put someone to such a test. Is this what faith was? Sub-mission to an insecure God with the hope that he'll say, "Just kid-ding," before it's too late?

"If I was God," Shulman said at the time, "I would've had a lot more respect for Abraham if he said, 'No, I'm not going to do it.' I would've been impressed with how much the guy loved his son."

"Oh, and I'm sure Abraham had nothing better to think about than how he could impress *you*," his mother could not have said more sarcastically.

And there Shulman sat. In the living room. Silently praying that the other shoe wouldn't drop. A ten-year-old boy who had little to his name but was willing to give it all just to hear his dad say that he agreed with him. That a father's love for his children was unequaled. And the mere suggestion of doing anything other than protecting those children, no matter whom the request came from, was unthinkable.

"Dad . . . ? How about you? How do *you* feel about this?"

Shulman was confident. He didn't plead. He kept it simple, not whiny. Babies whined. Not ten-year-old men. Shulman had teed it up perfectly for him. This was going to be easy. Sure, Dad was a man of few words. Words were Mom's department. But this really didn't require a lot of words. All he had to do was look at his son and say what he felt—that it was not a good thing to agree to pierce your child with a dagger no matter who asked you to do it.

Come on, Dad. Please stop staring at the floor.

Shulman's father lifted his head.

That's it. Now look at me.

His father's eyes blinked a few times before settling on his son.

Great. And then another encouraging sign. *He's smiling at me!* Now all that was missing were the words. *Come on, Dad. You can do it. Just a few words to make your boy feel a lot better. Please?* And then, finally . . .

"It's getting late. What do you say you go upstairs and get ready for bed?"

". . . Sure, Dad."

Alone in his room, Shulman felt like crying. So he did. And when he was finished, he closed his eyes and promised that if he ever had children he would make sure that they never felt as lonely as he did right then.

Mile 7

Shulman and Garfunkel

"Six hours and two minutes?" asked an incredulous Shulman. "How's that possible?"

Austin, the high school kid who worked at Shulman's part-time because he was saving up for a car, sat behind the counter with a pen and pad. And a small calculator. As well as one of those multiplication tables found on the inside cover of a black-and-white composition book.

"I'm sorry, Mr. Shulman," he said with corroborative certainty. "But no matter what method I use, it still comes out the same. That at your current pace of thirteen and a half minutes a mile, a person could watch the movie *Titanic* twice in less time than it will take you to complete a marathon."

"My God . . ."

"Or fly from New York to Seattle."

"Jesus . . ."

"Or, like, if I went to bed at midnight, and that was the exact time the race started, I could get a full night's sleep, wake up totally refreshed and maybe even have some orange juice, and you'd still be running."

"Okay, Austin."

"Maybe even a three-minute egg. As a matter of fact, during the time you're running, I can actually make a hundred and twenty consecutive three-minute eggs."

"Austin, I get it."

"Sorry, Mr. Shulman. I was just trying to give this whole thing some perspective. I mean, I think it's terrific what you're doing, but my grandfather had a heart transplant and the operation took only five hours."

Lately, the need for hired help in itself was questionable. There were days when Shulman had to actually invent things for the kid to do. But Shulman liked Austin. He was a sweet boy. And his dad had died about a year ago so . . .

"I appreciate it, Austin. Now can you please do me a favor and unpack the carton that came in this morning?"

"I already did."

"Really?"

"Those pens that still write even when you're upside down like the astronauts?"

"Yeah, the Space Pens."

"See?" Austin pointed to the glass display case that housed a wide variety of pens. A specialty at Shulman's. Modern and antique. Ballpoint and fountain. Some were simply writing implements. Others flirted with the status of jewelry. And there, in the corner of the middle shelf, Shulman saw a half dozen small pens invented by a man named Paul C. Fisher, whose nitrogen refills did not depend on gravity to operate, which made them perfect for the weightlessness of the *Apollo* missions or doing crossword puzzles while lying on your back in bed.

"I put the rest of them in the drawer underneath," Austin continued. "Is there anything else you'd like me to do, Mr. Shulman?"

"Just watch the store. I'll be back in a few minutes."

Despite having suffered the indignity of what everyone in all of the running groups were now referring to as "Vomit Day," Shulman still didn't make the commitment, that is, the total commitment, to his training for several more weeks. So until that time, just about every aspect of the program Coach Jeffrey urged all of them to follow went totally ignored. "Two practice runs during the week"? Shulman didn't do them. "Low-sodium diet"? Shulman loved salty food. "Keep drinking water until you hear sloshing in your stomach"? Shulman only drank water after he ate tons of salty food. The sole part of the training that Shulman was religiously adhering to was the Sunday-morning practice sessions, which under the ever-watchful eye of his buddy Maria, he managed to slog through. But as those runs grew incrementally longer, they began to present an unforeseen challenge.

In short, Shulman was now convinced that he was going to need some help surviving the *boredom* of a six-hour and two-minute run. All skeletal and muscular wear and tear notwithstanding, Shulman was at a loss as to what he should be thinking about while he was running—aside from wondering if each labored step he took was going to be his very last on this planet. Or if there was anything he could personally do to make time speed up during the three minutes of running and then make it stop altogether during those one-minute walk breaks.

But in the event that he would not be able to find any loopholes in those laws of relativity Albert Einstein so eloquently spoke of (pretty much cementing his reputation as being the smartest person who ever lived), Shulman knew he would need another diversion. Something to get lost in. A place for his mind to go while his body dealt with its own struggles.

So Shulman exited his store, turned right, and started walking. It had been a while since he'd been outside for any stretch of time during business hours. Even lunches had been reduced to a quick trip to the pizza place two doors down, and then eating the slices back behind his own counter. Or maybe sending Austin out to Squires, the kosher deli in the heart of Fort Lee, for sandwiches. But this mission was different. It was personal. Decisions were going to have to be made and he couldn't delegate. So, as rare a sight as it had grown to become, the same man who somewhere along the line had changed from "Shulman" to "the old guy from the stationery store" was walking. Past the 1 Hr. Photo that used to be a bakery, and the supermarket that used to be a grocery, and the Gap that was once a bookstore, and the Borders that was once a clothing store, and an ATM that used to be a bank, and a big Blockbuster that used to be a much smaller Blockbuster. For the most part, it was an anonymous walk, with only a few hints of recognition from those who noticed him. Those half smiles passersby offer when they think they know you but have trouble identifying you because you're not in the place they know you from. The place you're supposed to be. How strange, Shulman thought, to be just a few steps away and so out of context.

But he kept walking. Past the salon where women had their hair and nails done. Past the pet salon where dogs had their hair and nails done. Then past the window of Tower Records, up to its front door, through its front door, past the signs that said NEW AGE and RAP/HIP-HOP. Past the kid with pink hair and a ring in his lip. Past the girl with no hair and what he would've sworn was a small fire extinguisher in her neck. To the back of the store. Along the wall. The section marked ROCK, POP, AND SOUL. Where Shulman took out a blue spiral memo pad and one of the new Fisher Space Pens and started writing.

The idea of listening to music while running was not Shulman's. He'd noticed at the Sunday-morning sessions that an increasing number of the volunteers were showing up with headsets connected to a portable source. He even gave it a shot himself but his attempt to get lost in the sounds of a tiny FM radio proved to be something less than successful. The radio, one of those lightweight models about the size of a domino that Paula picked up for him at the Sharper Image (a high-tech novelty store where he once purchased a toenail clipper that had a compass) worked well in his house, with volume and tone clarity that were truly remarkable. How such a tiny instrument could actually receive songs coming from God knows where was a mystery that Shulman could appreciate but never understand. What was even harder for him to understand was how the only local station that wasn't blistering with static once he took it outdoors was a Spanish one that featured a Sunday-morning evangelist screaming *"¡Dios mío!"* like there was no mañana. Then after a number of spectacularly futile attempts to coax the damn thing into playing something audible from this side of the Atlantic by holding it at different angles, shaking it, and even smacking it a few times in the off chance that it would jolt the Spanish preacher into saying something in English, Shulman's next moment of audio-technological appreciation came when he saw just how far a small, lightweight radio could be sailed into a forest after hurled by a frustrated, overweight jogger.

So his decision to control the programming was a logical one.

The only question now was what to listen to. For so many years, he had tried so hard to tolerate, understand, and embrace the music his kids were listening to. Three white middle-class children rapping about ghetto life, cop killings, and "teaching that motherfucker a lesson,/by holding down his bitch and doin' some messin'."

"I don't get it," he would tell Paula.

"Stop trying," she told him. "It's their music."

"Oh, come on, honey. Didn't you want your parents to like what you were listening to?"

"Not really. I wanted them to respect it. And to not belittle it. But I didn't want it to go any further than that. I had no interest in Frank Sinatra. He was their music. I wanted to have mine and it made me cringe every time my mom would tell me how much she liked Bobby Stewart."

"Who's Bobby Stewart?"

"That's what she used to call Rod Stewart."

"Why?"

"I'm not sure," Paula answered while still shuddering at the recollection. "But my guess is that it was for pretty much the same reason my father insisted on pronouncing his name Bruce Springstine."

Shulman understood all too well. While growing up he lived through the horror of having a father who would seize upon a lyric and belt it out in situations where singing was, by all accounts, uncalled for. A kind of musical Tourette's syndrome that would fracture the silence of an otherwise peaceful dinner when, without warning, he'd look up from his meal, croon the words "Sugar Pie Honey Bunch," and then go back to eating. Or the times when the teenage Shulman would be studying for an exam and the bedroom door would fly open, followed by his dad sticking his head in, making eye contact with him, singing "Help me, Rhonda, help help me, Rhonda," winking, and then closing the door.

So Paula was right. His parents had theirs. As did his kids. So what better time than now to reclaim his own music? Shulman's Greatest Hits. Six hours and two minutes of pet sounds to be fed directly into his memory and heard only by him. The notes that scored the theme to all that's happened. In effect, his most secret biography. With assistance from two guys from Queens.

When Shulman first heard the story, he paid very little attention to it. He was far too young to appreciate it when his dad came home one night and told of the bar mitzvah a fellow worker had attended the previous Saturday in Forest Hills. Of a boy whose voice was so beautiful that a crowd had gathered on the steps outside the temple so they too could hear him sing. And since the name of the boy was hardly the relevant point, it was neither asked nor given. So it wouldn't be until many years later, when the anecdote was recounted in *Rolling Stone,* that Shulman learned that the boy with the voice was Art Garfunkel.

In the 1960s, certain people were cast as major characters in the ongoing drama that was the daily life of New York City. John Lindsay got to play the handsome mayor. Adam Clayton Powell the angry guy from Harlem. Gloria Steinem was the smart female role model who was pretty and wore big glasses. Bella Abzug was the smart female role model who was ugly and wore big hats. Nelson Rockefeller was rich. Mickey Mantle was God. Joe Namath was cool. The new New York Mets stunk. And comedian Alan King said the same things everyone's dad said except he got to say them on *The Ed Sullivan Show.*

All of them lived in, played in, represented, or joked about

New York. But to a kid growing up on Long Island in those days, Simon and Garfunkel *were* New York. Two friends from Queens. One was short. The other was even shorter. Homegrown and unashamed. Feelings set to harmony. Simon wrote them, he and his pal sang them, and an entire generation said that was how they felt too. The Beatles were more fun. And the Stones threw a much better party. But Paul Simon had the uncanny ability to accurately assign lyrics to every one of Shulman's moods. Lyrics that Shulman regarded as poetry. And plagiarized when he was on the verge of failing a poetry-writing class in college. All semester long the ancient professor, a Dr. Nora Rent who looked as if she'd had affairs with at least two Elizabethans, kept dismissing Shulman's poems as incoherent drivel unworthy of the red ink it took to write, "God, this stinks!" at the top of the pages he wrote them on. So, he handed in the words to Simon's "The Boxer" as his final journal entry, confident that the old crone wouldn't recognize the song and have him booted out of school with a thrust that would send his body hurtling toward the Mekong Delta. What he couldn't anticipate, however, was how awed she'd be by Shulman's sudden burst of brilliance. So much so that she insisted he come up and read his masterpiece to the rest of the class. Try as he did to beg off (at one point claiming he felt the onset of dyspepsia) the teacher ultimately prevailed and Shulman feared only the worst as he made his way toward the front of the room, the lyrics to "The Boxer" in hand, with Dr. Nora Rent's enthusiastic "Excellent!" written in the margin next to them. A quick glance at the time informed him, with forty minutes left in the period, that there wasn't even a glimmer of hope of his stalling and, in effect, running out the clock. No, it was obvious that nothing shy of an act of God (indeed a perfect opportunity for the Lord to reach into his old bag of tricks and yell, "Stop!") was going to save him from having to recite the words he'd copied from the liner notes on the cover of the biggest-selling album of the year. So he cleared his throat, took one last look over at Dr. Nora Rent, was disappointed to see that she was still alive, and began:

"I am just a poor boy, though my story's seldom told,
I have squandered my resistance
For a pocket full of mumbles, such are promises,
All lies and jest still a man hears what he wants to hear,
And disregards the rest," Shulman said.

Holding his breath, he then permitted his gaze to drift upward, over the top of the page, and out at the kids in the class. Some of whom were friends. All of whom were peers with record collections whose jaws had dropped considerably since he started reading. At the same time that Dr. Nora Rent was beaming. Prideful of her new find. This young poet whose gritty take of life on city streets that was making her students' jaws drop considerably since he started reading. Her expression also conveyed that she fully expected Shulman to keep reading:

"When I left my home and my family I was no more than a boy,
In the company of strangers,
In the quiet of the railway station, runnin' scared.
Laying low, seeking out the poorer quarters
Where the ragged people go,
Lookin' for the places only they would know . . ."

And that's when it happened. To Shulman's supreme horror, it was precisely at this moment that all the other students in the class, who'd obviously had more than their fill of this nonsense, spontaneously started singing the next lyric:

"Lie la lie, lie la lie lie lie lie lie, lie la lie,
  Lie la lie lie lie lie lie lie lie lie lie . . ."

Not even a fisherman would've been able to identify (much less tie) the knot that instantly appeared in Shulman's stomach. A twisted duodenal maze about the size of an avocado pit that would not only rival the diamond as the hardest element known to man, but would make it beg for mercy should the two ever meet in a dark alley. However, the most frightening reaction, by far, was the one that this musical outburst elicited from his esteemed professor.

"It's inspiring, isn't it?" said Dr. Nora Rent, whose fossil-like skeleton was now dipping and swaying and gyrating in what were either rhythmic movements or epilepsy. Either way, once the old lady finally stopped shaking, she gave Shulman an A for Paul Simon's efforts and encouraged him to continue with his writing.

So now, standing in an aisle in Tower Records, that's how Shulman's list began. With Simon and Garfunkel. And "The Sounds of Silence" and "I Am a Rock" and "Cecilia." And then Simon without Garfunkel and songs like "Slip Slidin' Away" and "American Tune." He then went up and down the Rock, Pop, and Soul aisles and picked lots of songs by the Beatles and "Start Me Up" by the Stones and tons of Motown songs and "La Bamba" but only by Ritchie Valens and not Los Lobos. There was "Hit the Road, Jack" by Ray Charles and there were Elvis songs but mostly before he got real fat, and Dylan because he started it all, and the Byrds because they sang Dylan's songs a lot nicer than the way Dylan sang them. Eric Clapton sang "Layla" and the Doors sang "Touch Me"; the Eagles sang "Lyin' Eyes," Fleetwood Mac did a lot from *Rumours,* the Who did all of *Tommy,* and the Beach Boys sang "Good Vibrations," which Shulman knew from when it was popular and his kids knew from a Sunkist commercial. Then up the Broadway aisle, with selections from shows like *Hair, Smokey Joe's Cafe,* and *Fiddler on the Roof,* then down the soundtrack aisle, where he chose themes from *The Godfather* and *Rocky,* and *The Big Chill* just in case there were any Stones and Motown songs he had missed. The classics aisle had Beethoven's Ninth Symphony and Lalo's Symphonie Espagnole and a bunch of Hungarian rhapsodies, and the "Toreador Song" from the opera *Carmen* pretty much because it was the only song from the only opera he really knew. Then back to the rock aisle because he remembered that Elton John's "Your Song" was the first song he ever made out to, then to the comedy section, where he selected Carl Reiner and Mel Brooks's *2000 Year Old Man,* Nichols and May, some of Richard Pryor's and Steve Martin's monologues, and Monty Python's "The Lumberjack Song," which was the second song he ever made out to.

Two hours later he was finished. The pages of his blue spiral memo pad were filled. And if he were to purchase all of the CDs that all of these recordings were on, it would cost somewhere in the neighborhood of $2,300. And necessitate his running the 26.2-mile marathon carrying a rather large piece of furniture to hold them all.

"I could burn some CDs for you," Austin told him when he finally got back to the store. Where the kid had done his usual competent job of holding the fort for Shulman. There'd been no calls. No customers. And the only person who had entered the place, a mailman delivering bills, did so while Austin was in the bathroom. The boy was seventeen. Shulman's carried *Playboy.* Ergo, he went to the bathroom a lot.

"That's not a bad idea," Shulman said about the CDs.

"Sure. Just give me a list of the songs you want and I'll pull them off the Internet for you. That way you'll be able to get everything you want on maybe five or six discs."

At last Sunday's training session, Coach Jeffrey had said that once they started doing longer runs, everyone should carry a water bottle to prevent dehydration. So Shulman had gone to a sporting goods store and bought a belt made especially to hold water bottles. It also had an extra pocket he was now thinking he could keep the discs in.

"Okay," Shulman said, handing Austin the blue spiral memo pad and fifty dollars that he'd grabbed from the cash register.

"Gee, thanks, Mr. Shulman," Austin said while making a fist around the cash that you couldn't cut through with pruning shears. "So I guess this means I got a raise, huh?"

"And why would you guess that?"

"Well, this should only take me about an hour to do, and for over a year now . . ."

For over a year now Shulman had been paying him $7 an hour to stock shelves, run errands, and jerk off in the bathroom.

"Austin, do you honestly believe that I'm giving you a forty-three-dollar-an-hour raise?"

"At first I couldn't, but then I remembered that you're a very generous man. And the math does speak for itself."

"Austin . . ."

"Then again, it may take me two hours to do this. And then my raise would then be up to twenty-five dollars an hour, which is still pretty splendid of you, Mr. Shulman."

Shulman didn't know Austin while Austin's dad was alive. One day he'd been talking to a customer who was buying a condolence card for a woman who had just lost her husband to cancer. On her birthday, no less. The husband was thirty-eight and the woman had three children. Shulman got her name from the customer, called the woman, introduced himself, and asked if there was anything he could do to help. A few days later, Austin started working for him.

"Tell you what," Shulman said. "I'll burn those CDs myself."

"But I was just kidding, Mr. Shulman," snapped Austin, who was suddenly afraid he'd pushed things too far.

"And as far as that money I just gave you is concerned—"

"I mean it, Mr. Shulman. I forgot to take my meds this morning, so my impulse control—"

"I want you to buy your mother something nice with it. It's her birthday this week, right?"

Mile 8

Howard Lights a Fuse

When Shulman slowed down to grab a cup of water at the mile marker, he was passed by a one-legged runner dressed in a tuxedo. Granted, the man was a lot younger than Shulman and looked like he was in fairly decent shape—although it was hard to get a true read as to how flat his stomach actually was because of the cummerbund. However, the fact remained that the guy was virtually hopping, holding aloft a small bar tray with a fake glass of beer taped to it, and was now beating Shulman in the marathon.

Shulman laughed. And then looked around to see if anyone else at the water station was taking notice of this absurdity. Apparently, they weren't. Or if they were, they displayed their appreciation by ignoring the one-legged hopper in such a way that completely eluded Shulman in its subtlety. So he drank the water, casually tossed the cup aside the way he'd seen marathon runners on television do, set out to catch up with the one-legged guy in the tuxedo, and made a note to tell Maria about this when he saw her again. Which was supposed to be now. Earlier, before the race started, Maria was worried that they were never going to be able to find each other when the men's and women's courses converged at Mile 8. But Shulman assured her that if they both kept up their pace and took the built-in walking breaks the way Coach Jeffrey insisted, they shouldn't have too much trouble getting to the same place at the same time.

Shulman consulted his Timex Ironman watch and did the math. According to the chronometer, it had been one hour and six minutes since *his* race started. And sixty-six minutes divided by eight came to just a little more than the thirteen-minute miles that he and Maria hoped would be their pace. So as he approached the point where Bayridge Parkway appeared diagonally off to his left, with a steady flow of women marathoners rejoining the men at the confluence of Fourth Avenue, Shulman started to look for his running partner.

Maria. Brown eyes. Brownish hair. She had slimmed down considerably during the months of training and become even prettier in the process. In an even more comfortable way. Week after week, as the Sunday runs steadily grew longer, they had gotten to know each other better. Maria would purposely run slower to keep Shulman company as he lagged behind the others. She did most of the talking (she had a lot to say as she ran toward a brother she would never see again), and he did most of the listening (because virtually all mammals are physically incapable of forming coherent sentences while gasping for air).

He now tried his best to spot her. He sped up in the event she was exceeding their prescribed pace and was ahead of him. He then took an extended walk break in case she was running slower.

Although they now ran along the same Brooklyn street, a median would separate the men and women for the next few blocks, giving him an unobstructed view as the women runners continued to pour into Bedford-Stuyvesant, home to the largest black community in New York. The setting of Spike Lee's *Do the Right Thing*. An extended path of urban blight interrupted by the hallowed presence of churches. Houses of worship where Shulman saw dozens of congregants exiting from this Sunday morning's services. Families dressed up. Wearing the look one tends to have after conceding to a higher power. The temporary loss of concern. The faith that no matter how bad things may be at the present moment, somehow everything is going to work out because of a relationship with God.

Shulman remembered when he once had a relationship with God.

When Shulman's daughter Erin was five years old, she came down with spinal meningitis. There were seizures. Her temperature reached 106 degrees. The doctor said she was going to die.

It was right there, in that hospital room, that Shulman dropped to his knees and gave God another chance to be a hero. Just as He'd done at the base of that mountain when He saved Isaac. To come in at the last second and say, "Just kidding," to those insidious bacterial agents He'd allowed to invade the body of an innocent young girl. Yes, Shulman had turned away from Him many years before. And called Him insecure because of what He'd put Abraham through. But now, with the full extent of human capability exhausted, Shulman launched an appeal. There were pleas. *I beg you.* Negotiations. *If you spare her, I promise I'll start believing in you again.* And even the most juvenile modes of prodding. *If you're so fucking almighty, let's see you prove it. Come on, Miracle Man! I dare you!*

And while there was ultimately a medical explanation to account for Erin's recovery (she was left with only an imperceptible
but lifelong slur)—Shulman decided he'd play the odds. Just in
case credit was indeed due elsewhere, he *chose* to believe. Out of
gratitude for Erin. It was only right. And not as lonely when he
was at a loss for answers. Sort of like having a constant compan-
ion toward whom you could shrug and say, "I don't know. Ask
Him."

But he drew the line at praying. This he couldn't do. For one
thing, he didn't think it was nice to use the Lord only when He
was needed. It seemed so impolite. Like phoning an old acquain-
tance only because you know he has tickets to the World Series. In
Shulman's mind, this arrangement seemed to be fair to both of
them. God would have Himself a new fan, but one who wasn't
going to keep pestering Him for favors. God would oversee the
health of those whom Shulman loved, and Shulman would handle
everything else by himself. This was the deal that Shulman ham-
mered out with the creator of the universe. For the most part, the
same agreement Vito Corleone would've made if he owned a
struggling stationery store.

So when his accountant told Shulman that he was broke, he
was at a loss for emotional options. Or where to go to vent. To
appeal skyward would be a violation of their covenant. Absence
of money was not absence of health, so this dilemma clearly fell
under Shulman's jurisdiction. And to share this news with Paula
was something he was not prepared to do. Not yet, anyway. His
role was to keep such burdens *away* from her. To provide security
and peace of mind. To create and, more important, sustain a life
they could comfortably live within. As opposed to telling her that
she should go rent the movie *Oliver!* so she and the kids could
bone up on how to beg for food and pick people's pockets.

"Define 'broke,' " he asked the accountant. Howard. Dedi-cated. Straightforward. Pure business. A nice guy who once sneezed and numbers flew out of his nose.

"Broke is when a person has no money," Howard answered.

"And you're telling me that I have no money."

"Why would this come as a shock to you? I've been warning you about this for—"

"Well, I knew there was a cash-flow problem."

"True. That's because you don't have any cash to be flowing. Or even to stagnate. And that's a problem if you have any thoughts about purchasing anything."

"Jesus . . ." was all Shulman was able to get out.

"*You're* in the retail business. You tell *me*. Don't you require customers to pay when they want to walk out of your store with the products you sell there?"

"Not all the time," Shulman answered with only a half smile.

"Yeah, I forgot who I was talking to," Howard replied, shak-ing his head. They'd been together for years. Before Shulman's be-came "Shulman's." During the glory years of multicolored paper clips and the invention of Post-its. And now. Howard had seen it all. And what he hadn't seen, what Shulman didn't tell him be-cause he knew he wouldn't approve, Howard suspected. The free-bies. The markdowns. All the careless examples of Shulman's belief that when goodwill is cast outward, it eventually circles back, carrying its own rewards.

They would argue about everything. Howard called him a dreamer. Shulman called him a cynic. Howard called him "Saint Shulman." Accusing Shulman of acting irresponsibly and saying that he resented being placed in the position of always having to say no to an adult who should know better. Of having to play fa-ther to a man who was only two years his junior. And now it had come to this. The two of them sitting across from each other in a diner. With an eight-columned ledger book reflecting Shulman's finances opened on the table between them.

"You should think about closing the store," Howard said. Without emotion. And with no deference to the irony that the ledger book he was referring to came from Shulman's. Second row. Third shelf. Next to the month-at-a-glance calendar books. Shulman had given it to him last tax season. Along with the Cross pen Howard was holding right now. From the display case to the left of the cash register. How unnerving it was to see them being turned against him to help deliver Howard's bleak message.

"Go out of business?" Shulman asked. He heard his words as they met the air and was surprised at how calm they sounded. Not matter-of-fact. No, more like the monotone of a computerized voice. Or of a prefrontal-lobotomy patient. Freestanding words placed in an order that made Shulman appropriately responsive without betraying any of the heartbreak they were attached to.

"I can't do that, Howard," he said. "I just can't."

"I'm not sure you have a choice anymore," Howard responded. "You're running on fumes as it is. Besides, what could possibly happen that could turn things around? To bring more people through your doors? Really, Shulman. Especially with that new place they're opening in Alpine."

Shulman was aware of this new place. Stationery Land? Stationery Planet? Grand Central Stationery? Something like that. A huge new store in a huge new mall the next town over. The noose was tightening. The final chokehold on the one spot in the world where he always felt safe.

And that's when it happened. It was at that precise moment that Shulman, his desperation swelling, felt the need to take control. Of *something*. A quick inventory revealed children who were doing great except they weren't children anymore. A marriage that was doing great except he stood a better chance of getting laid if his dick were attached to a feng shui catalogue. And a business that was doing great except for the fact that it wasn't doing any business. It was time to reclaim the power he'd assigned to others. After a lifetime of deference, he decided to try his hand at initiative, now that even he didn't buy into the illusion of his strength. With nothing but an excess of time on his hands, he felt his first need was to establish order. A discipline to adhere to. And a goal to strive for.

Running became Shulman's salvation. His escape. The centerpiece of his new order. So, after first pleading with Howard to figure out something, anything, that would keep him afloat while he himself tried to figure out what his next move should be, he ran. A lot. On Sundays with Maria, Coach Jeffrey, and the others. As well as the practice runs, even more often than the suggested two days a week. He ran before he opened the store and he let Austin close up so he could run before dark. And he was doing extremely well: losing weight, eating less, feeling better. Other than his ill-advised experiment when the Heimlich maneuver had to be called upon to dislodge the small flashlight he put in his mouth in an attempt to run after the sun went down, Shulman was quite happy with his new regimen.

Mostly he ran at Fort Lee High School. The same school his children had attended, graduated, and moved on from. How ironic it was that he was now voluntarily circling the same kind of cinder track he'd tried so desperately to get out of running around as a student. A quarter-mile ellipse around a field where summer-league games were being played. "Hit the fat guy and it's a double," a left fielder joked. But Shulman kept running and in just a few weeks was upgraded to a triple because "he's smaller and faster and harder to hit."

He was a lumbering spectacle in shorts, T-shirts from any of the institutions of higher learning he had written checks to, and a New York Mets baseball cap. He'd labored over that one. Not the affiliation. No, they were his team from their start. More human than the vaunted Yankees. No designated hitters to cheapen the game. Much better parking at their stadium. The question, however, was *how* he should wear the cap. Which direction it should point toward once it was perched on top of his head. Nearly a half century of life on the planet had programmed him to have the brim facing forward so it could reduce the sun's glare, display the team's insignia to all who were approaching, and to be just that, a baseball cap. To spin it around would make it a yarmulke. A woolen, one-size-fits-all skullcap replete with sweatband and Mets logo announcing who he rooted for to all who ran behind him. And given the speed at which he ran, the odds were that there'd be very few who would fall into that category. He gave it a shot, though. Once. He put the cap on backward, found a mirror, and determined that no matter how he angled the thing it looked like he was wearing a small frying pan on his head. So he turned it around and that was that.

He became a fixture down at the field. Even a mascot of sorts. One team considered it a good omen if they came to bat when Shulman was starting an odd-numbered lap, while a young girl actually calculated that her soccer team was undefeated on days when Shulman wore the University of Michigan shorts that had GO BLUE embroidered on the back. They watched him run for three minutes and walk for one. Slowly increasing his distance, as well as the amount of time he spent on the track, which they measured not in terms of hours and minutes, but by their own game's standard of innings or periods. And they saw him get smaller. Thinner. As if whatever was living inside of all that flesh was starting to emerge from its own internment. Slowly. Method-

ically. He would never be skinny. Or wiry, lanky, gaunt, lean, or
sinewy. Given his bone structure and basic body type, the most he
could realistically aspire to be was a large man who used to be a
larger man before he started running.

Though nothing in Shulman's nonrunning world was changing,
he began to feel a difference. It was hard to explain, even to himself, why things didn't seem as bad as they should have. But they
didn't. Perhaps it was this new sanctuary he'd created. Where
panic was tempered and fear was no longer quite as scary. Now
that he was shedding pieces of that Other Shulman, the running
was becoming easier. And as the running got easier, he ran longer
and his body chemistry kept changing. And though he had no answers to just about anything, he became more optimistic about
everything because the questions didn't seem as hard. And when
that young girl's soccer team made the play-offs, she asked Shulman if he could please come and wear the shorts that had GO
BLUE embroidered on the butt. He did and the team won the first
round. She asked again, he wore them again, and they won the
second round. Then the semifinals. But then his car broke down
on his way to the championship game. Something under the hood
that shouldn't have been spewing black liquid was doing just that
and it was raining and AAA said they'd only be twenty minutes
but after an hour they still hadn't arrived. An accident on the Pal-
isades Parkway either took precedence or inhibited their trucks
from getting through, depending on which dispatcher he spoke to
every time he called. All he knew was that the game must've been
in at least the second period by now and that he'd made a promise. And though he hadn't been naked in the back of a parked car
since his twelfth date with Paula (*Blazing Saddles* at the Westbury
Drive-in), that's where he went, changed into his running clothes,
and took off. In the rain. Along wet streets. Through someone's

yard and across a footbridge before entering the gates of the soccer field, where, like an overweight Phidippides barreling into Athens, he proceeded to circle the soggy cinder track with the score tied 0–0 with just a few minutes to go in the game. The young girl saw him, alerted her teammates, and despite the fact that a portion of his drenched University of Michigan running shorts found its way up his butt crack, causing the o in GO and the B in BLUE to virtually disappear so he now had the word GLUE embroidered on his ass, the girls got the message, scored a goal, won the game, climbed on their mascot like he was a playground structure, and kept yelling, "Thanks, mister," until the weight of the now champion Fort Lee Mustangs girls soccer team caused Shulman's body to pitch forward and landed him face-first into a puddle on the dirt part of the sideline.

Mile 9

The call came to the store. It was a Saturday morning in late August that was otherwise routine. Unseasonably chilly with a slight drizzle. The kind of dampness that would make Shulman's arthritic grandmother, though dead for several years, still wring her hands and curse the landlord. When Austin told him who was on the phone, Shulman thought he was kidding.

"No, really, Austin. Who is it?"

Austin, whose fascination with the Fisher Space Pen had escalated to the point where he now did crossword puzzles while standing on his head, didn't bother to budge.

"I'm telling you, Mr. Shulman. The guy said his name is Coach Jeffrey. If anything, wouldn't he be the person in this story who's make-believe?"

The little boy inside of Shulman was reacting as if a teacher were seeking him out at home. Sense memories ranging from *What did I do wrong?* to *Wow, I can't believe a person like that is actually taking the time to call me on the telephone!* flashed through his brain.

"Austin, do you really think it makes a good impression if customers walk in and see you upside down?" he asked while reaching for the receiver.

"Absolutely, Mr. Shulman. I can't even think of a better way to show the world how great these pens work."

"Interesting," Shulman said. "And here I thought I was asking a rhetorical question." Then Shulman picked up the phone, said "Hello?" and was surprised to hear sobbing at the other end. "Coach Jeffrey, are you all right?"

"Shulman? Did you hear?"

"Hear what?"

"That soccer team? The one you took the picture with?"

During the celebration following the girls' victory, someone snapped a picture of the team reveling on top of Shulman's fallen body. But how Coach Jeffrey knew about it was beyond him.

"Yes . . . ?" Shulman responded.

"Well, they've been telling everybody about you and the marathon and in the past two days alone we've received five thousand one hundred dollars of donations in your nickname. That's why I'm calling. To thank you."

Nickname?

And by the time the photo ran in the following week's issue of the local newspaper with the caption "Glue Sticks to His Promise," that amount had almost doubled and made him the anonymous darling of the North Bergen County charitable set. A fact made that much more ironic when compared with the paltry

$10 from Paula's dad's gardener (to whom Shulman had given a box of free pens) that had been donated under his own name.

"Honey, isn't that your ass?" Paula asked. They were in bed. At night. She was reading the *Fort Lee Record*—a periodical of perhaps thirty pages including a masthead filled with names of some very snoopy neighbors. He was watching television. *Law & Order*. On a cable channel. He'd seen this episode before. That afternoon. On the same cable channel. It was very shortly after Shulman put a small TV into the back room of the store that he came to the conclusion that this particular cable channel only had five or six different programs, which they kept repeating during the course of any given weekday, never suspecting that any gainfully employed viewer would notice.

"No. No way that ass is attached to me," he answered, hoping she would now drop the subject. Knowing full well she wouldn't.

"Sure it is," she insisted.

Please don't read it to me.

" 'The Mustang players said they were inspired,' " she read, " 'by an unnamed local man who's been training so he can raise money for AIDS in the New York Marathon. Twelve-year-old Lindsay Gilbert voiced the sentiment of her teammates when she said, "We just figured that if a chubby guy like that could have a dream, so could we. I just wish we knew his name so we could thank him properly." ' "

Okay, fine. Now please don't ask me why I didn't tell them my name.

"Why didn't you tell them your name?"

"Tell who my name?"

"These kids."

"I've never seen those kids before in my life."

"But that's your ass!"

"That's not my ass!"

He didn't like lying to her. And he hardly ever did. Okay, maybe an error of omission here and there regarding matters of little consequence. Or occasionally the more brazen falsehood (the time he told her he passed a kidney stone so he wouldn't have to go to her cousin's wedding), but that invariably presented a new set of problems (when he showed Paula the kidney stone and she recognized it as coming from their driveway).

But in this particular instance, well, the scene that Shulman kept replaying was the one when Coach Jeffrey was crying on the telephone—a gay man filled with emotion because people were sending in a lot of money to help a cause affecting his community so much more than their own. And that maybe the outpouring was indeed a gesture of inclusion. A measure of acceptance that said all the fag jokes were just jokes. Told by folks who, when the chips were down, actually cared.

Over the past few Sunday mornings, Shulman had found himself observing this thirty-three-year-old man who called himself Coach Jeffrey. A silhouette arriving at a park when the world was at rest, carrying an armful of placards bearing the names of world-class athletes. He'd lug them from an aged Datsun's trunk to their assigned spots along the grass, then head back to the aged Datsun, where he grabbed pamphlets and literature about the virus they were trying to defeat. Then he'd greet the still-groggy volunteers with an almost songlike "Good morning, my sleepy people" and would repeat it until he was satisfied that enough of them had responded, "Good morning, Coach Jeffrey." His pep talks described them all as heroes. He sent each running group on its way with words of encouragement and was there to offer hugs to every one of them when they returned sweaty and out of breath. And then, like the host of a party that had just ended, he would clean up after all his guests had gone home.

That is what Shulman knew of Coach Jeffrey. That, plus the fact that he himself ran marathons, which went a very long way toward bolstering credibility with the unspoken attitude of "If I can do it, so can you."

What Shulman *didn't* know was that Coach Jeffrey was HIV positive. A fact not revealed until conveyed somewhat off-handedly the previous week by a substitute coach who explained his presence by alluding to Jeffrey's having to go for a few medical tests.

"Did you know that?" he had asked Maria.

"Sure. Everyone knows."

"Oh . . ."

And then this morning. When the figure who set up signs at dawn in a park was sobbing on the phone. A softer, disembodied voice on temporary leave from the role of coach, which was now just coming from a sick man who was saying, "Thank you, thank you, thank you." This disease that never really existed within the guarded borders of Shulman's own world now had a face and a name and Shulman wanted to help *him*. Someone whose problems could not be solved by just adding more customers. Or with the money that continued to be donated in Shulman's secret new nickname. But as the amount kept growing (more than $22,000 by that week's end), Shulman felt that the fund-raising could be dramatically impaired if he came out too early. That there was something about the anonymity of whom they were all sponsoring that helped attract public interest and added a titillation to the collective spirit that was beginning to mount. And he wanted to see just how far this could all go. Suddenly, he was on a mission with a purpose outside himself.

So he lied.

Shulman had a secret. Known only by him and the man who was now scolding him. "Why are you finding this so hard to do?" Coach Jeffrey asked him. "Come on, Shulman. All I'm asking you to do is lean back a little."

They were in the park. About fifteen minutes before the other marathoners-in-training would be assembling for that Sunday's run, which featured a hill. Not dramatically steep. Yet severe enough to warrant a slight change in posture for the purpose of maintaining a center of gravity. But so far, Shulman had done little more than to reaffirm that Sir Isaac Newton was correct—that there *is* a force of gravity. Which he demonstrated twice by tipping over, falling onto the pavement, and rolling backward a few feet. And then a third time when he tipped over, fell onto the pavement, and rolled backward onto Coach Jeffrey's feet.

"Now let's try this once more," Coach Jeffrey suggested. Shulman was upright again. But for how long was debatable as Coach Jeffrey stood beside him with his right hand pressed firmly against the small of Shulman's back.

To Shulman's way of thinking, if Coach Jeffrey was going to be even the symbolic motivation for committing to the rather prodigious efforts he had in front of him, why not tap into the guy to learn the finer points of marathon running? So, at the tail end of their most recent conversation (when Coach Jeffrey called to say that the donations made in Glue's name had now passed the $30,000 mark), Shulman asked if he could have this private session to reduce the chances of his ineptitude being put on display once again. And a grateful Coach Jeffrey, who agreed they stood a better chance of raising more money if Glue's identity remained a mystery and was also a man who liked to undertake the impossible, was only too happy to help.

"The tendency when running uphill is to lean forward and that's wrong," Coach Jeffrey told Shulman as he bent him forward to illustrate his point.

"But I wasn't leaning forward," Shulman tried his best to interject as his upper body was suddenly being yanked in the opposite direction.

"Sit back just a little," Coach Jeffrey said as he steadied Shulman before he fell backward again. "Pretend you're in an easy chair."

"That's what I've been doing. . . ."

"Yes, but I don't recall saying anything about pretending your feet are on top of an ottoman. Listen to me. . . ." Coach Jeffrey said before looking around to make sure no one was within earshot. Shulman noticed that Coach Jeffrey did that a lot. Looking around when he already knew the nearest person was miles away and would need to have ears the size of satellite dishes to pick up what he was saying. But it was more than a mere habit, Shulman thought. It appeared to be a purposeful move. Used to convey something more emotional than confidential, as Coach Jeffrey, now satisfied that he wouldn't be overheard, leaned in to whisper, "Hills are your friends, Shulman."

"Excuse me?"

"They break up the monotony of the flat. But like any other challenge, you have to accept and learn to live with them. And then they'll make you stronger."

Another hesitation. Another glance around. Another whisper. "Shulman?"

"Yes?"

"Promise me you'll learn to love the hills."

Though Shulman had never even come close to entertaining a promise like this before, there was something about the passion with which Coach Jeffrey spoke about hills—spoke about everything, for that matter—that made it seem possible that a person could indeed love such a thing. So he promised. Then Coach Jeffrey further explained how a runner can go from hating hills to actually looking forward to encountering them and using them to his advantage. How to angle backward and take shorter steps to maintain an even cadence.

"And whatever you do, Shulman, I implore you to not look at your feet. That will make you hunch over, which tenses your muscles and hinders your breathing. Pick a spot twenty or thirty yards up the road and run toward it. Like you would with any goal."

Coach Jeffrey then grabbed Shulman's head and gently tossed it back and forth between his hands before tilting it upward. Shulman felt like laughing. He wasn't used to having his head handled in this fashion. As if it were a fresh melon Coach Jeffrey was thinking about buying.

"What kind of work do you do?" Shulman asked. "I mean, when you're not doing this."

"I'm a musician."

"Really?" Shulman said with his sights now trained on the very top of the incline and beyond. "What instrument do you play?"

"The piano. I was with the philharmonic for seven years."

"Oh, really?" replied Shulman, trying not to sound like he was suddenly impressed. "And now?"

Coach Jeffrey smiled before he answered.

"Now, I only do this."

The look in Coach Jeffrey's eyes gave nothing away. Still, something about it made Shulman want to know more. But then cars started pulling into the lot. The other trainees arriving on schedule. His next set of questions for Coach Jeffrey would have to wait.

Meanwhile, "Glue" became a rage. What began as a simple lark suddenly took on a life of its own and had a galvanizing effect on an otherwise fractured suburb. Newfound community pride displayed in the form of donations that kept driving a dollar amount (now at $41,736) higher and higher. Shulman's instinct had been correct. The town of Fort Lee, revived with an injection of common purpose, was abuzz with new conversation made even sexier by the intrigue surrounding the "mystery man's" identity. Theories were plentiful. Everyone had an opinion, or a hunch, or a friend who heard that . . .

As a result, the *Fort Lee Record* immediately launched into an impersonation of *The Washington Post* during the Watergate era by becoming the nerve center of all this activity. Their modest storefront window now sported a hand-painted thermometer that kept track of the growing sum donated in Glue's name. In addition, they spearheaded the effort to reveal his identity by dispatching reporters to the high school track, Glue's last known sighting, in hopes of his return.

Shulman was feeling more like Clark Kent than he'd ever imagined he would at this point in his adult life. But it was fun to have a secret identity. And to have caused something that actually yielded a tangible public effect, once again, on the town he always loved. It had been awhile. Its new vibrancy was his gift.

So to elude the hounds from the local press, he no longer did his practice runs at the high school or anywhere in Fort Lee, for that matter. Instead, he opted for a dirt track that encircled a private golf course about a half hour north on Route 9W. Twice a week he drove there. Then three times. Then four. By himself. This went on for the next few weeks and it was ideal. No one from the press bothered him and, in time, he actually grew to enjoy the process of retreating deeper into himself. Of allowing the music in his headphones to take him away. Strangely, he didn't miss being at the store, where Austin was logging more and more idle hours. Even stranger, he didn't miss the silent bed where the nightly pile of architectural and interior design magazines was now taking on Berlin Wall–size dimensions.

He worked hard at concentrating on what Coach Jeffrey insisted would one day come naturally. The proper breathing. Posture. Strides that lead with the heel. So much focus was aimed at his body's mechanics that, on this particular day, at first he didn't even notice the guy who was approaching. It was a runner coming from the opposite direction. Nothing remarkable on the face of it. Hundreds of joggers ran along that same beaten dirt path, and the fact that this particular person was running counterclockwise was also of little note as there was no designated correct direction to run. People ran whichever way they chose and simply stayed to their right so as not to collide with oncoming foot traffic. But as *this* particular runner came closer, what struck Shulman was the man's uncanny resemblance to him. His coloring. The same unfortunate body type. The stiff movement of the legs that made him look like a former ballplayer running out of the dugout after being introduced on Old-Timers Day. And as they narrowed the gap between them, detail contracted into focus, revealing the man to have eyes, ears, and chins that bore an uncanny resemblance to Shulman's eyes, ears, and chins. For a moment, Shulman, as if running toward himself, couldn't help but flash on the scene from *Duck Soup* where Harpo assumed Groucho's identity and tried to trick him by mimicking all of his movements as if he were merely his reflection in a full-length mirror. Because when Shulman moved to the right side of the running path, the approaching runner appeared to shift to his left, which placed him in a direct line with Shulman. And when Shulman veered to the left, the guy moved to his right. Back and forth this dance went, with no smile from the oncoming runner in acknowledgment of their coincidental movements. No nod from a fellow warrior, training in the same trenches, to tacitly convey his awareness of their situation and that, of course, he'd do whatever it took to avoid the disastrous. No. If anything, this runner seemed to be bearing down on Shulman. As if he had him in his crosshairs and would not be denied a direct hit. And as the two bodies got closer and closer, coming within mere steps of each other, Shulman, vehicles on his left and foliage to his right, found himself diving for safety into a cluster of nearby bushes just before the guy looked down at him, called him an asshole, and kept on running.

Mile 10

The Other Shulman?

"Are you okay?"

"Huh?"

"You seem really preoccupied today," Austin said. "Is something wrong?"

The next morning. In the store. Shulman's mind was still wrapped around the events of the day before. The physical damage, though minimal, was disconcerting. Cuts. Bruises. Scabs. Such kidlike markings, incongruous on his now grown-up limbs. But it was what occurred *after* his collision-averting swan dive that still had its grip on Shulman. Sitting up. Looking in the direction of the runner as he continued on. Noticing that the man's butt looked stunningly like his own. Struggling to his feet. Finding his car, then driving aimlessly along the unfamiliar streets of

Rockland County. Robotically his body steered, stopped, yielded, signaled, somehow effecting all proper rules of the road without any participation whatsoever from his brain.

His mind, on temporary leave from the rest of him, had the greater need to wander off on its own with the understanding that it would catch up to his body at a later time. Until then, it was free to dwell upon the man that Shulman thought looked like him. Perhaps this person was a slightly slicker version, but that was more of a hair-gel thing. And a capped-teeth thing. And an opal pinky ring thing. Still, why had this guy been so hostile? The purposeful lowering of the head and the downshifting to ramming speed. Shulman's instinct was to take it personally. But was it possible that he was not the intended target? That the coincidence lay solely in the resemblance and that the object of this man's anger could actually have been anyone unfortunate enough to be on the path at that time? Or *everyone* who was on the path at that time? Who's to say that after he sent Shulman sprawling into those prickly evergreens this lunatic didn't proceed to intentionally mow down every other jogger along his way, leaving the dirt path around the Nyack golf course littered with the bodies of innocent victims out for an unassuming jog?

Shulman found relief in the prospect that he might not have been singled out. And he explored the comforts of that possibility long enough to have no idea where he was when he finally got back to noticing that he was driving a car. Along with no knowledge as to whether he'd traveled only one block or if he was now on another continent. Yet he didn't allow the disorientation to throw him. He reassumed control and made his way along the neighborhood roads. Rural. Large homes set back a good distance from absent curbs. Old trees on either side providing a leafy canopy overhead. He was in Alpine. The character-driven, understated part of this New Jersey township. However, with one turn of the wheel, cozy turned to gaudy—homes that were newer and bigger and devoid of all charm. They were sprouting up all over this part of the state. On formerly wooded fields zoned into two-acre lots, people were building what looked like three-acre homes. And as these new communities became populated, their needs instigated the opening of new stores in new malls—not unlike the one he saw up ahead. An excellent place, he figured, to ask for directions back to the parkway. Maybe even stop into a pharmacy, if it had one, to get some Band-Aids for the battle scars on his arms and legs.

Shulman parked his car in the newly paved outdoor lot and walked toward the establishments that comprised the new Alpine Mall—many of which were still festooned with multicolored bunting commemorating their grand openings. His gaze angled upward and fell upon all the obligatory names and familiar logos. One sign did arouse curiosity, however. In his modest quest for a drugstore, Shulman couldn't help but notice Stationery Land—a store with ballpark dimensions, rows of stocked shelves, and long lines of back-to-school shoppers purchasing every supply imaginable. Including Band-Aids.

But it was the notice taped to the front door that drew Shulman closer. The twenty-four-by-thirty-six white posterboard that had the words "Pledge to Our Customers" in bold typeface at the top, followed by the founder's oath claiming that his store was a stationery mecca of unparalleled wonder and that this was just the first of many other meccas that he'd soon be opening in many other towns. Including Fort Lee.

However, the pit of Shulman's still-ample stomach didn't really start to sway until he saw the accompanying photo of this new chain's ambitious founder. The man who was doing this customer pledging was a dressed-up, business-posed rendition of none other than the same guy who had caused his need for those damn Band-

Aids in the first place. That guy who looked just like him. And in case there were any lingering questions as to where this man's ire was specifically aimed, the customer pledger's signature at the bottom of the twenty-four-by-thirty-six white posterboard read, in handwriting that looked far too similar to his own, "T. O. Shulman."

No. It wasn't possible. There had to be an explanation. True, there were approximately six billion people in the world. But, Shulman reasoned, only so many different ways that noses, eyes, ears, and mouths can be shaped and configured. So it was hard for him to believe that the permutations don't exhaust themselves at, let's say, the four billionth person so the same faces start repeating with the four billionth and first person.

As for names. Same thing. And while Shulman reasoned that the odds were certainly greater that two people who coincidentally looked a lot alike would coincidentally have similar names, it certainly wasn't impossible. And who was to say that the *T.O.* didn't stand for Theodore Oscar? Or Thelonious Oklahoma? Farfetched? Not any more so than the explanation that the Other Shulman was more than a one-line joke about his lost weight. That he was more than some mythical doppelgänger representing the malicious counterpart of his own existence. This guy was real! Alive! And he was mad!

As shaken as Shulman was about this occurrence, he was now certain the time had come for him to make a move. To take a proactive approach in dealing with this man who purposely attacked him on a jogging path and was out to destroy him by opening a rival stationery store in his own town. So he got back into his car, drove back to the same path where he'd seen the girl with the butterfly tattoo, vomited once again into those same hapless azalea bushes, then got back into his car and set out to learn all he could about this Other Shulman.

Williamsburg

Shulman, who had never received a high-five from a Hassidic Jew before, more than made up for lost time when an entire family (there must have been eleven of them) stood abreast and slapped his hand as he entered the Williamsburg section of Brooklyn. Bearded men with ringlets spiraling down the sides of their faces. Pasty-faced women standing demurely next to their matching daughters. One by one they cheered and gave Shulman five as if he'd just returned to the dugout after hitting a home run against the Gentiles.

Williamsburg. Originally a popular resort, this community's affluence faded with the opening of the Williamsburg Bridge in 1903, when immigrant families fled from overcrowded Manhattan to settle here. Among the varied ethnicities that carved their own enclaves into Williamsburg's landscape were the ultra-Orthodox Hassidim, whose wardrobe and strict adherence to Old World tenets served to isolate them from non-Jews and fellow Jews alike. Today, despite the bohemian touches provided by artists who'd opened galleries and trendy bodegas, Williamsburg was still the only location along the marathon route that Fred Lebow, the man who founded this race, used to rally crowds by yelling Yiddish through his megaphone.

It had been years (was it possible that it was actually forty?) since Shulman last visited this part of Brooklyn. His grandparents lived in the nearby Flatbush section and visits usually included a Saturday-afternoon movie at the Avalon Theater on Kings Highway. It was there that he saw his first movie. *Ben-Hur.* A biblical epic about two childhood friends, Judah and Messalla, who became estranged when Messalla went to Rome and returned many years later a soldier with values antithetical to those still held by his old pal Judah. They clashed. Became bitter enemies when Messalla imposed his punishing will on Judah and his family. Their hostilities escalated to the point where they could no longer coexist in the same world. And it all came to a head during a chariot race where Judah had no choice but to kill Messalla in order to assure his own survival.

The movie was still one of Shulman's favorites and when he recently watched it again its moral seemed to resonate more than ever. A bad man terrorizes a good man. But the good man's faith sustains him through even the most trying times. With the promise that, in the end, the good man will be rewarded for being good.

But to his surprise, the description of T. O. Shulman on the Stationeryland.com website did not make him seem like a *bad* man. Not that he expected that the short biography of the company's founder and chief executive officer would say horrible things about him. Still, a small part of Shulman hoped that amid such essentials as "spent his undergraduate years at Princeton" and "went on to earn his MBA in economics at Harvard Business School" there would be some tidbit about how T.O. was a big bully who "spends his spare time drop-kicking small kittens into shallow lakes" to lend insight into behavior that Shulman already knew about. Or suspected. There was no such entry.

However, one piece of information did jump out at him. It was the fact that he, like Shulman himself, was "born in Brooklyn and moved to Long Island at the age of eight." Though just a throwaway phrase within the larger context of entrepreneurial ventures and better-business citations, it was vital in establishing a link between the two of them. That their beginnings were identical served to reinforce the notion that the two of them started this life together but at a particular juncture there was a divergence. When? Sometime before they each left home for their respective colleges? And was there a seminal moment, after the Other Shulman had already renounced all affiliations with him, when the Other Shulman came to the conclusion that he had to destroy this Shulman? Like Messalla tried to do to Judah? But was it indeed comparable? Judah fought with a man whose hatred was fueled by the mighty Roman Empire's desire for dominance over the entire civilized world, while Shulman was up against a guy who merely had a bigger stationery store.

The next few days were marked by aftershocks of paranoia. A double take to make sure that it wasn't the Other Shulman who had just cut him off on the turnpike. Wondering if a phone hangup could very well have been the Other Shulman trying to taunt him. And bolting upright in bed at three o'clock in the morning with sweat issuing from almost every pore in his body.

"What's wrong?" asked Paula, whom his shouts of "Don't even think about it!" had just startled out of what had been proceeding along as a pleasant, uneventful sleep.

"Oh, man," he said, shaking his head. "I was dreaming that some guy who looks just like me was trying to poison our cat."

"We don't have a cat."

"That's not the point," he responded.

"Then what *is* the point?" Paula asked with an edge that was out of proportion to what had taken place so far in this conversation.

"Why are you so angry?" asked Shulman. "People don't have control of what they dream."

He smiled at her.

She didn't smile back at him.

He tried another approach.

"Go back to sleep, sweetie. I'm sorry I woke you," he added, hoping to deflect whatever heat-seeking dialogue might be launched in his direction.

"I'm not angry . . ."

Shulman's deflection was apparently successful.

"I'm frustrated and lonely . . ."

Shulman's deflection was apparently unsuccessful.

". . . and I feel like you're shutting me out."

Shulman's deflection was apparently a disaster.

Consequently, this conversation was destined to continue. The only question now was how it would do so. It was a question of tone. His tone. He knew that whatever spin he put on a response of "Why are you frustrated and lonely, and feel like I'm shutting you out?" would be insulting to both of them. The last thing Paula wanted to do was entertain another question.

Prior to this most recent event, he'd been fighting his stationery store wars single-handedly. He kept telling (and came very close to convincing) himself that it was to protect her. That the condition which had been so many years in the making was, in fact, sudden. And temporary. So why rock her sense of security by unnecessarily coming clean?

But now? Now that he had come to believe a different truth? No. Now he *really* couldn't let her in. Not when full disclosure would have to include encounters with another Shulman that would, in addition to affecting her security, herald his flirtations with lunacy. Still, the girl he married twenty-six years ago felt lonely. And she had every right to feel that way. They were growing apart—a hybrid of their respective conditions, given that she was growing and he was falling apart.

Shulman was proud of Paula. Her design business was starting to take off and he loved what it was doing for her. Her confidence. The wonder of her belated self-discovery. Feedback from friends who complimented her, and from satisfied clients who referred her. Most every call that now came to the house was for the artist who had patiently waited until the job of raising three children was behind her before starting to express her creativity with a different voice. He'd become her fan and was not, for even a moment, jealous. If anything, he enjoyed his newest role as her loudest cheerleader. Seizing upon any and all opportunities to brag about her accomplishments and still-evolving talents to anyone who asked how he felt about what his wife was doing.

The marriage part of their relationship was a different story, however. Most of Paula's clients worked during the day, so evenings and weekends were really the only times they were available to her. So Shulman was home alone. A lot. Which was convenient because it came with an implied geographical excuse for their lack of intimacy—which was so much harder to justify during those times when they were both under the same roof.

The choreography of their home life had settled into a synchronized routine of non-moments. She'd return from work, he'd ask how things had gone, she'd tell him, he'd praise her, she'd ask about his day, he'd shrug, get quiet, then go out for a run. He'd return from his run, she'd be on the phone, he'd shower, she'd ask what he wanted for dinner, he'd answer, "Anything," she'd prepare the "anything," they'd eat the "anything," she'd look at the clock, and go to Home Depot to shop for a client, and he'd clear the dinner table, watch television, then pass out on the couch. Sex? Downgraded to a nonissue. It had been so long since they'd touched each other that the detachment had become the prevailing condition between them. The new norm. *Not* having sex used to be awkward. Awkward for Shulman, who'd lie next to the mother of his children quietly fuming that he had to strategize like a sixteen-year-old looking to cop a feel in a movie theater. And awkward for Paula when she wasn't in the mood to be felt up in a movie theater. But during the past few harrowing weeks, Shulman's sexual desires had been compromised by indifference, and their bed was now strictly for sleeping. He on his side, Paula all the way over there on hers. With no threat that he'd encroach now that his penis was in repose.

And that's exactly where Paula was at that moment. On her side of their bed at three o'clock in the morning. Frustrated, lonely, and in need of reassurance that he was okay in spite of what was becoming increasingly obvious—that he wasn't okay. So Shulman ventured over to her (sort of rolled over to her side of the bed in a purposefully clumsy way that made her smile), reached up, grabbed her head, pulled it down toward the crook in his neck, and held her there.

"I'm worried about you," she whispered.

"Everything's going to be fine, honey. I promise."

"You're a good man, Shulman. But I'm worried about you and that's why I called. Are you enjoying your Cobb salad with balsamic vinaigrette dressing on the side?"

The day after Shulman's mid-night talk with Paula, the phone rang at the store. It was Roy Toy. He sounded upset. He wanted to meet for lunch. Shulman said okay. So now they were sitting in a Manhattan restaurant where Shulman watched as his old college roommate nervously chomped on a turkey leg pretty much the same way a steam shovel carves away the side of an old tenement it's leveling.

"The salad's good. Thank you."

"Don't mention it," said Roy Toy. He then removed the last shred of evidence that this erstwhile turkey ever possessed anything that even resembled meat, held its former leg bone vertically in his hand, and started to hit the table with it. Nothing overly dramatic or insistent. Just a slow, steady up-and-down tapping that looked as if, well, as if someone was steadily tapping a meatless turkey leg on a table.

Shulman recognized the look that was slowly making its way across his pal's puffy face. It was that faraway expression a simple man gets when his clear mind suddenly becomes burdened with a little bit of knowledge.

"What's wrong, Roy Toy?"

"I'm worried about your toenails."

"You are?"

"Very much so."

"May I ask why?" asked Shulman.

"Because you're going to lose them."

"I'm going to lose my toenails?"

"Shulman, I've been reading about the toll long-distance running takes on the human body. And it's very common for toenails to turn black and then fall off because they keep slamming against the inside of your shoes."

"I appreciate your concern. But I wear two pairs of socks when I run and they act as a cushion."

"But even if you do protect your toenails," Roy Toy continued, "what good will they be to you if you lose your foot?"

"I'm going to lose my foot?"

"Shulman, please don't act stupid. You know as well as I do that it's impossible for a person to have a foot if they don't have a leg."

"I'm going to lose my leg?"

"You could," Roy Toy responded. And to further illustrate this truly unique brand of reasoning, he called Shulman's attention to the turkey bone that he'd never stopped tapping. "Pretend this is *your* leg, okay?"

"Do I really have to?"

"Yes, you do."

"Fine. That's my leg."

"Okay. Now, I've been hitting it against this table for only a few minutes but look what's happened. See? The bottom of it is crushed and it's already starting to splinter. So just imagine if I kept pounding it against twenty-six miles of pavement for six hours and two minutes. It would be an unrecognizable mess. And this bone is a lot younger than yours, Shulman, because my guess is that this leg did not come off of a middle-aged turkey that weighs two hundred thirty-seven pounds."

During the past few months, Shulman had become increasingly aware of the injuries that could occur as a result of such a demanding physical commitment at this stage in his existence. The running magazines he now carried at the store warned about the shin splints. The damaged knees. The shift in the architecture of the lower back, yielding postures with Frank Lloyd Wright–type angles. (At one of the Sunday-morning training sessions, a story had started circulating about a runner from another group who had accidentally stepped into a pothole, which did something so horrible to his vertebrae that he could now see what was behind him without turning around.)

The fact that Shulman had dropped twelve pounds since he started training was somewhat helpful. In addition to shortening the amount of lag time between when the front of his stomach and the rest of his body entered a room, the reduced weight also eased the demands placed on his legs while they were supporting everything that was on top of them. He didn't get winded as easily. His pants could actually be gotten into without the aid of carpentry tools. And his smaller face gave the illusion that he had more hair on his head than he really did. Still, it was an undeniable truth that he was trying to defy the planned obsolescence of the body that housed him.

"We're not built to last," Roy Toy said. "All of our parts have expiration dates. They may not be stamped on us, which is really too bad because then we wouldn't be so surprised when they start to sputter and break down. But let's be honest here, Shulman. At this point in our lives, it's all about damage control. So why speed up the process by subjecting yourself to this kind of punishment? You want a hobby? Play checkers."

"Where?" Shulman asked. "In the park with immigrants? Or should I join a club where they go inside and also play bingo on rainy afternoons?"

"That was a figure of speech and you know it," Roy Toy responded. "Look, it's only human nature to seek some form of escape. I get it. The problem is that an escape is not really an escape if you come back to the same place you're trying to get away from. Prisoners who aren't caught have escaped. The ones who the bloodhounds tracked down and are dragged back to the big house have only attempted to escape. And trust me, Shulman, when they return, very few of them look around and say, 'You know, this penitentiary is cute. The food's tasty and my nine-by-six cement cell really *isn't* dank. The few hours away from here really has given me a much needed new perspective."

Shulman allowed himself a laugh that was disproportionate to the moment. It was the first time he had laughed since positively identifying the Other Shulman, and the release felt good.

"So, basically, if I read you correctly, you're comparing my little stationery store to Alcatraz," he joked.

"No I'm not," Roy Toy said, without helping himself to any of the levity Shulman had just invited to their table. Instead, he maintained his expression and patiently waited for Shulman to return from his little hiatus before continuing. It reminded Shulman of the days when his children had wanted to make a point and were afraid that even a momentary lapse in tone would subvert the gravity of the message they wished to deliver. He meant no disrespect. Quite the opposite. He was listening to every word Roy Toy was saying, and had mistakenly reacted to how they were being delivered rather than to the passions from which they sprung. So Shulman readjusted. He let his laugh, deprived of longevity due to lack of encouragement, come to an almost apologetic halt before taking a few seconds to fully recapture the tenor of the conversation they'd been having.

"Look, Shulman. I love your store. Your store is you, and I love you, so I love your store. I might even love your store if it wasn't yours but then it would be a different store because it wouldn't be you and probably wouldn't be called Shulman's so I don't know. That being said, I think it may be time for you to shift gears a little. There's nothing wrong with that. It's not a sign of defeat. If anything, it would be a positive step to stop, take a deep breath, look around, and see that the solution to all of your problems can be found at eight-thirty on Wednesday nights starting this fall."

Roy Toy stopped talking but held his pose. Shulman, fearing a replay of the breech he'd just committed with his Alcatraz remark, stayed firm awaiting further orders. They came a few seconds later by dint of a nod and the beginnings of a smile from his cherubic old buddy.

"What are you saying?" Shulman cautiously asked.

"I'm saying that I have a new television show coming on."

"Congratulations. What kind of show?"

"Well, it's called *Who Wants to Play Dots?*"

"Who Wants to Play Dots?"

"Yeah, it's based on that kids' game. Two contestants will take turns connecting dots and whoever makes the most boxes either wins a million dollars or gets to marry a woman named Dot."

"You're kidding?"

"Pretty wild idea, huh? We go on the air in October."

"My God, you're not kidding."

"And I want to know if you'd like to work on it."

"Work on a TV game show? Why?"

"Because it would be fun to work together. Like the old days when you used to do my homework for me. But this time I'd pay you."

"Toy, I don't know the first thing about your business. So what exactly would you be paying me for? To be your friend?"

Roy Toy's shrug summarily categorized Shulman's question as absurd. A waste of time even bothering to ask. But in the off chance that Shulman needed to be reminded, Roy Toy responded with the inflection of someone stating the obvious.

"You'd do it for me if I needed help."

Shulman, who had just been offered a job he hadn't applied for and that he was also unqualified to perform, was speechless. Partly because he felt grateful that at this point in his life he had an old friend who would make such an offer. And partly because he was embarrassed that at this point in his life he was in a position where an old friend felt the need to make such an offer. Almost like one of those good news/bad news jokes. The good news being that the doctors have located a new kidney that is a perfect match for your body. The bad news being that if locating a new kidney is good news, then there must be something terribly wrong with the kidney you already have.

"Thanks, Roy Toy," he was finally able to muster. "Really . . ."

"So you'll do it?" Roy Toy asked.

Again, Shulman recognized the look on Roy Toy's face. From the time his daughter Jenny ran toward him wanting to know if it was okay for her to have her ears pierced. She was only four years old at the time. And her excitement at the prospect of being like Heather (a little friend of hers who had just returned from the mall looking like a preschool fortune-teller) was so great that it was hard for her to contain herself even after she was at a standstill. The movement of her arms. The joy in her eyes. It would have been cruel to disappoint her at that particular moment. Just as it would have been had Shulman told Roy Toy exactly what he was thinking right now. So he smiled and gave him the same answer he had given Jenny.

"Let me think about it. Okay?"

Iced Coffee with Maria

"Have you heard about that guy called Glue?" asked Maria. "No one knows who he really is, but they've already raised something like fifty-one thousand dollars in his name. There's something so sexy about this whole thing, isn't there?"

It would be so easy, Shulman thought. As he sat across from Maria in a booth at the Fairlawn Diner, just the two of them after one of the Sunday training sessions, all Shulman could think of was how simple it would be to reveal himself right now. To merely stand up, say, "Could you please excuse me for one second?," pretend he was going to the men's room, sneak out to his car, drive home, change into his Michigan GO BLUE running shorts, fold the *o* and the *B,* insert them strategically, drive back to the diner, and show her that it was indeed he who had all of Bergen County abuzz. But he chose not to. Instead, he just sat there talking while silently trying to figure out the last time he was out with a woman who was not his wife or one of his daughters.

"And what exactly do you find sexy about it?" he asked.

Why the hell did I ask her that?

"Oh, come on," Maria responded. "You don't think it's really cool that some guy out there is raising a lot of money to help people like my brother and doesn't care at all about promoting himself?"

"Oh, I think it's really cool."

Jesus . . .

"You do?" Maria asked.

"Absolutely. I think it's supercool."

Supercool?

"My guess is that he's an older man," said Maria. "Some highly successful, confident businessman who doesn't need any pats on the back or bogus glorification from strangers."

"An amazing man."

Easy there, Shulman.

"Absolutely," she said.

"An amazing, amazing, amazing man."

Shulman!!!!

Technically, it was Maria who'd suggested they get something to drink. Not that Shulman objected or even made an effort to politely beg off. As far as he was concerned, there was nothing indiscreet about two people who had just been through a somewhat harrowing experience together winding down over a couple of iced coffees across from each other in a booth by the window in a very public place.

That morning's session was a particularly grueling one. Now that the summer was well into August and the Sunday runs were getting longer, Coach Jeffrey had them report to the site an hour earlier than they had been. At 6 A.M. The rationale being that they would finish before the temperature got really hot outside. Excellent logic. Unless a runner whose name was, let's say, Shulman got a cramp that literally took the efforts of two members of the Animal Rescue Squad to knead so his right leg could once again be regarded as a functioning limb.

Although Shulman didn't realize it at the time, his right-leg problem had actually made an appearance the night before. A painless warning shot in the form of a spasm that he discovered only because he happened to be looking at his right leg at that precise moment. In bed. Next to Paula. He watching a rerun of *Saturday Night Live*. She drawing a sketch to see how different the back of her sister's house would look if it had a different patio, different bushes, a different pool, and different windows on the house itself. At one point he casually glanced down and noticed that his right thigh muscle was moving. On its own accord. Rapid up-and-down twitches that looked as if a very small animal had somehow burrowed its way under Shulman's skin, scurried along until it reached his thigh, fell forward, then started doing push-ups.

"Honey, the top of my thigh is pulsating," he said to Paula.

"Maybe it's trying to tell you something," Paula said without looking up.

"It could be. Do you know Morse code?"

Then it stopped quivering. And didn't start again until just before the thirteenth mile of that Sunday morning's training run. Just after his heart went out to a young girl whose kitten was shivering on an upper branch of a tree he was running past. About the time he stepped onto the park bench, which brought him closer to a lower branch, which he climbed onto. And continued during those few seconds he was sitting on that lower branch. Then tightened into a cramp that would have felled Seabiscuit just as he reached up to grab the kitten. A cramp that lasted well beyond the moment Shulman dropped the kitten as he was handing it down to the young girl. A cramp that was eventually massaged back to whence it came by the boys from the Animal Rescue Squad who'd been called to rescue the kitten.

Despite the early start, by the time Shulman was able to put any reasonable amount of weight on his sore right leg it was close to noon. The August sun was directly overhead. Maria, who had stayed with him throughout this ordeal, suggested they walk the last mile back to the lot where their cars were parked. Shulman tried his best to cover his embarrassment with some old-fashioned, we-must-be-crazy-to-be-training-for-a-marathon-in-this-ungodly-heat levity by saying, "Sure, in about five hours," before he turned away from her and started to reclimb the tree. "In the meantime, I'm going to sit in the shade," he added.

Maria laughed. Then they compromised by going to a very public diner for iced coffee.

"That was real nice what you did back there," said Maria. "Helping that little girl with her kitten, I mean."

Shulman smiled, shrugged, and, for a fleeting moment, thought about saying "Shucks." He decided against it, however, because he felt it might call attention to his age. He knew that his children didn't use that word. So, instead, he smiled, shrugged, and rummaged for an expression that was more classic. Timeless. Less decade specific.

"'Twas nothing," he said.

Maria looked good. The many miles of training had helped pare away a fair amount of baby fat, revealing a striking figure that was hiding underneath. And the sadness in her eyes, though still a factor, had been reduced to a lesser role. What surprised

Shulman, however, was that despite the weight loss, Maria didn't look much younger. She managed to maintain that air of wisdom certain people have that transcends the sum of their calendar years. That suggested the knowledge she hadn't acquired, she somehow already knew. And when she did come to learn something, Maria wasn't surprised. Shulman's daughter Erin was like that. A girl who was born holding secrets. So was his maternal grandmother, an immigrant woman who gave advice without saying a word.

"How does your leg feel?" asked Maria.

"Oh, it's fine," he lied. Fact was, his right leg hurt. A lot. So much so that he was now contemplating a future that didn't necessarily include this particular right leg.

"Are you taking enough magnesium?"

"I wouldn't know. How can I tell? Why do you ask?"

"Well, from what I've been reading," said Maria, "one-sided leg cramps usually indicate some kind of mineral deficiency. If it's on the left side, you need calcium. If it's on the right, magnesium."

"And how do you take magnesium? Are there pills?"

"Sure. There are tablets that you can buy in any vitamin store or even a supermarket. It's also found in nuts, broccoli, spinach . . . most vegetables."

Maria took a sip of iced coffee. Through a straw. Shulman, fearing that he'd embarrass himself by making a slurping sound (an odd concern for a man who'd just spent the better part of the morning stuck in a tree), opted to forego the straw and then immediately embarrassed himself when an ice cube came tumbling out of his tipped glass, hit him under his left eye, dropped to the table, and slid along until it fell onto the floor before skidding to its final resting place at the foot of an elderly woman sitting in a booth across the aisle.

"That happens to me a lot," Maria said in a manner that not

only made it seem that it had indeed happened to her, but also made Shulman feel that he wasn't foolish for having done it. Because at one time or another it happened to everyone. With the possible exception of the elderly woman across the aisle who pointed toward Shulman, leaned over to her friend, and whispered the word "retarded."

"You've lost a lot of weight, haven't you?" said Maria.

"Some," answered Shulman with a shrug intended to casually slough off what he was actually excited about: at last count, there were seventeen fewer pounds of him than when he had started training, and he was particularly proud of the reappearance of a jawline last seen in his wedding album.

"Have you been dieting too?" Maria asked.

"Yes," Shulman answered. "I've become very conscious of what I eat. But have you also found that all of this running reduces your appetite?"

"Oh, absolutely," said Maria. "Sometimes I have to remind myself that I *should* be eating, even though I'm not really that hungry, because our bodies need the fuel."

"Me too. As a matter of fact—"

But just as Shulman was about to further expound on the hunger-suppressant virtues of his new obsession, he was interrupted by a waitress who approached carrying a plate heaped with representatives from approximately forty different food groups.

"Three-egg omelet with ham, mushrooms, green peppers, bell peppers, salsa, provolone, and Cheddar cheese. A double side of bacon. Sausage links. Hash browns. And a chocolate milk shake," said the waitress, who started to place this festival in front of Shulman.

"What's this?" he asked.

"A three-egg omelet with ham, mushrooms, green peppers—"

"No, no, no," said Shulman. "What I meant was, why are you giving this to me?"

"Because that's what you ordered." she answered.

"No I didn't."

"Sure you did."

"I'm sorry, ma'am, but I really didn't order that meal."

"Yes you did, sir," she insisted.

Shulman shot a look across the table at Maria. She smiled. He smiled back. They both knew he hadn't ordered that concoction. So he felt that made it okay to humor this adamant waitress. "Okay, then when did I order it?" Shulman asked.

"Please don't try to make a fool of me, sir."

"No. Refresh my memory."

The waitress looked at Shulman with the glare of a hired killer. She had a ton of other tables to serve, and to be put on display like this was (if the way she was brandishing his cutlery was any indication) just cause to strike again.

"When you came out of the men's room," she said.

"But I didn't go to the men's room," Shulman told her.

"Yes, you did. I was on the phone, you came barging out of the men's room, said, 'Honey, I'm so hungry I can eat a sorority,' gave me your order, and told me that you're sitting at this table. By the way, what happened to that snazzy little outfit you were wearing before?"

"What snazzy outfit?" asked Shulman.

"That maroon three-piece suit. The one that made you look like a big blood clot."

Maria laughed. Not so much at the waitress's joke but rather at the silliness of the whole situation. A simple, unencumbered, young girl's laugh that, for the first time since Shulman met Maria, actually made her look like a young girl. An infectious laugh that urged Shulman to join her. To accept this folly for what it was by giving it the appropriate response. And Shulman was about to when he saw him through the window. Outside. Getting into his car. Wearing a maroon three-piece suit and looking like he'd lost a few pounds since Shulman's last "run-in" with him.

A suddenly flummoxed Shulman reacted by standing. Pointing. And uttering a bunch of words intended to be "Is that the guy you're talking about?" but that, when ultimately deciphered, couldn't be answered with any certainty as the man had already pulled out of the parking lot and was driving away.

It was him. It was the Other Shulman who had ordered that sludge and had it sent to this Shulman's table. But why? As a prank? Like phoning the zoo and asking to speak to Mr. Fox? Or did it go deeper? Shulman wondered.

The Other Shulman looked fit. As fit as Shulman himself was aspiring to be, and, at least at this point, his own resolve was stronger than it had ever been. But would it last?

"Sir, do you want this meal or not?" the waitress asked.

The marathon was still seven weeks away and, as determined as Shulman was to adhere to his commitment, he had a history of allowing himself to get derailed. Of letting distraction subvert focus. In baseball parlance, what was commonly referred to as taking your eye off the ball. Or in stationery circles, leaving the cap off the pen.

"Look, Bozo, I haven't got all day," she now said loud enough to induce a head turn from the elderly woman across the aisle.

Was this part of the Other Shulman's purpose? To achieve domination, in part, by temptation? To have an overbearing waitress shove a plate of landfill in front of him with hopes that he'd let his guard down and reward what was now a strict discipline with a harmless taste that would be the first step back in undermining all that he'd worked so hard to control? Years ago, Paula had joined a group that helped people to quit smoking whose slogan was "You're a puff away from a pack a day." And while Shulman drew no parallels between withdrawal from nicotine and his controllable penchant for depositing calorie-laden treats down his gullet, he was more than familiar with the need for total abstinence if moderation was impossible to maintain.

"Hey," the pushy waitress said in a tone that would've made her next twenty words redundant had she actually said them. The woman wanted an answer. And whether or not he'd ordered the meal was now relegated to a footnote. The issue at this juncture was whether he *wanted* that meal, which he most certainly did not. It sure smelled good, though. Real good. And it wasn't that he didn't want it as much as he knew he shouldn't have it. No way. No matter how *great* it smelled. And looked. So the only thing left was to tell her. To say, "No, thank you. I don't want to eat this," even though, at that very moment, he was starving and the pile sitting on that plate was starting to look more and more like the best food he'd ever seen in his life. In any restaurant. In any country. But he couldn't eat it. Of course not. Not even a small taste. No way.

He turned his head and looked at the waitress, who was scowling at him.

Then across the table where Maria was smiling at him.

Then down at the plate where that three-egg omelet was now whispering, "Come on, big guy. You know you want me."

Shulman, himself curious as to what he was going to do, took a deep breath pretty much the way a ballplayer does before stepping back into the batter's box after he's called time-out. When all eyes are on him once again.

"Well . . . ?" demanded the waitress.

"Shulman . . . ?" whispered Maria.

"Eat me! Come on, eat me!" beckoned the three-egg omelet.

Like a chorus singing in rounds, the voices were continual and overlapping and insistent. Over and over again they sounded. A cacophonous blend of voices that united to form their own tune with an occasional "well" or "Shulman" or "eat me" rising from the din. And it kept building. And gaining momentum as it raced toward a crescendo that would climax only when Shulman willed it to do so. And when it got to that point when Shulman couldn't stand it any longer, not another second of this haunting, swelling polyphony, Shulman grabbed the plate from the waitress, set it in front of him on the table, picked up a salt shaker, unscrewed the top before dumping its contents onto the omelet, did the same with the pepper shaker, all of the packets of sugar and sugar substitutes, the ketchup bottle, the jar of mustard, and then topped it off by pouring his entire glass of iced coffee onto it—thereby rendering the three-egg omelet and its dastardly conspirators inedible.

And then it ended. The chorus came to a sudden halt. And there were no more voices. Only a restive silence astir in its wake.

Shulman leaned back and allowed himself the pleasure of his metaphoric victory. A smile and a self-congratulatory nod for identifying the enemy, decoding his plan, and thwarting his intentions with the only casualty being whatever they charged him for the breakfast he'd destroyed.

Would this be the end of it? His message that he would not succumb to the lures aimed at his own self-destruction? Hard to say. This Other Shulman appeared so intent on bringing him down that Shulman could only wonder if this was merely a short-lived, minor triumph in what had all the earmarks of a long war.

He did feel better, though. Emboldened. And he slowly emerged from his private celebration not quite ready to deal with the audience who had witnessed his three-egg-omelet massacre, unaware of its greater significance.

"Why'd you do that?" asked the waitress.

"Shulman . . . ?" said Maria, who was laughing.

"Retarded," whispered the elderly woman to her friend across the aisle.

Mile 13

Forest Hills Comes Alive with the Sound of Shulman

Queens. The largest of New York's five boroughs. First settled by Native Americans. Named in honor of the wife of England's King Charles II. Currently a massive urban complex with a population close to two million people. None of whom had ever witnessed a display like the one Shulman put on when he set foot onto their streets.

Perhaps it was the Pulaski Bridge, which linked Brooklyn to Queens. Shulman had looked down at the Long Island Expressway traffic below as he ran across it. Maybe it made him dizzy. Or perhaps it was the onset of dehydration. He'd neglected to stop for water at the last three or four mile-markers. Maybe that accounted for some light-headedness. Or perhaps it was the momentary rush of excitement he got when he saw a beautiful woman run past and thought that he had finally located Maria. Or maybe those fabled endorphins were now kicking in and mixing with these other chemical sensations to form a goofy brew. And allowing him, luring him, hypnotically lulling him into the world of *The Sound of Music* now playing in his earphones. That he sang along to. With *that* Maria. The Julie Andrews/Maria as she too crossed a small bridge and entered a town surrounded by children. Where now he too spread his arms and started to spin as he crooned the tale of "The Lonely Goatherd."

"*High on a hill was a lonely goatherd*
Lay ee odl lay ee odl lay hee hoo, ·
Loud was the voice of the lonely goatherd
Lay ee odl lay ee odl-oo . . ."

Shulman was yodeling! Whether he, himself, was consciously aware of it at that moment was doubtful—so lost he had become in the tune that now carried him. But what the crowd that lined both sides of 11th Street undeniably saw was the imponderable sight of a New Jersey man swirling into their borough with his hands on his hips and yodeling to them, as well as to the dozens of befuddled runners who were passing him.

"*Folks in a town that was quite remote heard,*
Lay ee odl lay ee odl lay hee hoo,
Lusty and clear from the goatherd's throat heard,
Lay ee odl lay ee odl-oo . . ."

And it didn't matter that he was turning heads. At that moment, nothing mattered. There were no other runners. There was no ailing store. There were no Other Shulmans. Right then, the only thing that was real was the plight of the Von Trapp family.

And the only thing that mattered at that point in Shulman's life was that he grab the hands of the uniformed parochial-school children standing on the curb and lead them to safety through the Alps before the advancing Nazi army captured them.

"*O ho lay dee odl lee o, o ho lay dee odl ay,*
O ho lay dee odl lee o, lay dee odl lee o lay . . ."

It would be difficult to determine whether it was the smack across Shulman's face from one of those uniformed parochial-school children or the shouts of "Officer, there seems to be something terribly wrong with that man!" from the nun who was jumping up and down and pointing her cotton candy at him that snapped Shulman out of his high-stepping musical reverie. Either way, it took him but a second to trade that Austrian mountain range for Vernon Boulevard and relinquishing the children's hands, uttering something about being sorry, then reinjecting himself into the sea of passing marathoners with every hope that that officer didn't take down the number pinned to the front of his shirt, run it through the system, and put out an Amber Alert.

Oddly enough, what had just occurred didn't startle Shulman. That little side trip away from coherent, civilized behavior he had just taken. Not at all. If anything, he was now feeling better than he'd felt thus far in the race. No aches. No pangs that the water cups and protein bars being handed out by those volunteers up ahead couldn't handle. No, Shulman was just fine. Laughing at the comedy routine Woody Allen was now delivering in his earphones about shooting a moose. And reveling in the thought that he had just completed half a marathon. That's right! According to the hand-painted sign being held by the yawning child sitting on his father's shoulders in front of Corwin's Tool and Dye factory, there were now a little more than thirteen miles between where the race started and where Shulman was at that very moment. So all he had to do was do what he had just done, one more time. *What?* That's right, all he had to do was run another 13.1 miles. *Wait a second!* Shulman checked his watch and saw that he had been running, walking, moving nonstop in a forward direction for three hours and one minute. God, even if he was able to keep this pace, that seemed like an incredibly long time that he would still have to be running, walking, and moving in a forward direction, given that he'd already been doing it for three hours and one minute. Somehow, when measured in hours and minutes, the distance ahead seemed longer than when done so in miles. So Shulman continued. Onward. And shook his head as he recalled a conversation he'd had a few months earlier about this very subject.

"I want to improve my time," said Shulman.

"No you don't," Coach Jeffrey told him.

"I don't?"

The groups had just finished that particular Sunday's training run. Everyone, including Maria, had already said their good-byes and left. Shulman, however, lingered and was now helping Coach Jeffrey carry the placards with the names of the pace groups on them back to his aged Datsun. That week they had all received e-mails describing speed-work sessions that were now being offered and they had aroused Shulman's curiosity. Roy Toy's turkey leg admonitions aside, he had been wondering if the wear and tear on his middle-aged carcass would be reduced if it took him less time to run the same number of miles. To Shulman's way of thinking, it would amount to that many fewer steps taken on unforgiving pavement, fewer heartbeats at NASCAR speeds, plus it would simply *sound* better if he, for example, could say that he finished the race in *five* hours and fifty-nine minutes as opposed to *six* hours and two minutes. Essentially, the same hollow logic Shulman had called upon after the only time he played golf. When he told everyone he shot a 99—neglecting to include that he left the course and went to a movie after fourteen holes.

"How come I don't want to run faster?" asked Shulman.

Coach Jeffrey took the last of the signs from Shulman, placed them next to the ones he had just deposited into the trunk, and turned back to Shulman.

"This is your first marathon and your goal is to finish. All twenty-six point two miles of it. That's what you're working toward."

"Oh, absolutely," said Shulman. "I was just thinking—"

"I know what you're thinking," Coach Jeffrey interrupted. "But what I'm afraid of is that if you put any of your energy into running any faster than your body wants you to run right now, you'll be denying yourself the full satisfaction of this experience, and I can't allow that to happen to you, Shulman. Understand?"

"No, not really."

Coach Jeffrey didn't look well. Shulman hadn't noticed it earlier when all of the groups were assembled. But here, with just the two of them standing closely in the slender shade provided by the still-open trunk of an aged Datsun, Shulman saw that he was talking to a man who appeared to be a bit wan and a lot more preoccupied than the last time he'd seen him.

Should he ask him if he was okay? Shulman wondered. It was one of those fragile dilemmas confronted only by healthy people. And in the instant it took him to deliberate, Shulman considered the net effects of both scenarios. To make the inquiry would say, "I care," but could very well be heard as "I'm asking you because you look really bad." While by not asking, he would run the risk of seeming not to care. Shulman cared. Enough not to make

Coach Jeffrey think that something which, up to that point, had gone unacknowledged was starting to become obvious. So he didn't ask.

"I envy the marathon you're going to be running," said Coach Jeffrey.

"Why?"

"First of all, you know you're not going to win . . . you *do* know you're not going to win it, right?"

"I know."

"You sure?" Coach Jeffrey asked with a smile that found its way into his tone. "Is it safe for me to presume that you're not harboring any secret fantasies about getting a real good night's sleep before the race or finding a pair of magic shoes that will lead to you becoming the new winged symbol for FTD florists?"

"Yes, it's perfectly fine for you to make that presumption," answered Shulman with the same smile.

"Okay. So if you're not running to win and since you've never done this before, there's no personal record you're trying to beat, you have nothing but the purity of the run to look forward to. Do you have any idea how beautiful and unencumbered that will be? Not to have to be concerned about the clock?"

Coach Jeffrey started to look better. With each word, life crept back into his eyes as if he were riding what he was saying to a higher, happier ground that he was able to lose himself on. A short excursion to a place he loved. A momentary reprieve from where he currently lived.

"Clocks are lies, Shulman, because there is really no such thing as time. The world goes on and on at its own pace and clocks are just our attempt to make things calculable. To take something we are not even remotely equipped to understand and bring it down to our level so we know when to wake up and how much longer it will be until the bus gets here."

Coach Jeffrey reached up, grabbed the open hood to the trunk, and purposefully closed it more gently than Shulman had ever seen anyone do so before. It wasn't a slam. In fact, neither gravity nor human energy made a contribution to the process. He just simply lowered it until it reached the bottom, then pressed lightly on it with both hands, snapped it shut, then patted it. Almost affectionately. Somehow, it made sense. As a gesture a car owner might make to the trunk of his trusty old Datsun. Or what a former pianist might do to the lid of a beloved Steinway.

"Running is an end unto itself, Shulman. An activity without a purpose. And the marathon, well, they may call it a race but it's not a competition. It's a challenge to push yourself further than you ever thought you could go. And you know what you're going to discover along the way? That clocks and other runners don't exist."

Coach Jeffrey took a moment to nod. As if he were using it as a silent, reflective punctuation mark to connect what he'd just said to his next point.

"And once you do come to realize that finishing *is* winning— then you'll realize that you'll only be running against yourself. So then it will be up to you, and only you, to do what it takes to win."

Shulman watched Coach Jeffrey make his way toward the front of the car and open its door as gingerly as he'd closed its trunk. He was a gentle man, Shulman decided. Probably always was. But in the few short weeks that Shulman had known him, he was able to detect a change. Was it possible that Coach Jeffrey was happier? Or, in the very least, more at home in a world that had penalized him for living by slightly different rules? Shulman then flashed to an episode that had occurred years ago. When all the kids were living at home and the family ate all their dinners together. As dialogue made its way around the table in waves of overlapping accounts of everyone's day and mixed opinions concerning the merits of the dinner Paula had prepared, Jake, a high school junior at the time, somehow broke through the din with a joke about two gay guys and a lawn mower. Jake played varsity baseball, one of his teammates had told the joke on the bus, and it was funny. Very funny. Yet, at this particular dinner table, they all turned to Shulman before anyone dared commit to laughter. He remembered Paula's eyes begging him not to endorse such insensitivity—especially in front of young children who could not yet make the distinction between off-color humor and malice. And then he remembered the dinner table he had sat at when he was a young boy and how he would never even *think* about telling such a joke. So he didn't laugh. Instead, Shulman assumed the role of responsible adult and told Jake why all jokes such as that were not at all funny. Back then it was the right thing for him to do. But now? So many years later standing in a parking lot with a man who seemed more comfortable with who he was than Shulman did? How odd, Shulman thought, that had he remembered the joke about the two gay guys and the lawn mower and told it to Coach Jeffrey, he'd laugh.

"Shulman, let me ask you something," said Coach Jeffrey. "When you were a kid, did you play any games in the street?"

"Sure," answered Shulman.

"Like what? Stickball? Kick ball? Tag?"

"All of those games," Shulman said. "As a matter of fact, during the marathon, we're going to be running pretty close to some of the streets I played on when my family lived in Brooklyn."

"It was a carefree time, wasn't it? Summer nights. Friends. Parents who tucked you in. The only concern in the world an occasional moving car that you had to get out of the way for, right?"

"Yes," said Shulman, smiling along with the memory.

"Think about it, Shulman. It was a time when your mind and your body were one. Integrated. It wasn't like you were doing one thing but your thoughts were somewhere else. Everything that you were, all of those ingredients that made up that young Shulman, was absorbed in the playing. That's something a child does naturally before he dies and becomes an adult. He plays in a world that has infinite possibilities. And that's what I want you to do for six hours and two minutes. Go back and play in those streets. Meet up with that kid and get to know him again. It will be even better this time. There won't be any moving cars to worry about."

Mile 14

Shulman's Horrible Morning

"You're not going to wear *that* outfit, are you?" Paula asked.

A startled Shulman nearly jumped. It was five-thirty on a Sunday morning. The sun itself hadn't given thought to being up at this hour. So, according to what could now be considered a weekly ritual, Shulman had tiptoed out of bed and was attempting to dress for that morning's training run without the benefit of light, so as not to disturb his hibernating wife.

That his thoughtful intentions were ineffective was not totally surprising. Paula had always had the uncanny ability to sense the absence of weight from his side of the mattress no matter how he performed the dismount. And it bothered Shulman that, despite their long history of bed sharing, he still hadn't found a method that allowed him to leave undetected without any bankable consistency. And he'd tried them all. Ranging from the sudden, "I'll do this in one quick burst" approach that bore the same rationale employed when attempting to painlessly remove a Band-Aid from a particularly hairy part of the anatomy, to the more delicate, infinitely longer "slithering to the edge of the mattress then slowly extending yourself over its side until the majority of your body weight is hanging down, making it that much easier to roll onto the floor" technique that he once saw a bear use when getting down from a big rock at the Bronx Zoo. This morning's effort featured him lying on his back and coordinating the movements between his heels and butt cheeks that eventually brought him down to the foot of the bed, and he exited that way. With apparently no success as well.

But what totally befuddled Shulman was how Paula was able to see what clothing he was putting on in the predawn darkness of their bedroom. Here he was trying to feel the difference between a blue and a green T-shirt, while she, from the other side of the room, had the capacity to critique his choices.

"What are you? A bat?" he turned and asked toward what he believed was her general direction. "How can you see anything? Do you have infrared goggles?"

Since that initial picture of Glue had run in the *Fort Lee Record* (what was now) six weeks ago, Shulman had purposely not worn those shorts to help maintain anonymity. Instead, he'd replaced them with a random assortment boasting the names of different universities and brands but had not yet settled on any particular pair to be their permanent successor.

"By the way," he continued, "it's not like I'm dressing for the inauguration. We're talking about shorts and a T-shirt that I'm going to be sweating in for the next several hours."

"Yeah, but still . . ." she said as she left the bed and made a beeline to the same dresser, and under the exact lighting condi-

tions, that Shulman had groped his way toward just a minute before. When Paula reached the dresser, she opened a drawer,
grabbed a pair of running shorts, said, "Here," as she handed them
to him, opened another drawer, said, "Here," as she handed him
a T-shirt, closed the drawers, and then quickly darted into the
bathroom.

Shulman remembered a rendition of this act that had been performed by his mother. How she used to hound his father about his
wardrobe. In particular, the cause célèbre was a red velour shirt.
A fascinating garment when considering that there was no pig-
ment in any crayon box or on any paint charts that even came
close to complementing it. Magically, whatever color pants it was
worn with ended up looking brown. It clashed with the uphol-
stery. Walls. Pets. It was shapeless. It sagged. And had a musty
smell. Probably because food crumbs were still clinging to the
shirt even upon its return from the dry cleaner and it always
looked like it needed to be flossed. Yet, Shulman's father loved
that shirt and he wore it on Sundays as if required to do so by law.
The kids knew it as Daddy's Shirt. The centerpiece of his weekend
uniform. Good for gardening. Napping. Moviegoing. And barbe-
cuing for unexpected guests. It also proved to be an excellent target for Shulman's mother, who was relentless in her assault on
both the shirt and the man who was wearing it.

"When you die they're going to have to peel that thing off of
you," Shulman's mother would say to his dad.

"Why can't you just let me wear my shirt in peace?" he'd respond.

"Because that shirt looks like my ass in two parts."

"Well, I happen to love it."

"That's because you don't have to look at yourself in it."

"Neither do you."

And then he left. He walked out the door, got into the car, drove to a Holiday Inn, and didn't come home for two nights. Not until she promised to stop badgering him about that shirt. She promised. He came home. And she kept her mouth shut. For about six months. When she started up again, he left again. This sequence kept repeating itself to the point where the desk clerk at the Holiday Inn would say, "She started badgering you about that shirt again, Henry?" upon seeing him. This sequence finally ended when the shirt disappeared with the lost luggage on a flight back from Paradise Island, although Shulman's dad would probably go to his grave still thinking that his wife had tipped the Bahamian skycap extra money to dispose of his suitcase.

Was this his and Paula's future? Shulman wondered. Was her telling him how to dress for a morning run the onset of their redirection? The next incarnation for what was once sexual energy, resurfacing as eye rolling and ridicule? As Shulman stood there in the Sunday-morning darkness, he tried to remember how old his father was when that red velour business had started kicking in. To determine how much time was left before he too would begin walking around mumbling displeasures about a condition he felt too powerless to change.

Shulman also wondered about Jake. Their twenty-two-year-old son who was in love. Was this in the cards for him as well? And what about their daughters? When Shulman first became a father, he had taken that private vow all new parents take to not do the things his parents had done that had driven him crazy when he was a kid. So he never talked down to them. Took all of their problems seriously, no matter how puerile or fleeting. And he never broke into song when their friends were around. But now Shulman was curious about the conduct between himself and Paula. The well-intentioned yet flawed example they had set as a couple. He wondered which argument, head shake, or slammed door subconsciously had biased his children's future choice of a mate. And he cringed when he thought about the nasty words, though later apologized for in private, they'd overheard and could very well reprise in their own homes some day.

But now the house was empty. No potential witnesses to behavior either civil or unkind. Life as it was before he and Paula made passionate love and gave birth to buffers. As the sound of faucets being turned off signaled his wife's imminent return to their bedroom, Shulman decided to take a stand. Just as he had done at the diner—but without the aid of the ketchup, iced coffee, and assorted condiments that played such a vital role in that display of independent thinking. Here, it was imperative as well. To thwart the arrival of their "Red Velour/Holiday Inn" years. So he quickly put on the shorts and shirt he'd originally chosen and purposely lingered until Paula emerged from the bathroom.

"See you later," he said while assuming a pose he thought he'd seen on a Dockers pants commercial.

"Have a good run," she responded without even looking at him as she headed back to the bed. "By the way, if you're looking for any of your toenails, there are two of them on top of the washing machine."

"Excuse me?"

"I found them in your socks when I was doing the laundry."

Shulman tried his best to maintain his Dockers pose but it was difficult. He couldn't help but feel somewhat incomplete given that 20 percent of his toenails were now sitting on top of a household appliance in another room. And the fact that this was the first he'd heard of it unnerved him as well. How did something like this get by him? Shouldn't he have noticed that pieces of him were no longer attached? That they were indeed missing? Of course he should have. Yet, he didn't. He didn't feel their loss.

And the thought of taking toenail inventory before putting on his running shoes never even crossed his mind. Still, in his quest to preserve whatever dignity one could actually have in a situation such as this, Shulman maintained his Dockers pose and searched for a tone that could pass for unfazed.

"Oh, that happens all the time to runners. In fact, they say the better the runner you are, the less toenails you have. That's why there are so few pedicurists in Uganda," he told her.

"I'm sure there aren't," Paula answered. Then she turned over and burrowed deep under the blankets. Shulman stood there and waited for more. But it never came. No punch line. No Paula-type parting shot. No new version of when she tattooed that butterfly to the small of her back. Her little joke that had made him laugh so much just a short while ago.

This endnote lingered. And Shulman kept thinking about it during his drive to the training site. So much so that he missed a turn, got lost on familiar streets, and wasn't even aware that the radio was on until they played that jingle. A chorus. Accompanied by full orchestration. Singing a song to the tune of "This Land Is Your Land."

> "*Stationery Land's your land,*
> *Stationery Land's my land,*
> *If you need supplies for,*
> *Your home or office,*
> *From pens and paper,*
> *To computers and printers,*
> *Stationery Land has even got TVs.*"

A pitchman's voice then proceeded to list, at breakneck speed, the products from *A* (address books) to *Z* (zippered address books) that Stationery Land carried in all of its stores—including the one that was due to open in Fort Lee that fall.

That the Other Shulman's newest store was soon going to exist in Shulman's hometown certainly came as no surprise to him. Nor did the fact that his nemesis had the means to advertise it on the radio. But the song was a violation. That people were singing about a place that could very well spell the end of his own livelihood, to the tune of one of his favorite songs, no less, was a cruel blow. A form of taunting that, had this been an NFL football game, would have drawn a penalty for unsportsmanlike conduct.

Shulman purposely slowed down so he could stop at the light when it turned red. He needed a moment. According to the dashboard clock it was only 6:04, but he felt like he'd already put in a long day. First Paula. Then that song. And now this street he was driving on. This must have been the third time he'd seen those same houses. And that stop sign up ahead. The one he'd turned right at because he thought that was the way to the park but had somehow ended up back here. So the next time he'd turned left but had somehow ended up back here. Or had he accidentally made a right turn the second time as well? Or had he, indeed, made a left turn both times? The light changed to green but with no other cars on the street at this hour, Shulman stayed put, rolled down his window, and shouted to another early riser, who was walking his dog. A Great Dane that was bigger than the house Shulman grew up in.

"Excuse me. Could you please tell me how to get to Linwood Park?"

The man tugged at the dog's leash, took a few steps toward the car, and leaned in through the open window.

"It's real easy. Just go up to that stop sign and turn . . . Shulman?"

Oh, Jesus.

"You really fooled me there for a second. What a funny thing to do."

Oh, Jesus.

The man was Marty Gordon. The family physician that Shulman now hated more than Hitler. Marty Gordon's house was on this street. Shulman had been there many times. Marty Gordon's house was only a few blocks from Linwood Park. They used to take their kids there to play together. So it was understandable for Marty Gordon to think Shulman was joking by asking for directions to a place he obviously knew how to get to.

"How've you been, Shulman?"

"Not bad, Marty. And yourself?"

As if I give a flying shit.

"Great. Just great."

"Good to hear, Marty."

Now tell me where the fucking park is.

"Still training to run a marathon, Shulman?"

"Yep. In fact, I'm on my way to the park right now."

"Linwood Park?"

Isn't that the park I just asked you about, you mongoloid?

"Yeah. Good ol' Linwood Park," said Shulman.

Now where the hell is it?

"That's so funny."

"What's so funny, Marty?"

"I just came from Linwood Park."

"No kidding?"

So you went up to the stop sign and turned which way?

"That *is* funny," Shulman added.

Left or right? Goddamn you!

"Yeah, Snickers took a huge dump there."

"Really?"

A Great Dane named Snickers?

"He was constipated all week. So I ended up giving him a laxative I brought home from the hospital, and I'm telling you, within two hours he dropped a load that, well, you'll see when you get to the park."

I will?

"Yeah, whatever bug he had in his system is now sitting in a hefty pile between third base and home plate."

What!!!

"It's a real wet one."

You miserable lowlife!!!

"Well, I'm glad Snickers is feeling better, Marty."

"Thanks, Shulman. Have fun at the park."

"You bet, Marty."

God, this is a horrible morning.

By the time Shulman regained his bearings and finally arrived at the park, he found all of the marathoners seated on the grass writing on little strips of paper.

"What's going on?" he asked Maria while taking a seat next to her.

"Here. I grabbed one for you. Fill it out," she said.

It was an ID tag that had spaces for a runner to write his name, blood type, medications being taken, and the phone number of someone to call in the event of an emergency.

"When you're finished, slip it through your shoelace and then snap the ends together so it doesn't fall off when you run," Maria added.

"We're supposed to run with these things on our shoes?"

Maria nodded.

"In the event something happens while you're running—" she started to say.

"They know where to ship my body?"

"Well, in the very least, who to call to come pick it up."

Shulman took a quick moment to laugh before he automatically went back to thinking about the way things were with Paula. The distancing. The lapses in kindness. Marriage by rote. And how, a few days earlier when Paula had caught him staring while she was getting dressed, she covered herself with a towel and politely asked for privacy. As if it was now inappropriate for him to stare at the same naked body he'd been staring at since college. Was it only last Christmas, at a neighbor's party, that Paula had joked to a few friends that "my husband still can't believe that he's married to someone who's got breasts that he's allowed to see anytime he wants"? Everyone laughed because they knew Shulman and thought it was cute. And Paula felt good that her immature husband was still excited about her.

But now Shulman was wondering if he should even put Paula's name on his emergency ID tag. Now maybe she wouldn't want to be bothered with burying anyone whom she wouldn't allow to see her naked. Shulman then played with the thought of whom else he would designate for this role. One of his children? No. It would be an unfair emotional burden. His parents? No. To let his mother know that he chose her over his wife was a satisfaction he wasn't willing to give her, even posthumously. Then who else was there? Shulman remembered when he was in college; he and some friends went on a school-sponsored ski trip that required their filling out an emergency medical form. Everyone put their parents' names. Except for Roy Toy, who wrote "Prince Charles" and gave the Buckingham Palace address. It was hard to pinpoint exactly when Roy Toy became so fascinated by the Prince of Wales that he would mail him postcards (*Dear Chuck, Just a quick note to let you know that I had a great time visiting the Amish country with my family over spring break,* or *Dear Chuck, Thanks for the Beatles. They're fab!!!!*), but by the time Shulman came into his life,

Roy Toy was more than ready to have his lifeless remains shipped to the heir to the British throne.

"And you really think that Prince Charles will take the call and say what? 'Sure, feel free to send me that American idiot who keeps hounding me with his nonsense. I'll have a bunch of my Royal Guardsmen meet the plane at Heathrow'?" Shulman remembered asking him at the time.

"I know it's a long shot," Roy Toy reasoned. "But if he says yes, I'll get to go to London."

Shulman then heard Maria saying his name in a tone that implied she'd called it before and was repeating herself.

"Yeah?" he responded.

"Are you okay?" Maria asked.

"Sure. Why do you ask?"

Maria smiled. She looked *especially* pretty this morning.

"Oh, I don't know. Maybe because I've said your name four times and haven't been able to get your attention," she answered.

They hadn't spent any more extracurricular time together since that day they'd had iced coffee. Yet it had added a subtle dimension to their relationship. That innocent secret kids share when they've sneaked outside their usual perimeters.

"I'm sorry," he said. "I was just thinking about something. What's up?"

"All I was trying to tell you was that I like what you're wearing today."

"You do?"

Shulman was afraid he might have asked that question with far too much incredulity. That he had placed an extraordinary amount of emphasis (particularly on the word "do") that could be interpreted to mean, "You *do*? That is so refreshing to hear because my wife of twenty-six years absolutely hates it."

"Yes, I really do," Maria said.

— — —

After that morning's practice run, they hugged. In the parking lot. Shulman walked Maria to her car and they bade their good-byes when Maria suddenly turned, threw her arms around him, and said, "See you next week."

On its surface, nothing worthy of headlines. Just a spontaneous, almost reflexive gesture between two people who'd become familiar by virtue of time and exigent circumstances. Pretty much the same way football players embrace teammates after a close game. Or how an airplane pilot might hug the air traffic controller who guided him to a safe landing during a thunderstorm.

It would be a much bigger story, however, if the memory of that hug lingered for a few days and the football player started looking forward to those postgame hugs. Or if that pilot purposely started wearing a particular shirt and pair of shorts because he knew the air traffic controller thought they looked good on him. But that's what Shulman did in subsequent weeks, when a hug just naturally became part of his and Maria's greeting when they first saw each other and their farewell before going their separate ways at the end of the training session.

Was he falling in love with her? he remembered wondering at the time. Or was this just an unfortunate commentary on how needy he'd become to have physical contact with someone, anyone, who wasn't always pissed off at him?

Shulman shuddered at the prospect of either possibility. He still preferred to be in love with his wife and held on tightly to the hope of their marriage rekindling. On the other hand, Maria's revised status would now give him something else to think about until then.

The Man in the Blurry Picture

"I see you've decided to come out of the closet," Coach Jeffrey joked through his end of the phone. "Isn't that supposed to be my area of expertise?"

"But I'm telling you that's not me," Shulman told him. "That's what makes this whole thing so odd. I haven't run at that high school in weeks."

The photo was of poor quality. Reminiscent of the ones that appear every so often when there's a sighting of Big Foot. Black-and-white. Grainy. A large person's distinctive features were blurred against a gymnasium wall in the distant background. Still, the *Fort Lee Record* had chosen to run the picture on its front page under a headline that read: IS THIS GLUE?

Because the amount of money donated on his behalf was now

over $72,000 with still no hint as to his identity, the very concept of "Glue" had swelled to mythical proportions. Editorials were written about "the benevolent ghost of Bergen County," clergymen delivered sermons about the man who embodied the true spirit of charity by anonymous giving, and local business was on the upswing as curious folks from surrounding areas, when given a choice, opted to eat at a Fort Lee restaurant or to go shopping at one of its stores.

Shulman had put his beloved town on the map and couldn't have been happier despite the irony that he seemed to be the only one who wasn't garnering any tangible benefits for doing so. Yet he enjoyed the power of his silence. And its ability to influence the movement of people in their quests for answers without his having to lift a finger. Shulman wondered if this was what God did whenever human beings were confronted with something new and inexplicable. If he simply sat back and observed how everyone behaved in their exercising of free will.

It was a position of quiet nobility. A secret space he was confident would not be threatened by exposure. And to a man who saw most every other aspect of his existence unraveling, such a retreat was becoming more and more essential. Plus he enjoyed the role of spectator to the sport he'd created. The guessing games his neighbors were playing. The debates between callers on local radio shows. Even the impostors—any of those attention-starved persons who would put on Michigan gym shorts and walk backward into the *Fort Lee Record*'s offices claiming that *they* were the guy everyone was talking about.

But this blurry picture on the front page of the paper was of a different order. Candid. Seemingly random. According to the accompanying article, the product of sheer happenstance. A young boy leaning out of a moving car's window indiscriminately snapping away at anything that just so happened to show up in the viewfinder of a camera his grandparents had just given him for his eleventh birthday. The result was a symphony of blur. Soupy images including a dog that looked like a bear, a cop who looked like Europe, twin girls conjoined with a bus, and the shadowy image of a large man on a running track wearing shorts that might very well have had the letter *G* on the rear.

"This picture is great for us," said Coach Jeffrey.

"I know."

Shulman fully understood the reasoning behind Coach Jeffrey's excitement. This photo would only promote more intrigue around town. Shulman understood that communities, like the individuals who comprise them, are vulnerable to seasonal rhythms. This "Glue" business had certainly been an unexpected and highly welcomed summer diversion. But with Labor Day quickly approaching, attention was likely to veer back toward the pedestrian. Kids home from camp. Shopping for school clothes. Bedtimes reinstated. Recess would be over. But the timing of this picture was perfect. The marathon was still several weeks away and this new plot beat might hold its audience until then. Let people think that that blurry man was Glue. Let the hounds from the *Fort Lee Record* stake out the high school in hopes of bagging their prey. Let them have their headline. Shulman already knew how the town's interest would be charted. With a spike upon finding that blurry man. A dramatic drop-off when he was revealed to be the wrong blurry man. And then shooting to even greater heights once the search resumed.

All the while Shulman would be maintaining his nonexistent public profile and focusing his attention on the business of trying to stay in business.

"Run that by me again," said Shulman's exasperated accountant.

"Come on, Howard . . ."

"Seriously, Shulman. Repeat what you just told me, and real slowly this time, so when I'm on trial for strangling you, I can tell the jury exactly what you said to provoke me. And you know something? My guess is that it will not only be enough to get me acquitted, but I'll also have the thanks of the court for taking a maniac off the streets."

Shulman was trying to figure out whether Howard had ever yelled at him in this particular diner before. The list of restaurants and assorted eateries where Howard had deemed it appropriate to unleash his vocal chords and take them out for a run during the course of their two-decade association was endless. A veritable Zagat's guide of financial lectures and humiliating reprimands. But the only recollection that Shulman had of having previously been here was when he and Maria had shared iced coffee a few weeks before. The day that the Other Shulman had ordered him breakfast from a waitress who, as luck would have it, was not only working at the moment, but Howard's voice had also managed to turn the head of the same elderly woman who'd been sitting across the aisle from him that last time.

"Listen, Howard," Shulman began. "I know how this must sound but please hear me out. Okay?"

The silence that followed was uncomfortable. One of those pauses where both people in a dialogue know that the words about to be spoken will do absolutely nothing to draw them closer to similar thinking. If anything, Shulman was aware that whatever he was about to say would do little more than provide Howard with time to reach into his arsenal, pull out a mouthful of fresh invectives, reload, then ready himself to hurl them in Shulman's direction once his brain gave the order.

And it was more than understandable that the man would assume this posture. Sitting on the table between them were the papers

Howard had drawn up. A contract between Shulman and Rolling Fields Shopping Plaza, Inc. Once it bore his signature, it would essentially release Shulman from the two years remaining on his rental agreement with them. In return, they would be allowed to assign his lease to another storeowner.

And then it would be over. By simply writing his name, there would be no more Shulman's.

"Ordinarily, there'd be some kind of penalty for early termination," Howard had explained to him. "But because of the history you've had with them—and they know things are only going to get worse with all these Stationery Lands cropping up all over—they're not going to make a big deal about it. This gives you until the end of this month."

Howard had looked like he was expecting a thank-you. When Shulman politely placed the pen down on the table without signing the document, Howard had looked like he was expecting an explanation. But it was when Shulman explained that he wanted to keep his store, at least through the Labor Day weekend, that Howard had started yelling at him for the first time in this particular diner.

"Howard, kids are going to need school supplies, the Jewish holiday cards always bring in more street traffic, and I think I've found a cheaper supplier for next year's daily diaries, which people usually start placing orders for in the fall."

If anything, Howard seemed insulted by the lameness of Shulman's argument. Please tell me that there's more, his glare was saying. Please tell me that you're just getting started. That you're building toward giving me solid reasons why that clinically dead store of yours should not be put out of its misery. And you had better tell me soon, very soon, or you'll leave me no choice but to throttle you in front of this waitress and that elderly woman who already thinks you're retarded.

"I can't do it, Howard," said Shulman, his voice cracking. "I just can't throw in the towel without putting up a fight."

Howard softened when he saw Shulman dab at a tear with a napkin. Neither of them had expected this moment and they both pretended not to be embarrassed by it. Consequently, its only acknowledgment was Howard leaning in and subtly relaxing his tone.

"Shulman, to put up a fight you need ammunition."

"I know."

"And you don't have any."

"I know," Shulman answered. "But I will."

"You think so?"

"I know so."

Howard leaned back and looked at Shulman. A reaction not so much to the words but to the tone with which they were delivered. The quiet assurance. And its unfathomable alienation from anything that Howard knew to be reality. So, with the same caution the boys from the bomb squad use when trying to talk down some lunatic with explosives strapped to his body, he leaned forward once again and gently whispered to Shulman.

"What do you plan on doing?" he asked.

"Expanding."

Mile 16

The Tall, Scary Buildings

It would have been wonderful. Poetic, even. But it wasn't meant to be. Too bad, because Shulman was really looking forward to hearing Simon and Garfunkel singing "The 59th Street Bridge Song" as he ran across the 59th Street Bridge. But because of either an error by Austin when he programmed the music, or a miscalculation by Shulman himself when trying to determine exactly what time he would reach the foot of this structure that linked Queens to Manhattan, he was hearing Martin Luther King's historic "I Have a Dream" speech through his headphones instead.

Perhaps this was more appropriate. Because despite its opening lyric (*Slow down, you move too fast*), Shulman thought there was a fundamental fraudulence in running to a song also known as "Feelin' Groovy" when, in fact, he was feelin' like shit and now, like Dr. King, also had a dream of reaching the promised land on the other side of this bridge before his heart exploded through his chest and went flying over the railing into the East River below.

The three miles they ran along the streets of Queens had been uneventful. Bland. And comparatively quiet due to the smaller crowds than in Brooklyn. But Coach Jeffrey had told them that there would be stretches with lower fan turnout. The middle miles, in particular, where people found it less exciting to cheer slower runners as they trudged along breathing heavily. The physicality of any location along the marathon route itself also played a role. So it was understandable that there wouldn't be any spectators on an old bridge with a very narrow walkway and a gradient that made Shulman feel like he was trying to run up the side of the Chrysler Building.

"Was this bridge always this steep?" he asked a woman runner. She was walking. Everyone was. A feeling of mass resignation had come over the hundreds of marathoners (both in front of and behind Shulman) who paid similar deference to this insidious incline, so it was just understood that this was the part of the journey where everyone walked. As a result, Shulman, who'd given some thought to "embracing the hill," as Coach Jeffrey had instructed, came to the quick conclusion that he was too tired to embrace anything and decided to walk as well.

The woman runner, who had dark hair and brown eyes, smiled. Polite. But not exactly an invitation for further dialogue. Then again, his question *was* somewhat rhetorical and the woman *was* breathing somewhat heavily so Shulman cut her some slack and figured he could take his mind off what he was doing by engaging her in conversation.

So he told her that his earliest memory of what was also called the Queensboro Bridge was of Penny Maidenbaum—a high school classmate whom he had a fierce crush on. And how, after finally gathering the courage to ask her out, he borrowed his father's car to celebrate his newly acquired driver's license with a trip to the city. And opting for the bridge instead of the more conveniently located Midtown Tunnel because the bridge didn't have a toll. And spending about six weeks' worth of allowances at a trendy restaurant called La Fondue, where he watched Penny dip chunks of bread into bubbling hot cheese and continually shovel them into her mouth with the abandon of someone whose tongue and palate were lined with asbestos. And how, when they drove back over this bridge, they got stuck behind one of those slow-moving sanitation trucks that had a big round swirling brush on its bottom that cleaned the road as it went along. And how they made believe that the truck was doing it just for them the same way European streets were swept just before the royal carriage came through. And how they kissed in Shulman's father's car and how Shulman began to refer to this bridge as "our bridge" and how Penny Maidenbaum began to refer to La Fondue as "our restaurant" and how Shulman had asked her if they could please look for another "our restaurant" because that one was so darn expensive. Then how Penny insisted and how Shulman went along with it because he didn't want to spoil things between them so he kept dipping into his savings account so she could keep dipping chunks of bread into hot cheese. And how, after his money ran out and after his mother caught him going through his father's pants, they suspended all car privileges and how it broke his heart when Penny Maidenbaum found another boyfriend to take her to La Fondue. And how apparently she'd found a number of other boyfriends to take her to La Fondue because during their senior year Penny Maidenbaum grew to the size of a Half-Dollar Maidenbaum and had to wear a special gown at graduation.

Shulman and the dark-haired woman were now at the middle

of the bridge. That point where it flattened out for about twenty yards before starting a downward slope on its way to the city. It would be easier now. Already his body felt lighter and in a matter of moments would join the people up ahead, who had resumed running. He looked over at the dark-haired woman he'd just spilled his guts to. All along she'd seemed less than intrigued with Shulman's reminiscence. Unresponsive. Still, he wanted to thank her for listening and for helping to pass the time.

"I hope I didn't bore you too much with my little story," he said.

"Yes."

Yes?

"But it did help take your mind off of that hill, no?"

"No."

No?

"Well then, I guess I should apologize," Shulman said. "Sorry. And good luck with the rest of the race."

"*Buena suerte,*" the dark-haired woman replied.

That Shulman hadn't placed any significance in the fact that the dark-haired woman's shirt was red, green, and white was understandable. Thirty-two thousand runners were wearing clothing combinations better designed for comfort than for fashion or affiliation. But how Shulman had missed the words on that red, green, and white shirt that boldly read TEAM MEXICO was harder to explain. Especially when he noticed that she was flanked by a group of approximately twelve other runners who were all wearing the same shirt. Was this testimony to his power to stay within himself and focus on the task at hand? Or simply evidence that those pills he took for his adult ADD were wearing off and that it would be in his best interest to take his afternoon dosage at the next water stop? Either way, he felt like an idiot. But the dark-haired woman's smile softened the blow. A gesture of international kindness to which Shulman shook his head and started laughing. And then she started laughing. And then the group of approximately twelve other runners who were all wearing the same shirt started laughing. It slowly grew louder among them. And even louder when Shulman asked, *"¿Donde esta la biblioteca?"*—a sentence that he remembered meant "Where is the library?" from both years that he'd taken Spanish I. Team Mexico answered by pointing toward the skyline off the left side of the bridge. Shulman said, *"Gracias,"* waved, then started to pick up speed as they all made their way downhill to Manhattan.

Just before he ran onto the 59th Street Bridge's lower roadway, when he was still in Queens, Shulman had seen a billboard. On it was an ad for a running shoe whose campaign slogan was "Why Do You Run?" The answer to this question appeared to be specific to today's marathon and was printed at the bottom of the sign, under the picture of the shoe: YOU'LL SEE ON THE OTHER SIDE OF THE BRIDGE. While somewhat vague, Shulman thought, he could only assume it was referring to the greatest city in the world. And there it was. Across this river. Framed within the steel girders that attached the bridge's upper and lower roadways. The Empire State Building. The United Nations building. The slanted roof of the Citicorp building. The tallest cement characters in a cast of thousands. They looked lonely. Office buildings on a Sunday usually do. A sign on the front door that says, PLEASE USE SIDE ENTRANCE. A dark lobby. A man with a mop who takes you up in the service elevator provides a slim reminder that life does take place here, but not right now. The place is eerily dormant. Like a stadium when the team is out of town.

This is when Shulman started to feel lonely. And afraid. Even more so than most men with marital and business problems who just happened to be running toward empty office buildings on a

Sunday afternoon would feel. Granted, the song he was listening to at that moment didn't help. Bob Dylan's "Knockin' on Heaven's Door." A great hymnal ballad from the movie *Pat Garrett & Billy the Kid,* though not exactly a tune that inspires joy and merriment. However, it was the very sight of those buildings that stirred the uneasiness now swirling in one of the darker recesses of Shulman's skull, as it made him recall a dream that had been haunting him for many years.

As a rule, Shulman paid little attention to symbolism in his dreams. Whether it be Freudian, Jungian, wet, or otherwise. It didn't matter. If anything, he found their cryptic and interpretive natures to be annoying and cowardly. As far as Shulman was concerned, if his subconscious felt the need to send him messages while he was asleep, it should make things obvious so he could get the information, deal with it when he woke up, and then move on. But to flippantly encode matters of importance with the use of phallic icons and other debatable representations was a waste of time and disrespectful to all people who had better things to do than wrack their brains to decipher the meanings.

The strong feelings Shulman held about the overemphasis placed on dreams was also enhanced by an experience he'd had three years earlier with one of his older brothers, a boastful, self-proclaimed Park Avenue psychiatrist who had a nasty habit of neglecting to explain that *his* Park Avenue office was on the same block as a Jiffy Lube auto parts store in Freeport, Long Island. Simply put, one day Shulman off-handedly told this older brother about a dream he'd had where he showed up naked to the christening of an ocean liner. The older brother said it meant that Shulman hated their mother, saw fit to tell her, and she responded by not talking to Shulman for the next six months.

"Why would you tell her such a thing?" Shulman asked. "It

was a dream. I had no control of it. Besides, I don't even know how you came to that idiotic conclusion."

"There's no reason why I shouldn't have told her," answered the older brother. "I'm not treating you. So I wasn't bound by any doctor-patient confidentiality rules."

"That's not the point!" Shulman yelled into the phone. "I'm talking about common sense! You had to know that if you told her something like that it was bound to upset her!"

"Well, I can't get into that with you."

"Why not?"

"Because Mom *is* my patient so whatever she and I discuss is privileged," said the older brother.

"You're treating our mother?"

"Yes."

"You're treating our mother because she went nuts after you told her that I hated her?" shouted Shulman while reaching a decibel level he had never achieved before with any one of his siblings. "There's something wrong with this! There's also something wrong with you! You fucking quack! Did you also sell her some snake oils?"

"Look, I fully understand how this can be disconcerting—"

"Disconcerting!"

"But trust me, little brother, this will all work out. By February everything will be just fine between you and Mom."

"February?" asked Shulman. "Why February?"

"Because February is six months from now and that's how long I told Mom not to speak to you while she is under my care."

But now, as Shulman was running on the downslope of the bridge, he found himself shocked by the feelings of the recurring dream that had plagued him since he was a young boy. A devastating forecast Shulman's father made about his son's future when an extra-innings game he was playing in had caused the nine-year-old Shulman to show up a half hour late for the family's pre–Yom Kippur dinner. A traditional feast in anticipation of the daylong fast that began at sundown.

"So I'll eat quickly," Shulman responded when questioned by his father. "Besides, I'm not even going to fast so I don't see what the big deal is. We won our game, by the way."

"Why won't you be fasting?"

"Because boys don't have to fast until they're thirteen."

"Your older brothers started fasting when they were seven."

"My older brothers also started drinking out of the toilet when they were nine so you'll understand if I'm a little hesitant to follow their lead."

To a little boy whose life was lived in a series of isolated moments, the infraction was nothing more than a fleeting episode. But to a father fearful that he was losing control, such renegade behavior required a warning.

"You know, if you keep this up, this caring about strangers more than you do your own family, you're going to lose everybody who's *really* important. You'll die a very lonely man. And no one's going to come to your funeral."

The bad dreams started shortly afterward.

And were replayed sporadically throughout the balance of childhood and the entirety of adolescence almost as often as his father's admonitions—delivered whenever an anniversary card arrived a day late, or when a Christmas break was spent skiing with college buddies instead of being bored to tears at home. Then years later, Shulman was horrified to discover that the dream had somehow survived the jump to adulthood.

"Whatever this dream is," Paula told her new husband upon

finding him in the other room, literally shaking, "I assure you that your father was wrong because I know that *I* plan on coming to your funeral. Want to see what I'll be wearing?"

And before Shulman even had a chance to respond, his new bride quickly ran back to their bedroom and returned seconds later completely naked with the exception of a black hat and mourning veil she'd bought at a thrift shop since the last time they'd had one of these conversations.

"What do you think?" she asked while striking poses young widows don't traditionally assume during such somber occasions. "Too understated?"

Shulman's laughter at the sight of his beautiful wife's attempt to put his mind at ease was boundless. A temporary salve. Therapeutic in its ability to deaden, if not eradicate, the images in that dream, which would disappear, sometimes, for years at a time. Yet somehow always managed to worm its way back into his emotional line of vision, as it was doing right now, while he was attempting to make his way across the 59th Street Bridge.

The dream was stark. Literal. And without any room for equivocation in its depiction of Shulman being alone. Sometime in the future. Ten years from now? Five years from now? Tomorrow? Everyone he ever knew was either dead or not talking to him. He saw himself panicked. Out of breath. Running from building to building. To all of his old houses, schools, and neighborhoods looking for a familiar face. For someone to say, "Hi, Shulman. It's good to see you." But the dream always played in total silence. The only responses he got were the blank stares or locked doors that fueled his desperation. His father's prediction. His greatest fear. Total estrangement. And now, as he ran toward the tops of those empty office buildings on this particular Sunday he pictured the people he loved and wondered where they all were. Paula?

The kids? Friends? He thought about all the detachments. His old customers. His parents and siblings. And how close his actual life was to resembling the one in that nightmare.

Shulman also thought about Maria. Here he was nearing Mile 16 of this marathon and he still hadn't seen her. Where the hell was she? Wasn't this supposed to be their day? The culmination of all their hard work and everything else they'd eventually gone through together?

As he got closer to the scary-building side of the bridge, Shulman's body informed him that he was frightened. Sweating a different kind of sweat than someone who was running a long race. And breathing shorter, quicker breaths as his central nervous system made no distinction between the dream and whatever it was that lay ahead of him.

The noise added to the mystery of it all. That dull pounding. At first, Shulman thought it was merely the sounds of the traffic above him on the upper roadway. The weighty whir of tires approaching on pavement, their almost palpable presence when directly overhead, and then their fading pitch as they receded into the distance behind him. A perfect example of the Doppler effect. From his high school science class. Good old Mr. Omerza! A man who gargled with mouthwash and spit the remnants into the lab sink. Only problem was that Shulman soon realized that that wasn't the noise he was concerned about as he refocused on the clamor that was emanating from in front of him. And staying there. And growing louder with each step he took. An insistent drone that was looming. Beckoning. And that he obliged by running toward. Deeper and deeper into the gloom. Toward the mysterious hum that was now captioning those scary buildings.

Sweating, head bent, and with a mouth feeling dry enough for the Hopi to set up pueblos in it, Shulman gingerly followed the road as it dipped down through a slight, dark passageway before

emptying onto the Manhattan side of the bridge, where he was
stunned by sunlight and the greetings of thousands upon thousands of excited, cheering people as the runners entered their borough. "Welcome to New York City!" "Way to go, marathoners!"
"You're looking good!" "You can do it!" Clapping, shouting,
holding signs, waving flags, these droves quickly identified themselves as the source of that indiscernible roar Shulman had been
hearing. That all of the runners had been hearing. After dragging
their butts in the gray shadows of an ancient bridge for close to a
mile and a half, the weary travelers were now being embraced by
a tumultuous crowd whose volume was still mounting with every
step they took along 59th Street and through their turn onto First
Avenue. And the crowd offered gifts. Of water for the thirsty. Of
granola bars and bananas for those who needed a dose of carbs.
Of music from a band playing on the sidewalk in front of a bagel
shop. And the resounding answer to that sneaker ad's question on
that billboard back in Queens. *They* were the reason why you ran.
Because they appreciated what you were attempting to do and
were celebrating it with abandon along the streets of a city that
could easily be perceived as scary to a nine-year-old man who was
now crying because he wasn't alone. As were his new compadres
from Team Mexico, who were simply touched by the warm reception from so many strangers. Though they were now connected
by the universality of their tears, Shulman also felt the desire to
verbally communicate with his non-English-speaking brethren
and share the moment in a more coherent fashion. So amidst the
surrounding commotion he called out to them loudly in an attempt to welcome them to his city.

"*Nueva York! Esta es mi cuchara!*" he exclaimed. "*Esta es mi
cuchara!*"

Team Mexico responded with nods and thumbs-up gestures
before disappearing into the swarm of runners heading uptown

on First Avenue. Shulman felt good again. Relieved and excited. Even several blocks later when he realized that what he'd actually announced to Team Mexico was, "New York is my spoon!" Though hardly the sentiment he was looking to express, it was also okay. The November sun felt good on his face. The city's buildings were no longer scary. Yes, New York was his spoon. For about fifteen blocks. Until that muscle in his right thigh started pulsating again.

Shulman Has a Plan

Shulman's plan for how to resuscitate his comatose store was inspired by Paula.

Things between them were getting better. Not because of any action they'd taken with each other, as much as what was developing in the new worlds they were forging away from each other. And were keeping to themselves. In those mental niches that are visited when two uncomfortable people are living together. The hidden spaces that allow for the return of smiles and flashes of pleasant dialogue because all of the charged energy is being secretly directed elsewhere.

For Shulman, it was Maria. Although they had not yet advanced from their sixth-grade hugging stage, his private thoughts now included movements far more acrobatic. As for Paula, it was a new account she had landed. A client with money to burn. New to the area, he said he'd gotten Paula's name from a neighbor whose landscaping he admired. They met, he loved her ideas, and he hired her to decorate the huge new home he'd just built in the upscale town of Katonah, New York. Rustic. Estate-size properties. Neighbors whose last names could also be seen on product labels. The pictures of quaint opulence on the pages of architectural magazines that could wind up being a fantastic opportunity for a designer looking to showcase her talents.

And now that the space between them was relieved of tension, it was easier for Shulman to observe his wife as she embraced her opportunity. The setting of a goal. Charting a course that would lead to it. And the summoning of the determination she would need for her journey there. She made lists. Drew up floor plans. Researched styles and genres to discern what might be appropriate. Spent countless hours sketching. Then even more time at the computer, where she had posted a picture of the client's home and then dropped in overlays to see how it would look with different options. Would a row of poplars look better here? Or should it be dogwood? What if this wall was knocked down and replaced with French doors that would look out onto a pool similar to one that had caught her eye when she had lunch at a small hotel in Saddle River?

Shulman noticed how she was also redesigning herself. How Paula had taken the retainer the client had given her and bought new clothes. And how she was now dieting and had blown off the dust on the treadmill so her already beautiful body might look better in them. She experimented with variations of a hairstyle she'd worn since he met her. Would it look better if it were parted here? Or not parted at all? What if it were cut shorter and coiffed the way Hilary Clinton wore it during her run for the Senate? All things once sacred were now subject to reevaluation. Anything to help Paula blend in and, at the same time, stand out in her new milieu.

One night in the car.

"You know what's so amazing about the cockroach that very few people are aware of?" Paula asked.

"It can hit a baseball four hundred feet?"

"Do you want me to tell you or not?"

"Sorry," said Shulman. "But in all the years we've known each other, I really can't remember you ever starting a conversation this way. So excuse me for thinking this was a riddle."

They were on their way home. From a movie that had nothing whatsoever to do with cockroaches or vermin of any kind.

"The remarkable thing about them is their adaptability," Paula stated, almost as if reciting. "Scientists say that they've been around for millions of years—since the beginning of life on this planet. But they survived the Ice Age and somehow managed to outlive the dinosaurs and a lot of other species that are now extinct. Think about it. Whether it was extreme temperatures, changes in the terrain, or even natural disasters, the cockroach did whatever it took to keep on existing and that's why they're still around today. In fact, most experts agree that cockroaches would survive a nuclear holocaust and be around long after all of us are gone."

Shulman took his eyes off the road and glanced across the front seat just to make sure that this was indeed the same woman he married and had three children with. He looked at her hands. Recognized the bracelet and wedding ring. This person was either Paula or a jewel thief.

"That *is* fascinating," he said with an inflection he hoped sounded sincere. "Where did you learn all of this?"

"From my new client."

"Is he an exterminator?"

"No. Steven owns a very successful construction company that's been in his family for three generations. But he used the cockroach as an example when I asked him how his business has managed to keep thriving while so many of his competitors have come and gone over the years."

Once again, Shulman looked over at his wife, wondering if she was trying to make a point relevant to his own situation. Her tone had borne no indication. And now her face appeared to be just as neutral. At ease. Jaw slack. With her eyes probably not seeing whatever they happened to be looking toward at that very moment.

"What's this Steven's last name?" he asked, merely to keep up his end of the discussion.

"Snipper."

"Steven Snipper?" The name sounded vaguely familiar. "Is it possible that I've seen his ads or his name written on a sign somewhere?"

"Did you know that there's one species of spiders that hides from its enemies by camouflaging itself to resemble bird dung? This helps them avoid detection from their predators, like birds and wasps," Paula responded. Apparently the dialogue part of this conversation was over.

Shulman was getting worried. Because oddly enough, he knew about this phenomenon. A few months earlier, he had found himself watching a nature show on the Discovery Channel. It was late at night and he couldn't find the remote—so the thought of getting out of bed to change the channel lost out to his learning about the Bolas spider, which was described as one of nature's prime examples of an organism that employs both protective and aggressive mimicry to survive. Protective mimicry is the act of blending in. The changing of appearance to become indiscernible to predators wanting to seek and destroy. However, the Bolas spider also has the capacity to release a sex scent that attracts male moths, which it kills with its strong front legs once they are lured to it. This is an example of aggressive mimicry. The duplication of another animal's behavior for the purpose of deception and destruction.

To the best of Shulman's knowledge, he did not give off any kind of scent that would aid him in his encounters with the Other Shulman. Nor did he wish to. Because the reality was that even if he were momentarily able to trick the guy with some fancy footwork or aromatic splendor, it was obvious that in the long run he wouldn't be able to marshal the resources needed to take the offensive against so formidable an enemy. So Shulman decided to make a few new rules of his own. He would make like a cockroach and adapt. By digging in. Fortifying his store. Fully stocking it with the products he'd been carrying all along, as well as expand his inventory to include items he never had before. He would stretch the definition of "stationery" just a bit to make Shulman's that much more personal than the frosty hollows of his competition. This way, when the time came for people to rediscover Shulman's, Shulman's would be ready for them. Welcome them back with coffee and today's pastry. And a couch and a comfortable chair or two in a lounge he was thinking of creating toward the back of the store. A television would also work well—so that any of the Sunday regulars who wanted to stay to watch a football game or the World Series together could do so. Or catch a movie on a DVD player. For those who wanted to read, there would be books, magazines from the racks in the front, and music would play throughout.

On the face of it, Shulman knew it was hard to imagine why anyone would want to spend this kind of time in a stationery store. Any more than they'd wish to kill a few extra hours at a dry

cleaner once they were handed their shirts. Or at a pharmacy after
their prescriptions were filled. Those were merely stops that people made on their way to another temporary stop. Commuting to
their errands. And then home. Where family members looked at
television and computer screens instead of at one another. Shulman felt the need for busy folks to gather. To occupy the same
space, share the same experience, or simply breathe the same air.

Essentially, Shulman wanted to build a living room in his store.
An oasis where everyone could slow down, yet not feel like they
were falling behind those who were racing around outside. Where
the very items on his shelves would not only be purchased but also
used. Where you could buy a card, then sit down and write the inscription. Where art supplies could evolve into art projects. And
where school supplies just naturally segued into study halls.

There had always been a common lament among the customers whom Shulman developed photos for. That they took
dozens of shots of their families on vacation, their kids playing
soccer, and their formally dressed teenagers posing with dates and
friends before the prom. But then, after looking at the pictures
perhaps only once, they remained permanently stuffed in the envelopes Shulman delivered them in because people had neither the
time nor the know-how to put them into albums. To lend a coher-
ence to a past they could revisit by turning pages. Wouldn't it be
great, Shulman thought, if that service could be provided for
them? Or, better yet, if they could be instructed how to do it themselves? In the living room in his store? Shulman knew that he was
incapable of imparting such knowledge. Despite his own talent
for being able to double-click on any given moment of his life and
replay it at all speeds and camera angles, his ability to organize
their print images and paste them into a scrapbook was nonexistent. But what if he were to have someone who did know what he
was doing come in once a week and give a class? To a group of

neighbors seated on his floor, helping each other arrange memories while having drinks and snacks? Scrapbook parties. The thought of it excited Shulman and inspired ideas as to how his store could be the host for other gatherings. He made a list of the possibilities. Book clubs. Calligraphy lessons. Computer classes. If anything Shulman's carried even hinted at a reason for people to get together, he would start a club and invite them over. Conversely, if he wanted to have a particular kind of club but didn't happen to carry that product, he would order it, put it on a shelf, and *then* invite them over. Granted, this did not always translate. (While Shulman understood why many of his male customers enjoyed spending a quiet afternoon freshwater fishing with a few close buddies, the prospect of selling bait and building a pond stocked with live trout in the back of a stationery store was plainly wrongheaded.) However, the spirit of his vision was crystal clear.

Shulman's was once at the heart of a town that was now in need of a new heart. And it would be so again. These were just the middle miles of the store's marathon. The ones that Coach Jeffrey always described as the toughest to get through because they were without the enthusiasm of the start or the anticipation of the finish. The daily grind of the Tuesday-Wednesday-Thursday miles that connected the two. When motivation often had to be self-induced and minor hurts tended to be overemphasized.

"You have to run through the pain," Coach Jeffrey had said. "Remember your goal and have respect for the distance that has to be covered to reach it. So don't give petty annoyances more importance than they deserve because they will only blur your focus along the way."

Whether the pain Shulman felt in his right thigh as he neared the Mile 18 marker was petty or not was hard for him to diagnose.

The one thing he was certain of, however, was that his pulsating muscle was starting to hurt. And if it was destined to follow the same pattern it had that day he wound up sitting in a tree, it was just a matter of time until it would start to *hurt*.

Where the hell are those endorphins? he wondered. Wouldn't this be a perfect time for them to make an appearance? What were they waiting for? An engraved invitation? Shulman started to giggle at the thought of someone actually sending an engraved invitation to an involuntary bodily secretion. However, he was aware that it was something he would ordinarily never find funny. He'd think it was infantile. Bordering on moronic. So why this sudden lowering of humor standards? Why here and why now? Could it mean that the endorphins had indeed arrived and were making him giddy? Or did the very fact that he was conscious of his present state mean that he wasn't under their influence? Sort of like the Catch-22 paradox that claimed a person couldn't be insane if he was sane enough to think he was insane. Shulman then realized that whichever explanation was correct really didn't matter as much as that when he looked up he was delighted to see he was three blocks farther along than he'd thought. His little endorphin/nonendorphin debate had gobbled up a small portion of this race that he'd missed entirely. How wonderful, he thought. Too bad it was so short-lived because he suddenly felt his thigh hurting again. It had probably been hurting all along but his thoughts had been otherwise engaged and he was simply oblivious to it. So, like a kid closing his eyes in an attempt to return to the great dream he'd just awakened from, Shulman tried to become giddy again by posing the conundrum *If a thigh pulsated during a marathon but no one felt it, would it still hurt?* The conundrum didn't work. Not only was he not laughing, but also his thigh was hurting more than ever. The result of either the continual pounding his leg was taking or punishment for the lame jokes he was trying to force-feed himself. Shulman knew that if he was going to prevail over his truculent thigh muscle, he would have to try another approach. So he turned his attention away from the pain by looking outside his body. To anesthetize his raw nerve endings by focusing externally on the race's most raucous spectators.

The Upper East Side of Manhattan. A twenty-block epitome of perception where high-priced restaurants become harder to get into every time they raise their prices. And where modest shops create an aura by calling themselves boutiques.

These crowds *were* different. Indeed living up to their billing as being more vocal than the ones in the other boroughs. But not without other differences as well. Shulman heard fewer dialects in the mix as the numbered street signs did nothing more than delineate one street from another, as opposed to one Old World neighborhood from another. He noticed that there were fewer children sitting on top of grown-up shoulders. And almost no people in work uniforms. It was a less gritty version of urban fanfare. Not as streetlike as it was on those other streets. As excited as they were, these people somehow seemed more appreciative than emotionally invested. Like the difference between an audience of theatergoers and the fans in the cheaper seats at a ballgame. Brooklyn and Queens was a tailgate party, while most everyone lining both sides of First Avenue looked as if they'd just stepped out onto the sidewalk after finishing brunch.

The refreshments made available to the runners were also different. The officials who organized this marathon really have this thing down to a science, Shulman thought to himself. At the mile markers that were now behind him, mostly water and Gatorade had been handed out to restore the fluids the runners were either sweating away or peeing into strategically deployed Port-A-Potties. But now, as the runners were well into the more serious, double-digit miles, the curbside tables also offered snacks designed to replenish a number of other nutrients the body was starting to run a little low on. The salt from the pretzels was a good source of sodium, important for hydration and electrolyte levels. Granola bars and tiny envelopes filled with a gooey substance called Power Gel provided the carbohydrates to replace whatever had already burned off from the race-sponsored Ronzoni Pasta Party the night before. And Shulman could only assume that the bananas were being offered as a source of potassium. That's the only thing that he really knew about bananas. And though it would have been somewhat of a stretch to say that Shulman had been running through the streets of Manhattan independently thinking, What I could really go for right now is a good banana, it was a bit uncanny when he saw they were actually available.

Shulman slowed down, veered to his left, grabbed a banana from a young girl, and gingerly worked his way back to the middle of the avenue, being careful, being extra careful, not to suffer the indignity of injuring himself any further by slipping on any of the discarded banana peels that coated the pavement in front of the tables. It was an explanation he didn't want to have to give—that all was going well in his quest to complete a 26.2-mile marathon until he launched into his Curly of the Three Stooges impersonation. So he walked to where the street was drier, and then slowly began to run. One tender step at a time. Each just a little more confident than the preceding. Eventually looking up and scanning the field he was a part of once again. To his left were runners who had stopped to talk to friends and family members standing on the other side of the wooden police barriers who had come to cheer them on. To his right he saw that he was being passed by someone dressed like a polar bear. And about half a block up ahead, he saw Maria.

"Maria!" he yelled. From what he could see, she was running at about the same speed he had been doing before his quaking thigh got into the act.

"Maria!" he yelled louder. He knew she wouldn't be able to hear him. Not with this crowd being as loud as they were. But there was a chance, he figured, of catching up to her if she was indeed maintaining the three-to-one run/walk ratio they had both started the race at. His plan was sound and simple: he would continue to move at this slower pace but without stopping. That way, he could make up the ground between them while Maria was taking her walk break and hopefully be at her side (or at least close enough to get her attention) by the time she started running again.

Shulman kept going and was encouraged when it appeared that his leg could withstand the stress that came with a little more speed. And he was encouraged even more when he saw Maria slowing to a walk. He now had a minute, probably *only* a minute, to get within earshot of her because he knew that he wouldn't be able to make up the distance if she got to add another three minutes of running.

He tried to lengthen his stride but couldn't. His pulsating (ticking?) leg made that perfectly clear. So he pulled it back to the edge of what was tolerable and did the same with his speed. Slower than a jog but hopefully faster than Maria's walk. At first, it was hard for Shulman to determine if he was gaining on her. He was in a line directly behind her, so the perspective offered little information. He swerved to get a more revealing angle, but that proved difficult because the rube wearing the polar bear costume had somehow managed to insinuate himself between them and was doing some swerving of his own. How ridiculously frustrating! As if attached by an invisible towline, whenever Shulman swayed to his left, the polar bear went left. When Shulman swayed to his right, the same thing happened.

"Maria!" he shouted, but she was still too far away to hear him above the excitement in these streets.

He kept advancing. The beep on his watch signaled that it was time to walk for a minute. But Shulman stayed on task and kept advancing.

"Hey, Polar Bear!"

Shulman couldn't believe that those words actually came from his mouth. According to his estimation, there were about twenty seconds left before Maria would start running again, and at this rate there was no way that he was going to catch up. So perhaps the next best thing was to get word to her that he was in the neighborhood. At first, Shulman entertained the notion of asking a nearby runner to put aside his or her own exhaustion and do him a huge favor—run faster than you are right now and tell that beautiful woman in the green shorts that Shulman is about fifty yards behind her—but under the circumstances he felt it might be a tad ballsy and insensitive. Instead, he called out to the only figure whose attention he thought he could get.

"Hey, Polar Bear!"

This time the guy (Arctic-dwelling mammal?) turned around and, at this point, the casual observer was treated to the rare Manhattan sight of a stationery-store owner miming to a polar bear in the middle of First Avenue on a Sunday afternoon. However, after a number of futile attempts to convey his message, Shulman did seem to get his point across to what proved to be a well-trained bear that danced his way over to Maria and tapped her on the shoulder. Maria turned around, saw a polar bear, laughed, turned forward, and started to run her next three-minute segment.

"No, no, Polar Bear!" Shulman yelled. "Please, stop her! Please!"

The polar bear nodded, danced up to Maria a second time,

tapped her on the shoulder and pointed back in Shulman's direction. Maria stopped, turned around, and just missed seeing Shulman, who disappeared into the wave of oncoming marathoners after the muscle in his right thigh knotted up and he fell to the ground, clutching his leg in agony.

This time Maria's smile told the polar bear that the joke was over and that she'd like to get on with the race. She then turned forward and disappeared into the same wave of oncoming marathoners as she resumed running uptown.

Mile 18

Shulman's Favorite Joke

When Austin popped up from behind the counter and shouted "Surprise!" Shulman was indeed surprised—primarily because he had never been given this kind of reception for simply returning from the bathroom to the main part of the store before. "What is this?" he asked when the kid handed him a small package wrapped in paper Shulman recognized from the second shelf about halfway up the third aisle; that could barely be seen under the much larger blue, self-adhering bow that sat on top of it; that could barely be seen under the even larger greeting card envelope that sat on top of *it;* resulting in something that an insane person might wear as a bonnet on Easter Sunday.

"It's your marathon music," Austin answered at the exact time that Shulman was reading the handwritten inscription he'd scrawled inside the card that read, *It's your marathon music.*

"I chose a card with a picture of two very old people on a see-saw because I couldn't find one with a picture of an iPod," he explained, as if that made sense.

"An iPod?"

Shulman was now surprised for the second time this afternoon, as he was under the impression that Austin was going to be burning all of his selections onto CDs. He was resigned to carrying his compact disc player in one hand throughout the course of the race, with about six discs crammed into the pockets of his running shorts or in a jogger's pouch made especially for such purposes. A bit cumbersome, but a small price to pay for the musical accompaniment. Yet, when Shulman opened the box, there it was. A thin, white-framed contraption about the size of a pack of cigarettes.

"I got you thirty gigabytes, which was more than enough to hold your entire music collection," Austin said. "In fact, if you want to add songs you can, because thirty gigs has a capability of holding about five hundred hours of music, which would come in handy in case something goes wrong and it takes you a week and a half to finish that race. Now, this is real easy to use. Just use the scroller to flip from song to song. See? I put them in the order you gave me. But if you want, you can divide everything by artist or category, or you can design your own subfolders to create different playlists."

It was about this time when Shulman's eyes began to glaze over. Not so much because he didn't understand a word that Austin was saying, as much as he was astounded how a boy who had trouble grasping all the challenges of unloading a carton of pencils could have the organizational acumen to master such a complex and confusing machine.

Although Shulman's own children were somewhat older than Austin, they too lived in a universe that moved at a faster clip than his own. He remembered back to when he and his son, Jake, who must have been twelve years old at the time, spent an evening together when Paula and the girls were out of town visiting her parents. So it was guys' night at the house. Shulman and Jake drove to the local video store, perused the Action aisle, where Shulman selected a movie called *The Magnificent Seven,* drove home, ordered a pizza, put the tape in the VCR, sat on the couch in the den, and farted the way guys do while watching a movie. Afterward, Shulman asked Jake how he enjoyed *The Magnificent Seven*—a film about a group of gunslingers recruited to defend a small Mexican village from desperados who are constantly attacking, pillaging, and setting fire to their homes and loved ones. Jake said that he enjoyed it very much, but did have one question.

"Why was this movie in the Action section of the video store?" he asked.

At first Shulman was stunned into silence. To his way of thinking: horses, gunfire, raiding, lynching, looting, and the decimation of entire communities were more than enough reasons for this to be termed an Action movie. But on second thought, he realized that to a kid primarily exposed to high-tech special-effects movies where plot was merely an excuse for the array of dazzling visuals that surrounded it, *The Magnificent Seven* was like watching *My Dinner with Andre* by comparison.

Shulman remembered how afterward he'd tried his best to slow things down for his son. Just a little. He introduced him to the silliness of the Marx Brothers. The intrigue of Alfred Hitchcock. And the flawed humanity of Frank Capra's characters. At best, Jake was polite. He was a good boy and Shulman appreciated his respect. But he also knew better than to press the issue. Shulman wondered if he should have shown him these things earlier—to have cultivated the boy's taste for some of life's simpler pleasures before the outside world took over. He also wondered if Jake would eventually find his own way to these simpler pleasures later on in his life, when he needed to take a break from the outside world. As for that particular moment, however, Shulman decided to follow his son's lead into the faster-paced worlds of video games and organized sports.

"Austin, can I ask you a question?"

"Sure."

Shulman, still staring at the iPod as if it were Kryptonite, was careful in his selection of the following words.

"Whose iPod *is* this?"

"What do you mean?" Austin asked back.

"Well, when you handed this to me you said, 'I got *you* thirty gigabytes.' "

"Right."

"So is this mine?"

"Well, I suppose it could be interpreted that way," Austin replied. "Another way you could look at this is that I got it for you to use in the marathon but afterward you give it back to me because you'd feel badly about accepting such an expensive gift from a young kid who toils in your establishment."

Oddly enough, that was exactly what Shulman had in mind. And though the notion that even a tiny part of his brain was wired similarly to that of Austin's frightened Shulman immensely, he *was* curious as to where the kid had gotten the money for an iPod. But when Shulman asked, Austin's posture tightened. His face turned red. And the quavering of his bottom lip betrayed a child who had been caught doing something he had a feeling might have been wrong but, because he was tempted by opportunity, went ahead and did it anyway.

"I'm sorry, Mr. Shulman. I didn't mean to lie to you."

"About what, Austin?"

Shulman recognized this as one of the distinct advantages a person who rarely makes sense has over everyone else—that it was hard to sift through their sea of drivel to determine which parts were actually untruthful.

"I didn't get you thirty gigabytes."

"Oh?" said Shulman, trying to match Austin's outpouring with the appropriate amount of surprise. "How many gigabytes does this iPod have?"

"It has thirty."

"Austin . . . ?"

"But I didn't get them for you, Mr. Shulman. That's where the lying part comes in. This was a present that someone else gave me."

Shulman's heart went out to Austin, who was visibly upset for having passed along a gift he'd gotten from someone else. A move that he and Paula practiced every Christmas upon receiving bottles of bad wine and tins of inedible shortbreads they never even bothered to open. Apparently others partook of this Yuletide tradition as well. Two holiday seasons ago, after a neighbor had given them a block of fruitcake that could have kept a cement truck from rolling backward, Shulman tested this theory by taking a red marking pen and drawing a small dot on the corner of its cellophane wrapping before attaching his own card and handing it off as a gift to his dentist, who lived two towns away. And though the dentist appeared to be more than appreciative after Shulman nearly threw his back out transporting the fruitcake from his car to the man's office without the aid of a dolly, it didn't really surprise Shulman that the following Christmas the fruitcake boomeranged back in the guise of a gift from an aunt who lived just outside of Chicago.

"There are only about twelve fruitcakes in the Western Hemisphere," he'd told Paula. "And it's just a matter of time until everyone gets a chance to touch it. It works pretty much on the same principle that says we're all descendants of Thomas Jefferson."

So now, with a full understanding of "hot potato" gift-giving, Shulman's immediate mission was to calm the shaken nerves of his dim but well-intentioned assistant, who needed to hear that he hadn't done anything wrong.

"Don't worry about it, Austin," said Shulman. "It's really the thought that counts."

"How weird," Austin answered, starting to compose himself. "That's exactly what that man said."

"What man?"

"The man who gave me this iPod. I never got his name."

"Wait a second," said Shulman. "Someone you don't know bought you a present like that?"

"Yes."

"Austin . . . ?"

Shulman's tone combined incredulity with a request for elaboration. This was when Austin started getting nervous again.

"At first, I thought that man was you. I saw him in Radio Shack and I said, 'Hi, Mr. Shulman.' Then, when he turned around, it was the oddest thing because he wasn't you—but he said he gets mistaken for you a lot."

"The Radio Shack next door?"

"Yes. I was checking out these iPods," said Austin. "Then he asked how I knew you. And after I told him that you were my boss, he laughed and then offered me a job in his new store when it opens."

"And what did you say?"

"I thanked him. But said you've been real nice to me and that I wouldn't feel good about leaving you even though he said he'd pay me four dollars an hour more than you do."

Shulman believed him. Not for one second did he question why anyone would offer a less than remarkable space cadet like Austin a higher wage than Shulman himself was pulling down at the moment. An incidental detail. He knew there was a greater message being delivered here by the Other Shulman.

"That's a lot of money, Austin. And I would certainly understand if you—"

"No, I would never do that," said Austin, cutting him off. "But then the man said you wouldn't be in business much longer. I told him he was wrong. And then he laughed again and bought me this iPod and said the only thing he wanted in return was for me to say hi to you for him. He said you'd know who he was. And that's also when he said that it's the thought that counts."

"Are you okay, sir?"

It wasn't another runner or anyone even associated with the marathon that helped Shulman get back onto his feet. It was a spectator who'd left his position on First Avenue's sidewalk once he saw Shulman go down.

"Yeah, I'm all right. Thanks," said Shulman, who knew he wasn't really all right. His left leg was only slightly bruised and had no problem supporting the northern regions of Shulman that sat above it. Its counterpart on the right, however, was doing a miserable job keeping up its end of the deal. So Shulman suddenly found himself doing something he was certain he had never done before—hopping in front of thousands of people with his arm around a strange man who was wearing a sweatshirt that had the words WHAT IF THE HOKEY POKEY IS REALLY WHAT IT'S ALL ABOUT? on the front.

"You want to sit down?" the man asked.

"Yeah. But only for a second," Shulman heard himself saying. He wanted to get back to the race. He wanted to somehow catch up to Maria.

So he hopped the curb and was now on the sidewalk, where the spectators respectfully parted, allowing Shulman and his escort to pass through.

"Where are we going?" he asked.

"This is me right here," the man said.

The man reached into his pocket, found a set of keys, and opened the door to the storefront of a real estate office. He then flipped the light switch and led Shulman to a couch, where he took a seat and then propped his foot up on a chair that the man pulled from behind a desk.

"I closed early today because of the race," he said. "You want anything? Ice for your leg? Something to drink?"

"No, thanks," said Shulman. "This is really nice of you, though."

"Hey, I know what it's like to run in this thing. I tried doing it about six, seven years ago. Started in Staten Island with everyone else, got as far as the street out there, said, 'Fuck it,' then came in here, plopped my ass down, and went to work. I have a lot of respect for what you're doing."

What a nice guy, Shulman thought, to extend himself like this to a stranger. Making him and his unruly thigh muscle feel as much at home as one could feel in a room like this. Even more so, what a curious sensation Shulman started to feel as he sat there. Although it was just the two of them, the air itself seemed thick with the energy of a group. There was something about this place. Shulman looked around. Five desks along the wall opposite from where he was now sitting. Thick binders filled with current market listings. Pictures of choice properties pinned to bulletin boards. But for some rea-son it felt familiar. In a different way.

"Was this place always a real estate office?" Shulman asked.

The man smiled. "How far back are we going?"

"I'm not sure. But I have this sense that I've been here before but can't quite put my finger on it."

"Before I moved in, this was another real estate office," the man explained.

"Oh . . ."

"And before that, this was a nightclub called Catch A Rising Star."

That was it. Catch A Rising Star. Between 77th and 78th streets on First Avenue. He and Paula used to come here all the time. The late 1970s. The early 1980s. To see young performers showcasing their talents at the beginning of their careers. A sand-lot where unknown comics with names like Billy Crystal, Robin Williams, Steve Martin, and Jerry Seinfeld would come to hone their craft. An arena where pros with household names like Robert Klein, Rodney Dangerfield, Bette Midler, and Richard Pryor stopped in to try out new material or just say hello to their roots. Dozens of their signed photos had hung on the walls of this very room—which used to be a bar. The comics would hang out here, waiting their turns to go on the stage that was over by that water cooler. How wonderfully bizarre that Shulman could still hear them now. As they spoke back then. To baby-boomer audi-ences about the world they had inherited from a generation that included the Borscht Belt comics who preceded them.

He recalled one voice in particular. That of a thin, bushy-haired kid named Steven Wright, who planted himself in one spot and spoke in a droll, barely audible monotone. One understated joke after another delivered without any more force than was needed to get the words out of his mouth. And he was funny. Ex-tremely funny. Audiences roared at the brilliance of his material coupled with the persona he'd created. But there was one joke that Shulman had personally taken to heart, and to this day its suggestion still resonated.

Steven Wright said that two babies were born on the same day, in the same hospital, and were lying next to each other in the nursery. The next day, they were each taken home by their parents and didn't see each other again until, by some amazing coinci-dence, they were both eighty-five years old and lying next to each other in beds at the same old-age home—when one of them looked over at the other and asked, "So, how did it go for you?"

That the network of events, moods, and details that comprise an entire lifetime could be casually distilled to a single conversa-tion fascinated Shulman. That the daily hiccups, which included things like flat tires, allergy shots, overflowing dishwashers, missed flights, tonsillectomies, sending back cold soup, and bank errors, would've been long forgotten. And even the more pro-found determinants like SAT scores, broken hearts, mortgage re-jections, hospital stays, deaths of pets, and misplaced trust would end up as mere footnotes in the retelling of the overall. Each episode came with its own dramas and side issues. But what *was* important, what any such conversation would begin with, were the bullet points of a life's résumé. Accomplishments achieved in spite of complications and long odds. Explanations and excuses, whether tragic or humorous, were purely anecdotal. And, more often than not, boring. Coach Jeffrey had stressed this when speaking about the marathon that was still going on outside. Every runner out there, in particular the ones who were only at Mile 18 at this point in time, would have their own story to tell about this race. However, each of those stories would begin with whether or not they finished.

Shulman took his right leg off the chair, took a deep breath, and stood without incident. He then flexed, using the same caution one would employ if opening a canister of plutonium. The leg was a bit tender but endured the full weight of Shulman's body when he took the few steps to the desk and back.

"Thanks for everything," Shulman said to the strange man.

"Good luck with the rest of the race."

Shulman smiled, opened the door, and then slipped back into the New York City Marathon.

Shulman Runs from the Cops

While he was driving to work that morning, it occurred to Shul-man that this was going to be his first job. Aside from the paper-boy, lawn-mowing, car-washing, and snow-shoveling stints of his boyhood. As well as the summer he took the Long Island Railroad to the city every morning to run errands for his father—when the earmarks of Shulman's future business prowess made their ominous debut.

"Why didn't you buy me a birthday present?" his father had asked after the small party he'd thrown for himself was over.

"Sorry, but I don't have any money."

"What about the salary I pay you?"

"Dad, you don't understand. Between the railroad ticket, subway tokens, and lunches, I'm already losing over five bucks a week. By the end of the summer, I might have to sell my bike just to break even."

"Would you like me to loan you some money?" his dad asked.

"Loan me money to buy you a birthday present?" Shulman asked back.

"There's a shirt at Macy's that I've had my eye on, but I would never spend that kind of money on myself. Here's a hundred dollars and this is real thoughtful of you, son. I am truly touched by your generosity and will be more than happy to help you figure out a schedule about repaying me."

Though not perfectly analogous to his current plight, it was not that much of a stretch to imagine how that same young boy grew to be the man who to date was anonymously responsible for more than $63,000 of donations to AIDS research, but had to take a job because his own fund-raising efforts had fallen far short of the $2,600 each participant was required to raise.

"Welcome aboard!" shouted a jubilant Roy Toy.

Shulman had just reported to the labyrinthine Midtown offices of RT Productions for the start of his first day as a creative consultant on the forthcoming television show *Who Wants to Play Dots?* On the phone the night before, he'd made it clear to Roy Toy that this would be temporary. A month. Two at the most. Until he earned enough to fulfill his marathon obligation. To finance the redesigning of his store. And to cover a raise for Austin. While Shulman wouldn't be able to match the Other Shulman's offer, he did want to show the boy appreciation for his loyalty. He also knew he was going to have to count on Austin to spell for him during those hours he was working for Roy Toy—although Shulman didn't tell him that he was doing so. Shulman hadn't told a soul. Not even Paula, who probably wouldn't have noticed anyway. The two of them were becoming increasingly remote. She

just wasn't around that much. Her days were spent up in Katonah, where she was dedicating herself to the myriad demands of
the job she was doing for Steven Snipper. And her nights were
spent preparing for the next day up in Katonah. Shulman's greater
objectives had become a full-time commitment as well. His new
day job was merely a sidebar that fed into them. A pit stop to re-
fuel so he could keep going. His nights were spent worrying.

"What does a creative consultant do?" he asked Roy Toy. An
unusual question considering that Shulman already had the position. Yet, during the course of his many years of television watching, he had often wondered what the actual division of labor was
among the seemingly endless list of executive producers, coexecu-
tive producers, supervising producers, consulting producers, pro-
ducers, coproducers, associate producers, and assistant producers
that he'd see on a show's credits. And according to the staff list
they had sent him, this show was not going to be any different.

"Basically," said Roy Toy, "you'll be working for the producers."

"Which ones?"

"All of them."

"Really?"

"That's the way it works," explained Roy Toy. "Given that
you're the only one here who isn't a producer."

Shulman smiled. "I didn't realize I needed that much supervi-
sion." In this setting he was going to be Austin.

"It's all horseshit," said Roy Toy. "But if you'd like, I can very
easily make you the coordinating producer. And then your first
chore will be to go out and hire a creative consultant so everyone
will feel good that they have at least one person they can boss
around."

"No, that's okay," Shulman begged off. "I'm not sure that I've
earned a promotion quite yet."

"I'm impressed with your modesty." It was Roy Toy's turn to smile. "Now the first thing we *are* going to need around here is stationery. Paper, envelopes, buck slips, poster boards—anything that we can print the show's logo on. And I was just wondering if you knew anyone who, let's say, owned a stationery store and could fill the order."

Shulman looked at his oldest pal, heartened by the possibility there was something in his world that might never change.

"While you're at it," Roy Toy continued, "this place is going to be using all kinds of supplies. You know—pens, legal pads, bulletin boards, computer paper, all that stuff. Why don't you look around, figure out where we're short, and add them to the list."

There is an inherent flaw in the very concept of friendship; that is, as soon as money comes into the picture, which is often at a time when a man is in most need of a friend, it somehow damages the friendship. But, whether it was conscious or instinctual, Roy Toy was handling the situation with a special brand of sensitivity. By identifying money as their common enemy. And then adopting the attitude that this lack of it was getting in the way of their doing other things together, *so let's figure out how to make it a nonissue so we can move on.*

"By the way," said Roy Toy, "I expect to pay full retail for everything."

"Toy—" Shulman started to protest.

"You hear me? This network does very nicely for itself. It doesn't need any bargains on office supplies."

"Yes, sir," Shulman told his new boss.

Shulman was shown around, introduced to everyone, and given an office. A desk, a couch, a chair, and a phone that he picked up, dialed 9, then the number of his supplier to fill the show's stationery order. This took all of five minutes. So, because the show's bevy of producers wouldn't be reporting to work until later in the week, he spent the rest of the day sketching out what he thought his store could look like once he made some changes. The new-and-improved Shulman's.

It wouldn't need much, he figured. No major reconstruction or anything that would send inordinate amounts of plaster flying. Perhaps moving the back wall a few feet. So what if his office was a little smaller? Nothing that required that much space went on there anyway. By and large, it would be a matter of redesigning—a term he'd heard Paula use in regard to some of her clients. It meant shifting whatever was already there to give the place a new look. Reconfiguring some of the aisles. Maybe a rug on the floor of what was going to be the lounge. And he could always bring in any of the furniture from his basement at home that had been collecting dust ever since the kids had become old enough to have premarital sex elsewhere.

Decorating was Paula's domain. This was the gift she'd been given and was now cultivating. What Shulman was laboring to do—envision what the space would look like if he put a couch here or hung a drape there—Paula could accomplish in no time at all. She'd draw a dozen versions of the same usable square footage, each one offering a distinctly different look with options that Shulman could never come up with. Years ago, she had done it with their backyard. Created a beautiful environment that looked far more extensive than the dimensions it sat upon. Tricks with sight lines. Forced perspectives. Feng shui. Paula was a master at doing what Shulman needed right now but he opted not to ask for her help. Part of the reason was because she was so busy with her own projects. She was feeling her oats, in particular because of the time-consuming Steven Snipper account, and he didn't want to distract her. The other reason was, well, he felt uncomfortable. As proud of his wife as Shulman was, he had begun to feel threatened by what she was doing. The company she was keeping and the grandeur of the success she was being exposed to on a daily basis. Nothing she said or did caused him to feel this way. It wasn't a change in her but the fact that he hadn't changed that caused his discomfort. Shulman knew this. And he was embarrassed.

After work, Shulman drove back over the George Washington Bridge and went to work. There was much to do. To start with, send Austin home.

"I thought you gave me a raise," he responded upon being told that he should enjoy the summer night in the company of friends.

"I did give you a raise," said Shulman.

"But what good is a raise if I work less hours?" Austin fired back. "In the end, it comes out to be the same amount of money."

"That's very true," said Shulman, "if you, indeed, worked less hours. But today you put in more hours than you ever have—so you made more money than you ever have."

"I know," Austin immediately conceded. He then paused long enough to shake his head a few times before continuing. "I'm sorry, Mr. Shulman. I guess I'm still a little upset from all that stuff that happened with those cops today." The kid shook his head one more time, grabbed his jacket, mumbled, "I'll see you tomorrow," and started for the door.

"Austin?"

Austin stopped and turned back toward his boss. "Yes, Mr. Shulman?"

"What cops?"

"The ones that came here looking for you."

The best Shulman was able to do with this information was repeat it back in the form of three small questions.

"Cops came here? To the store? Looking for *me*?"

"Yes," said Austin. "Sergeant Monday, I think the main guy's name was. Something like that. Maybe it was Wednesday. He left his card. It's on the shelf behind the cash register."

Shulman picked up the card. The cop's name was Sergeant January. Underneath his name was the Fort Lee Police Department insignia. And underneath the insignia was a telephone number.

"What's this all about?" asked Shulman.

This was after Shulman had dialed the number on the card; and the officer said it'd be better if they discussed this in person; and Shulman had Austin come back to close the store; and Shulman drove down to the police station; and Sergeant Leonard January, a cop who Shulman thought looked far too young to be a sergeant or to have the name Leonard, gestured for Shulman to take a seat on the chair beside his desk.

"A complaint has been filed against you, Mr. Shulman."

"A complaint? By whom?"

"A Martin Gordon," the sergeant answered.

"My doctor? My doctor complained to the police about me? Why?"

Because I didn't take that steaming pile Snickers left in the park and have it bronzed?

"Unlawful entry and destruction of private property," said the sergeant.

"What? That's nuts!"

Hopefully, whoever did do it had the good sense to write I AM A SCHMUCK *in big letters on the walls of that waiting room he makes his patients wait an hour in before he sees them.*

"Well, it did happen," said the sergeant. "Last night. Someone broke into the doctor's office and wrote, I am a schmuck, on the walls in his waiting room."

"Excuse me?"

"Also smashed about a dozen statuettes of the doctor's prized dog, Snickers," January added.

"And Marty Gordon thinks *I* did this?" asked Shulman.

"Yes, Mr. Shulman. He does."

"And that idiot thinks it was me because . . . ?"

"Because he has a surveillance tape that *shows* you doing it."

"He what?"

"I've seen the tape, Mr. Shulman. It was you."

"No it wasn't," Shulman protested. Vigorously.

"Mr. Shulman, I know what I saw," said January. "And if you don't mind my saying so, unless you *wanted* to get caught, you certainly could've done a much better job of concealing your identity."

"Oh, is that a fact?"

"It sure is," January continued. "Not only didn't you wear anything to cover your face, at one point you actually looked straight into the camera, pointed to yourself, and mouthed your name. No offense, but you're a horrible criminal."

"That wasn't me."

"It was so."

Shulman paused to think of what he'd say next.

"That wasn't me."

"It was so."

Shulman paused again. This time, to think of just how much about his situation he actually wished to share with this cop. Of course he didn't do those things to Marty Gordon's office. Yet if there indeed was a tape and the guy on it looked like him, then there was only one explanation.

"That wasn't me."

"It was so."

"You're wrong," protested Shulman. "Sure, the man on that

tape might look like me and have the same name as me but I'm telling you, Sergeant, it's not me."

There's an incredulous expression a person has when he's got proof positive of someone's wrongdoing and just can't believe that that person still has the audacity to try to lie his way out of it. Many years ago, when Shulman was in the sixth grade, his mother's face had that expression the morning she discovered seminal fluid on his sheets and he told her it was his father's. And now, despite Shulman's innocence, Sergeant January had that look on *his* face.

"Would you like his address?" Shulman asked.

"Whose?"

"The guy on that tape. I don't know where he lives but he's building a new store right over on—"

"So I should just assume that you're going to keep on denying that that's you?" Sergeant January asked, interrupting.

"Yes, sir. That would be an excellent assumption."

The sergeant leaned back in his chair, rolled his eyes, and now looked at him with the same expression Shulman's father had after he was told who his son said was the source of those stains.

"Well, here's what I suggest," said the sergeant. "Call your friend Dr. Gordon and try to work this out with him directly. The guy's pretty upset and is threatening to press charges and I'm sure you don't want that. Okay?"

"Okay."

This was an episode that Shulman effortlessly recalled when he noticed those New York City police cars behind him.

First, he'd heard their presence. The booming voice coming through the loudspeaker. Then he looked back—shocked to see the three patrol cars spread out across the width of First Avenue with their lights flashing.

Although it was something Coach Jeffrey had told them about, Shulman never thought it would be an issue considering the pace he was running. His projected running time of six hours and two minutes would have been easily achieved by maintaining his speed (speed?) of thirteen and a half minutes per mile. However, the fall he'd taken, compounded by his unforeseen layover in the strange man's real estate office, added about two minutes to that overall rate. Fifteen and a half minutes per mile. A person could arguably walk (stroll?) that fast—which was precisely what Shulman was doing as he tried to ease his bum right wheel into going faster. The problem was that the City of New York had other plans for those who were maintaining anything slower than a sixteen-minute-per-mile pace.

"Attention, all runners. These streets will soon be opening to vehicular traffic. If you are behind this police line, please proceed to the sidewalk and continue the race from there. Thank you."

The announcement was either a recording they were playing over and over again, or was being spoken by a cop with an uncanny ability to sound like a recording being played over and over again. The blue and white police cars were about fifty yards behind him. Rolling at what Shulman determined to be motorcade speed. He took a second to imagine what it would be like to be one of those Secret Service men who ran alongside the president's limousine wearing a suit. He then took another second to imagine that he was O. J. Simpson's Bronco the day the police were in pursuit during that slow-speed chase everyone saw on television. How odd it was for Shulman to pretend he was an SUV. Especially one that had a Heisman Trophy–winning murderer inside him. But, once again, his mental wanderings made it that much easier to pass the time. And he probably needed to lose himself in them now more than ever. He was getting nervous. The cops were shutting down the roads. His sore leg necessitated the revising of his three-to-one run/walk ratio to a three-to-one limp/limp slower one. And the crowds at First Avenue and 90th Street, though sparse, outnumbered the marathoners at this point. The hordes Shulman had been surrounded by were now far ahead of him. He looked around and saw runners who now only numbered in the dozens. Running alone or in pairs. Chasing the party that had moved farther uptown.

So while Shulman's body continued limping its way toward the upper extremities of Manhattan, his thoughts found their way back to that night after he'd left the police station. Driving. Debating whom he should deal with first. And quickly coming to the conclusion that the suggestion about speaking to Marty Gordon would be a colossal waste of time. Unless Shulman was willing to lie by saying that it was he who'd broken into Marty's office, had done that damage, apologize, and offer to settle this privately, the conversation would essentially be the same as the one he'd just had with Sergeant Leonard January. With Shulman denying that he was the one on the surveillance tape, which would piss Marty Gordon off even more.

No. Shulman's entire focus had to be on the Other Shulman. To strike back against that revolting son of a bitch who'd framed him for this. He even knew what form of aggressive mimicry he was going to retaliate with.

Mile 20

Shulman Hits the Wall

In 1639, a man named Jonas Bronck and his family were the first European settlers of the area north of Manhattan. And when people were traveling to visit them, they would say they were going up to "the Broncks'." Later on, the spelling changed but the phrase going to "The Bronx" stayed the same.

The Bronx. No matter what its derivation, the "The" had always annoyed Shulman, who personally thought it must have been named by someone who had the gout. For a boy who grew up on Long Island, however, The Bronx meant only one thing. Yankee Stadium. Home of The Bronx Bombers (although, technically, they should have been referred to as the The Bronx Bombers). Before the Mets brought the National League back to New York, Mickey Mantle and Roger Maris were the young Shulman's reason for waking up early every morning, opening the paper to the sports section, and checking the box scores to see how the M&M Boys had done the day before. Their dual assault on Babe Ruth's exalted home-run record in 1961 was his earliest baseball memory. A bit young to fully understand all the facets of the intrigue that was gripping the city, yet impressionable enough to get caught up in the prevailing excitement as Mantle and Maris were going for the Record.

But today, more than forty years later, The Bronx was presenting Shulman with a far more imposing phenomenon that also had the article "the" in front of it. The Wall. A legendary condition that all marathoners dread.

In short, there is really no physiological explanation as to how the human body can keep moving once it has run approximately twenty miles. By then, even the best-conditioned athlete has burned his supply of glycogen, a runner's primary fuel source. To make matters worse, its waste products have a nasty tendency to accumulate in the blood and muscle tissues faster than they can be eliminated. At that point, for those elite runners who are well prepared for this eventuality, the body starts to rely on fats to keep going. But for someone like Shulman, despite his more than ample supply, it becomes a problem because fatty acid metabolism requires a plentiful amount of oxygen—something that Shulman, if the heaving in his chest was to be taken literally, did not have at the moment. So, just in case there was any doubt about his current condition (which also included stomach cramps and a headache of seismic proportions), about midway across the Willis Avenue Bridge, next to the marker for Mile 20, Shulman spotted two young girls holding up a sign that said, WELCOME TO THE BRONX! HOME OF THE WALL!

He felt like stopping. Every instinct he had lobbied for him to slow down, walk over to the side of the road, and join the other runners who were stretching the muscles in the legs they'd propped up on the bridge's guardrail. As he watched them lean their bodies forward to get full extension, he envied the looks on their faces, visibly showing the release of the lactic acids that had caused the muscles to tighten. And he longed to make the sounds they were emitting—the "oohs" and "aahs" that accompanied the onset of relief. But something told him that he shouldn't. That if he didn't stay in motion, if he stopped for even a second, he would never be able to move again. That his legs would instantly fill with molten buckshot and, once it cooled off, render him a permanent fixture that all vehicles using this bridge to cross the Harlem River would have to tool around.

The police cars appeared not to be gaining on him, which led Shulman to believe that he too was miraculously maintaining the same speed despite the rather unorthodox strides he'd been taking for the past half mile. Sideways. How this had come about was easy to trace. To alleviate the stress on his aching right leg, Shulman started favoring it. So his body just naturally assigned more responsibility to his left leg. Which had been doing a laudable job of compensating until it too started to hurt because of the extra stress that was now being placed on it. So to alleviate the pain *it* was feeling, his body just naturally shifted weight back to his sore right leg, which sent it back to the now equally sore left leg, which sent it back to the right, and this sequence kept continuing—causing Shulman to rock back and forth. From side to side. At the same time doing his darndest to thrust each leg forward at least a few inches so his body would advance. In effect, he was waddling. Is this what Phidippides looked like when he entered Athens with news of its defeat of the Persian army back in 490 B.C.? Shulman wondered. He had always envisioned that mythological figure to have run with classic posture and long, effortless strides over the twenty-six-mile terrain that linked Marathon to the Greek capital city. Never before had Shulman even considered the possibility that this ancient messenger had stomach cramps and was trying his Olympic best to hold back a torrent of vomit as he waddled into Athens, shouted, "Victory!" and then dropped dead in front of the Parthenon.

Ironically, that also described how Shulman was feeling when he got out of his car, crossed the street, and furtively headed toward the Englewood Post Office carrying the package he'd hoped would even the score with the Other Shulman. Nauseous. Faint. Yet determined. He knew the move he was about to make was necessary.

There was one thing that Shulman couldn't seem to shake from his meeting with Sergeant Leonard January. Because it had occurred in a flash and went unmentioned in their conversation, it could easily have been dismissed. Or forgotten altogether. But for Shulman it was still lingering. The moment when he found out that the person who'd trashed Martin Gordon's office did so in exactly the same manner Shulman was secretly hoping he'd done it. (*Hopefully, whoever did do it had the good sense to write* I AM A SCHMUCK *in big letters on the wall of that waiting room he makes his patients wait an hour in before he sees them.*) The way Shulman would have done it had he, in fact, done it. Coincidence? Perhaps. Sure, Shulman knew that Marty was a schmuck. So the thought that someone else, even a schmuck like the Other Shulman, would feel similarly was not that far-fetched. But choosing a can of spray paint as the implement of expression (in addition to the assault on the pewter likenesses of that detestable mongrel Snickers Gordon) leant credence to the possibility of another explanation—that the Other Shulman was the version of him that came with bigger balls. That the two Shulmans were similar in taste and desire, but at that point where this Shulman applied the brakes, either in accordance with a moral compass or for lack of temerity, the Other Shulman kept going. In a higher gear. All of the dealings he'd had with this guy supported that theory. From their initial encounter on the running path, to the Other Shulman's attempt to poach Austin, to the stunt he pulled in Marty Gordon's office. Textbook examples of an id permitted to run amuck without the constraints of fear or conscience. Even that ridiculous omelet the Other Shulman had ordered for him at the diner. It was exactly what Shulman would have ordered, then picked at until it was all gone, and then hated himself for having done so afterward. And that's what Shulman came to conclude was at the core of all this. That the Other Shulman hated Shulman. And was out to destroy him.

Just how Shulman was going to prevent such an unfortunate occurrence from taking place was another story. The only thing he was immediately certain of was that if he and the Other Shulman were fundamentally the same person, give or take a few kegs of serotonin, then Shulman had no choice but to deal with the guy on those terms. To hell with manners. Or appeals to reason. People like this horrible Other Shulman spoke only one language and interpreted any approach that even hinted of civility as a sign of weakness.

But going toe-to-toe with a person like this was without precedent for Shulman. For the record, the only time Shulman had ever stood up to a bully was back in the seventh grade when Ralph Krulder knocked Shulman down and then stood him up again before stuffing him into a locker. (The same Ralph Krulder who, a few years later, bet another kid that he could swig a can of varnish and eventually had his photo appear on the "In Memoriam" page in the high school yearbook with the big joke around town being

that it should have been a glossy photo.) So taking the initiative—
in this case the rather unadventurous act of snapping pictures of
Stationery Land's gas-guzzling, noxious fumes–belching fleet of
vans—was, for Shulman, tantamount to just about anyone else
storming the beach at Normandy.

He respected the delicacy of the situation from a public-
perception standpoint. He knew that the important thing was not
to make this look like a typical case of a local businessman trying
to strike back against an inimical competitor. Hence, the decision
not to mail this in Fort Lee. A hometown postmark, Shulman figured, could result in fingers pointed in his direction, for he was a
person who had the most to gain by whistle-blowing. However,
any evidence that it came from a place too far away might make
it appear that a local person purposely did it to avoid identifica-
tion and could result in fingers pointing in his direction, for he
was a person who had a lot to gain by whistle-blowing. But Englewood, just one town to the north, felt like an effective compromise that would not turn any heads. The hope was merely to put
the information out there that the newest Stationery Land, once it
was open for business, would be launching no less than twelve
Bavarian-manufactured SUVs located at the bottom of every En-
vironmental Protection Agency list onto the neighborhood streets
of Fort Lee, the surrounding towns in Bergen County, and beyond. And then let everyone else shout their collective objections.

It was the perfect scenario, Shulman figured. The cause was
just and he knew that the town's outcry would be emphatic. Clean
air was of paramount concern to the communities along the tree-
lined bluffs of the Hudson. An issue not subject to compromise.
It's why they chose to live where they did. And willingly overpaid
for their homes in the process. To be away from the grime on the
city side of the bridge. Or the smoke from those factories down
along the turnpike. Those who commuted to work had little

choice but to accept those indignities as uncontrollable. The magnitude of those violations was so overwhelming most people felt that, while their objections were duly noted, there were so many other political and back-room corporate factors in play that they had little choice but to defer. And to reluctantly tolerate. But when it came to where their families swam, where their children rode their bicycles, or where they themselves didn't think twice about walking down their driveways in their bathrobes on Sunday mornings to grab the paper or to check out their garden—it was a different story. When the subject turned to their own streets, they not only had a say but were not at all bashful about circling the wagons to make themselves heard. Want to clear some land so the yard will be bigger? The fine is $500 per tree. A new fireplace requires building another chimney? Good luck getting that variance. And those were only examples of how they policed *one another.* Neighbors whom they'd broken bread with and had known forever. But just let a newcomer, someone not of their own, attempt to step out of bounds and the entire town perceived it as an assault. Two years ago, the local citizens delayed the opening of a Starbucks when someone notified the fire marshal that it didn't have an auxiliary water tank for emergency fire service. Exactly who reported this was never really known. Nor did that seem to be of any concern to those who took out ads, circulated petitions, and threatened to picket when the owner balked at installing the $1,500 tank.

So Shulman had every reason to believe that people would react similarly about Stationery Land when provided with the damning literature he was about to mail to the *Fort Lee Record.* Without a return address. In a mailbox that stood at the curb outside the Englewood Post Office—as opposed to him going into the building where he could be seen, recognized, and later remembered as the guy who mailed an eleven-by-fourteen single-clasped,

self-adhesive manila envelope that could very well have contained
the EPA reports and those photos of Stationery Land's nefarious
vans with the words "Is This What We Want Roaming Our
Streets?" Shulman had scrawled at the top of the page. With his
left hand. That had a latex glove on it lest anyone dust the thing
for fingerprints. People who mailed anthrax took fewer precau-
tions to hide their identities.

That night. In bed. Shulman was glad Paula wasn't home yet. She
had called from Katonah, said she was going to grab a quick bite
with Steven Snipper, asked Shulman if he wanted her to bring him
back anything from the restaurant; he said he wasn't hungry, and
she said she wouldn't be too late. All of which was just fine because there was much to think about and Shulman needed to be
quiet without having to wonder if he was being boring or behaving like a guilty man.

   He thought about the day, and the letter, and wondered if this
was what it was like to be slowly going mad. The way some of the
characters in Russian literature did. The thought was chilling, but
from the little that Shulman remembered about Tolstoy (or was it
Dostoyevsky? Didn't matter. They were the same guy, anyway) it
wouldn't have shocked him if he'd already written a classic about
an alienated man, Shulmanakov, who tried to exact revenge on his
evil doppelgänger, the Other Shulmanakov, by taking close to an
hour to mail an anonymous letter to the local newspaper before
plunging into the depths of despair. Is this how far he had fallen?
Shulman wondered. What had happened to all of the joy? Would
he fall farther? Was it only a matter of time until Shulmanakov
lost his shop, his home, his family, and became the village idiot,
who babbled to himself on the streets of Fort Leeningrad, New
Jersey, begging for morsels?

   Shulman did stumble upon a modicum of joy later that

evening, however, when he checked his e-mail. He had gone downstairs to get something to eat and became even more dejected when he went looking for food. Lately, Paula's hectic schedule as well as Shulman's own extracurricular obsessions had relegated grocery shopping to a forgotten pastime, so what was now sitting on the refrigerator's shelves was, at best, nostalgic. A shriveled exhibit of half-eaten and never-touched former food that had looked eminently more identifiable when it had been originally delivered days or even (in the case of the fossil he was fairly certain was once a roast chicken) weeks ago.

Then, at the computer. At first he wasn't even going to open the message because he didn't recognize the address of the lone item in his in-box. CJTurns34@yahoo.com? No. No one he knew.

For so long he had abstained from this form of communication altogether. As a stationery-store owner, he regarded his participation in this practice as an act of heresy. Treason. Comparable to a shoe salesman advising his customers to go barefoot. He would be contributing to the demise of the more personal art of letter writing. An endangered custom where each sentence, each word, written with a hand on a pen, was given thoughtful consideration before committed to store-bought paper, which was eventually folded and inserted into a store-bought envelope, sealed, and then posted with stamps that could also be bought at his store. At face value. Without the markup. As a service to his customers who, like him, hadn't written a letter in years because it was so much easier to e-mail.

CJTurns34@yahoo.com? Shulman was about to hit the DELETE button. But he was curious and he was alone in the house and what the hell, he figured. What's the worst that it could be? Another mass-mail communiqué selling diet pills or penis elongation from a nameless, faceless company that somehow caught wind that Shulman was heavyset and not overly endowed? (Funny,

Shulman noted, how they knew not to include him on the lists tar-
geting businessmen with lots of disposable income to spend on
travel and luxury cars.) So, rationalizing that this would most
likely be the only exercise he got that evening, Shulman double-
clicked on CJTurns34@yahoo.com and suddenly saw a picture of
Coach Jeffrey smiling at him from the screen—with the words
COACH JEFFREY TURNS 34! above it in big colorful letters in what
Shulman soon realized was an invitation to a surprise birthday
party. A nonmilestone celebration to be held at a restaurant Shulman never heard of and on a date that he would make sure he was
available.

　But it was the pictures of Coach Jeffrey through the years that
grabbed Shulman's attention. The ones at the bottom of the page
that had the handwritten captions. Parents cradling a newborn
baby who was "Home From The Hospital." A six-year-old boy
seated at a piano labeled "The Next Van Cliburn." A twenty-two-
year-old concert pianist dressed in tails on a stage at what was,
apparently, "Lincoln Center!" And a recent photo of him wearing
jogging shorts and an AIDS Marathon shirt above the caption
"Your Coach Jeffrey."

　Shulman studied the pictures. Going from one to the next, not-
ing how the little baby's features evolved into the version of the
Jeffrey he knew. The current model. Then rewinding back to the
infant, then forward again to the boy and the young man who, at
those points in time, had no way of knowing that he would one
day become a coach ("Your Coach") who was HIV positive. Shulman was riveted by the pictures and then found himself equally
intrigued with their captions. The first three were clearly written
by the same person. A woman's penmanship. The proud mother
in the first picture? Could have been. Shulman remembered a conversation in which Coach Jeffrey told him how his mom used to
brag to the world about her son's talents, and how his father, an

elementary school music teacher, had worked overtime giving students private piano lessons so he could afford to pay for Jeffrey's
private piano lessons.

The fourth caption had a different author, however. And since
the letters that spelled "Your Coach Jeffrey" had a left-handed
bias, Shulman immediately eliminated the birthday boy as a possibility because he knew that Coach Jeffrey was right-handed and
this handwriting bore no resemblance to the way he had signed
his name at the end of the letters he'd been sending to all of the
volunteers during the course of their training. So who did write
this? Shulman wondered. A significant other who knew that
Coach Jeffrey relished his current role as much as he had being
Maestro Jeffrey? Shulman also wondered if this person had been
there for that transition and helped him make the adjustment. The
cool front Coach Jeffrey presented: Was it his inherent nature to
take the world in stride and handle each surprise by stoically embracing the hill? Or did he secretly need the strength of this phan-
tom caption writer to support him through the scary parts?

Somehow two hours passed before Shulman, finally tired
enough to take another shot at sleep, turned off the lights in the
family room and went back upstairs. It was now eleven o'clock
and Paula still wasn't home.

Mile 21

Shulman Comes to Harlem

Shulman had never even heard of the Madison Avenue Bridge. Yet, there he was, power-walking across it on his way back to Manhattan. The fifth and final bridge the marathoners would be crossing that day.

His one-mile visit to The Bronx had been a short but recuperative stay as his nausea abated without incident. Which is to say that the combo platter of liquids and undigested solids percolating inside his stomach had quelled and eventually flattened to a mild simmer. Likewise, everything around him appeared to have settled down. It was approaching four o'clock on a Sunday afternoon in November. Skyward, what had been blue was quietly turning gray. The shadows cast by this neighborhood's buildings were creeping farther out onto the road. And the temperature was dropping accordingly. The "race" had turned lazy. In fact, the word itself was now a misnomer; for those who indeed "raced" had already completed the race and were currently partaking in post-race activities. But for Shulman and the dozens of other marathoners turning south for the downtown trek toward the finish line, the operative word was "casual." Some were strolling. Chatting with well-wishers in the crowd. One woman was on a cell phone ("Tell Daddy to change the reservations to seven-thirty. This thing is taking longer than I thought it would."). Still another had lifted her shirt and pulled down the top of her shorts as she showed the runner she was talking to what looked to be a scar from a cesarean section.

Life in these parts had temporarily slowed to half speed. Even the chronometer on Shulman's Ironman watch seemed lackadaisical in ticking off the digits informing him that it had been five hours and thirty-four minutes since he'd taken those first steps onto the red mat on Staten Island. Which meant that, according to the printed time breakdown on his wristband, Shulman should have been at least three miles ahead of where he was right now. And that unless he suddenly morphed into a taxicab or a cheetah, there was no chance in hell that he was going to finish in the six hours and two minutes he'd been hoping to. So why not take it easy along with everyone else? If finishing, as Coach Jeffrey had always maintained, was the essential goal of this undertaking, what difference did it make if he did so a bit later? Probably none.

And Shulman would've loved to slow down. For two reasons. First, so he could finally experience a part of Manhattan that to him had always been more mythical than actual. Harlem. A place that most people from the suburbs never went to on purpose. A scary corner of the city that you nervously found yourself in if you made a wrong turn or accidentally got off at the wrong subway stop.

Throughout the years, the romance of Harlem was something Shulman had appreciated only from safe distances. A photo of New York Giants centerfielder Willie Mays playing stickball in the street with a group of awestruck kids. Grainy footage of some of those legendary jazz musicians who had played at the Cotton Club. And laughing hysterically at the antics of the Globetrotters when he saw them on television. Generally speaking, that's as close as he'd gotten. Otherwise, Harlem had always been an uptown curiosity that even the most veteran cabdrivers were hesitant to travel to after a certain hour.

Therefore, it had been that much easier for the young Shulman and his friends to bring Harlem out to their Long Island suburbs. Buffered by the East River, which served as a moat, they were able to graft what they liked and incorporate it into their own geography, protected from any possible dangers from where it came. Words like "man" and "dig it" found their way into Shulman's vocabulary and became strange bedfellows with the ones that were already there (e.g., "Hey, man, my sister's having her tonsils taken out. Can you dig it?"). Hebrew-school kids were not only speaking the language of cool but helping themselves to some of its more colorful names as well. Picture if you will the seven-year-old "Blind Lemon" Shulman, wearing sunglasses while wailing "Hot Cross Buns" on the clarinet in his elementary school recital. Or the nine-year-old "Meadowlark" Shulman putting on a show for the crowd with a display of fancy dribbling while whistling "Sweet Georgia Brown" during an intramural basketball game against the fifth graders. Mere preludes, however, to the gravel-voiced performance of the fourteen-year-old "Satchmo" Shulman holding a prop trumpet and occasionally dabbing at nonexistent sweat on his forehead when he took fifth place in a summer camp talent contest for his rendition of "Hello, Dolly!" This long-distance relationship continued throughout his most idealistic college years. The late-night-marijuana-influenced discussions about how the government should scrub just one space mission and use that money to clean up the ghettos. Taking a Black Studies course because a really hot-looking white girl was in that class. And the wad of cash he won in a bet with Roy Toy, who'd insisted that the X in Malcolm X stood for the Roman numeral ten.

"So you're saying his name is Malcolm the tenth?" a stunned Shulman asked.

"Sure," a confident Roy Toy responded.

"The son of Malcolm the ninth?"

"Of course."

"You're wrong, Toy. X is his last name."

"No, it's a number. Like in Pope John XXIII or *The Godfather Part II*."

Then, after graduation, Shulman's entry into the real world he was carving for himself precluded any time for hands-on contact with this wellspring of Afro-American culture. A wife, new business, and growing family required his presence on the Jersey side of the bridge. And evening entertainment, when not found in a suburban cineplex followed by a quick bite at a Route 4 diner, generally implied a trip to the city via mid- or downtown tunnels and arteries that bypassed this part of Manhattan. Nothing personal, by any means. Yet, once again, it was appreciation at arm's length. The occasionally stumbled upon jazz station that was never awarded its own PRESET button on the car's radio. Making sure that Shulman's carried *Crawdaddy* and *Downbeat* magazines, which were routinely returned every month to make room for the following month's issues. And imparting to his then teenage son, Jake, the cautionary life lessons to be learned from some of the more tragic characters who played in that Harlem institution known as the Rucker Tournament.

Located at the corner of Eighth Avenue and 155th Street, Rucker Park is the fabled playground where every summer the "Asphalt Gods" of street basketball show off their moves against one another, as well as the multimillionaire NBA stars they aspire to be. Tagged with names like Richard "Pee Wee" Kirkland (who once scored 135 points in a game) and Earl "The Goat" Manigault (who jumped high enough to grab a quarter off the top of a backboard), their on-the-court exploits have become their own form of urban street theater. Unfortunately, drugs often kept literally dozens of these men in the ranks of the greatest unknowns to have ever played.

One in particular, Herman "Helicopter" Knowings, was renowned for a shot he called "the double-scoop sundae with a cherry on top"—where, with basketball in hand and street shoes on his feet, he would become airborne between midcourt and the top of the key, make two complete revolutions representing both scoops of the sundae, then stuff the ball backward through the hoop (aka "cherry on top"). As a kid, Shulman would marvel at the superhuman motor skills, in addition to the inventive imagination needed to devise and perfect such a move. But as the father of a fifteen-year-old very athletic son who'd been caught smoking dope with three of his varsity teammates, Shulman made a point of emphasizing the part of the story where Helicopter dies from an overdose. And though Shulman would later find out that Helicopter was indeed killed when the cab he was in was hit by another car, he never bothered to tell Jake. The point of his story had been made. His parental duty aptly fulfilled, especially after Jake was reinstated on the team and tested negative for drugs the rest of his high school career.

And Shulman never felt guilty about it. Hadn't even thought about it. Until now. In the real Harlem. Running on a Manhattan street that a sign identified as . . . Fifth Avenue? Was it possible? Decrepit buildings with boarded windows. Shells of cars parked at their curbs. Iron gratings protecting what used to be stores. Maybe this was another Fifth Avenue. Not the one that had the Guggenheim and Tiffany's and the apartment where Jacqueline Kennedy used to live—but an ancillary street that would soon converge with some other road and take *its* name so there'd be no confusion between this and the real Fifth Avenue. At least that's what he hoped. Otherwise, it was a rather cruel trick. Similar to the one his older brother tried to pull every time he passed himself off as a "Park Avenue" psychiatrist. Except in that case, it was simply a matter of an insecure turd attempting to impress anyone unfortunate enough to be standing within earshot of him at a dinner party. On the other hand, the folks who lived in these "Fifth Avenue" housing projects were merely the victims of an ironic mislabeling. Unintentional, but inherently sarcastic nonetheless. Comparable to calling a fat kid "Bones" or referring to a person with no legs as "Skippy." When children do it to other children, it hurts their feelings and makes scars they carry into adulthood. But when adults are diminished by other adults, it has the potential to make them feel awkward in front of their *own* children. Which hurts them both, no matter how old they are.

Yet, when Shulman looked for the pain he couldn't find it. Not on the faces of the children or in the posture of their parents. Instead, he saw families, united, happy families, who were as vocal in their enthusiasm for the runners as the crowd at any other location along the course thus far. Positive. Animated. Seemingly free from any of the doldrums he had unilaterally placed them in. Clapping. Celebrating. Some were even playing instruments— little Dixieland and jazz bands—filling the streets with that by-gone era young "Blind Lemon" Shulman had been so enchanted with. He loved what was going on. And started laughing when four black women, singing a capella, directed their homemade lyrics, hand gestures, and choreography to him the moment they saw him lumbering down their street:

> *Up in that Bronx you met the Wall,*
> *You crushed that wall, ran through that wall,*
> *In that Bronx, you beat that wall,*
> *Welcome to Harlem 'n have a ball.*

Shulman smiled and gave a thumbs-up gesture to signal that they too were doing a good job. And he would've liked to stop here. To take in all that was going on in a place he suddenly felt safe in. And for another reason. So he could allow the slight breeze coming off the Harlem River to fan his sodden body. He could have used it. Something smelled. Badly. And had for about three blocks now. After eliminating the possibilities that he was neither in the vicinity of a smokestack spewing sulfur or that he had been running next to a three-block-long herd of wet sheep, he was confronted by the frightening prospect that this was what five-hour-and-thirty-four-minutes-old sweat smelled like. *His* five-hour-and-thirty-four-minutes-old sweat. Liquid that his body se-creted. No wonder. It smelled. Badly. So he more than understood why his body didn't want to have this stuff inside of it anymore. So now it was his problem and what was he supposed to do? Run through a car wash? Hope that the volunteers at the next mile marker were handing out those deodorizers people hang from

their rearview mirrors so he could wear it around his neck? Shy of
that, the thought of taking it easy and giving Mother Nature the
onerous task of fumigating his fetid carcass was both attractive
and logical. Especially before he reached those housing projects
up ahead that would undoubtedly intercept whatever relief the
winds off the river were offering.

But as much as he wanted to, Shulman wouldn't allow himself
to slow down. Not after he saw all the signs. For "Maria." Six,
no, make that seven homemade placards congratulating Maria,
urging her to KEEP GOING! saying YOU'RE OUR HERO! and so forth;
accompanied by the shouts and exhortations of the people holding them. At first, Shulman started looking in all directions for
"his" Maria. Two complete revolutions he had made, right there
at the intersection of 133rd Street and Fifth, spinning like a smelly
top, looking for his beautiful running partner. He didn't see her.
But when he followed the group's line of vision to determine
whom it was they were cheering for, he did manage to catch a
glimpse of *their* Maria. Their three-hundred-pound diabetic Maria.
Who was wearing New York City Marathon running shorts even
though she was lying on top of a hospital gurney. Being pushed by
two equally jumbo-size runners dressed as a nurse and a paramedic. All three of whom were beating Shulman in this race. By at
least fifty yards. And this was unacceptable. Yes, Shulman had
heard every word Coach Jeffrey had said when he told him he
wouldn't be racing against anyone other than himself. And after
slogging along the pavement of five boroughs for close to twenty-
two grueling miles, it was becoming clearer to Shulman that this
was true. That the marathon was a very personal challenge with
the sole purpose of pushing yourself farther than you ever thought
you could go. No one else mattered. No one else even existed.
Wise words that Shulman had been taking to heart. However, in
the case of an incapacitated patient in a rolling infirmary, he just

had to make an exception. During the last few months, his own life and confidence had taken so much of a beating that the last thing he needed was to lose a footrace to three people who had a combined weight greater than his car, with one of them, unfortunate as it was, being an intravenously fed woman who lived on a table. That self-assured and focused on his own task, Shulman was not. So, Harlem or no Harlem, breeze or no breeze, his pride kept him running.

Still, despite the rather stunning discrepancies between the two Marias, it wasn't too much of a leap for Shulman to start thinking about his running partner of the same name. And where she might be about now. Probably the same three miles ahead where he'd be had he stayed on pace. Which meant that she'd be finishing in about a half hour. Too bad. He had always envisioned the two of them crossing the finish line together. Would she at least wait for him? he wondered. So together they could applaud their achievements? Take a walk? Sum things up? Or would she go straight home, take a long hot bath, maybe a nap, and then send him an e-mail asking how his race went? Like the one she'd sent that completely changed their relationship: *Want to go halfsies on Coach Jeffrey's gift?—Me.*

This message appeared on his computer screen six days after he'd mailed his package to the *Fort Lee Record*. Although there still hadn't been any reaction to it—no mention of Stationery Land's armada of offensive vehicles in the paper's most recent edition— Shulman wasn't upset. He knew it would take time. And that the delay was, in effect, a homage to him. The widespread excitement created by the paper's coverage of Glue had proved to be a boon to the tabloid's stature in the community. Circulation more than doubled. Each issue was six pages longer to accommodate the increase in ads. The newsstand price went up a nickel. And as a result, the snoopy neighbors whose names appeared on the *Record*'s masthead began taking their roles as journalists more seriously, given their current responsibilities as a credible news agency. They now subscribed to a national wire service. Adopted the Woodward and Bernstein practice of seeking out two sources to corroborate a story before they printed it. And were even rumored to be changing their slogan from "The Voice of Fort Lee" to "If You Didn't Read It Here, It's Probably Not True." Consequently, Shulman knew that they would not hastily run with such an indicting story until fully investigating its veracity.

So there Shulman sat. Staring at Maria's e-mail. Feeling awkward. She had never sent him one before. Probably got his address off the roster Coach Jeffrey had distributed to everyone in their running group. That part was fine. It wasn't even the word "halfsies" that bothered him—although truth be told, he always thought it was a rather silly word that now looked even sillier when he saw it spelled out.

The "Me" was the problem. It was ten-thirty at night. Paula was out. He was in his underwear. And another woman casually writes a note and signs it "Me"? It was the assumed intimacy that unnerved him. Yes, he really liked Maria. He thought about her a lot and they hugged. But when did she become his "Me"? Wasn't Paula his "Me"? A married man cannot have more than one "Me." No. Even in those societies where men are polygamists and have dozens and dozens of wives, only one of them, the special one, would be "Me." Otherwise, it would be confusing. Especially if more than one of them left a message that read: *Dinner at my mother's. I'll see you there at 7:00. Me.*

"Me" was an intimate code between two people so familiar that there was simply no need to use the names that the rest of the world knew them by. And surely Maria couldn't think that she was Shulman's "Me." Maria knew that Shulman was married, so the only way she could even justify referring to herself as "Me" was if they were having an affair. Which they weren't.

Shulman read her e-mail one more time before clicking on REPLY.

"Sure," he typed.

Then clicked SEND.

Three days later. Shulman showered far more thoroughly than someone who was simply going birthday shopping for his running coach. Not that he wasn't an excellent showerer to begin with. However, this particular cleaning was so meticulous that there wasn't any part of him, including those that rarely saw the light of day, that the Health Department wouldn't rate as high as some of New Jersey's finest restaurants.

Unsettling as it felt, Shulman fully understood the implications of what he was doing. He was showering for a date. And, more to the point, for the ultimate possibilities of what can transpire during the course of a successful date. This was not going to be an impromptu encounter. An ad-libbed iced coffee after a sweaty run. Or an explainable outgrowth from an activity organized by a third party. No, this was different. It was premeditated. They had made arrangements that were freestanding and with a life of their own. Independent of anything other than the singular intention to land them at the same place at the same time.

"What do you think we should get him?" she'd written.

"He was a pianist," Shulman e-mailed back. "Something to do with music?"

"Or with running."

"Why don't we just go to a mall and look around. I'm sure we'll know what's right when we see it."

Shulman's nerves were nostalgic. High school nerves. Fraught with the tensions associated with the unknown. What was Maria thinking? Was this just a shopping trip to her? Or did she take a special shower as well? She did sign her notes "Me," did she not? Surely that meant *something*. Still, the realities of Shulman's current life couldn't help but intrude and made him a bit paranoid.

"Any thoughts where we should go?" she wrote.

"I hear Dover Mall's got tons of great stores to choose from."

"Dover Mall? Where's that?"

"In Dover. Delaware."

Maria just assumed he was joking. But Shulman was, indeed, a married man and New Jersey was, indeed, one of the smaller states in the union so it increased the possibility of them being seen together by someone who knew him. And knew that the woman he was with was not Paula. Not that it couldn't easily be explained and pass as innocent. Two fully clothed people walking through a crowded mall on a weekday evening? Hardly a rarity. So to the naked eye, he wouldn't be doing anything wrong. No one had to know about his shower.

Mile 22

Shulman Makes a Bath

About an hour later, Shulman kissed Maria. Passionately. In Willowbrook Mall on Route 46 in Wayne, New Jersey.

And he didn't feel guilty about not feeling guilty because the night before he had tried to kiss Paula. Passionately. In the privacy of their bedroom. After she had taken the hot bath he had waiting for her when she'd gotten home late. But she wouldn't let him.

Paula had called with regrets. He wanted to take her out to dinner. Just the two of them. It had been a while and he told her it would be fun to catch up. He didn't tell her he was secretly hoping they'd have a good time so he wouldn't feel the need to kiss another woman in a mall. But the Furniture and Design Show was in town. She was running late and traffic was ridiculous and she was exhausted and he said, "Don't worry about it."

Shulman's day had also been rough—but in his case it was because absolutely nothing had occurred. The second issue of the *Fort Lee Record* since he sent his letter hit the stands without a single allusion to its content; Roy Toy had given everyone the day off so he spent the morning at Shulman's, where the most dynamic transactions he had were with the three customers who stopped in to exchange the AAA batteries Austin had sold them for the portable pocket fans that took AA batteries.

"I thought it would help business," he'd told Shulman.

"You mean, you sold them the wrong batteries on purpose?"

"Sure. This way they might also buy other things when they came back."

They didn't.

And later, when the same heat wave that increased the demand for such items broke in the form of a thunderstorm, it washed out all thoughts Shulman had about breaking the boredom with a practice run. So he went home, looked forward to his and Paula's dinner, and when she called from the flooded parkway, he rerouted all his energy into the preparation of her bath. Both faucets going with an emphasis on the warm. A mixture of four different selections from the Bath-of-the-Month Club subscription he'd given her a few Valentine's Days back. The dimming of the lights. The lighting of a scented candle. The placement of a glass of red wine on the lip of the tub. And the deployment of a towel in addition to what she would wear to bed afterward. This was always the tricky part as Shulman preferred she wore nothing. Or just a large, colorful feather, like she'd once done on a vacation to the Caribbean. Alone. Without the kids. After seeing him gawk at a native woman who was dancing in a holiday carnival. They were dressing for dinner, Paula stepped out of the hotel bathroom totally naked with the exception of a much smaller feather that she'd Scotch-taped to her cleavage, said, "We better hurry or we'll be late," and the two of them had sex for hours and laughed about it for years. But this was a much different time and as much as Shulman would've loved to have her melt at the recollection of that ancient moment, he didn't dare risk its obvious suggestion. No, in deference to the prevailing conjugal climate, it was best he tread lightly. Nothing so sexy that she'd think this whole thing was just one big seduction. On the other hand, nothing so plain that she'd *know* this whole thing was just one big seduction. Consequently, anything mesh, diaphanous, lace, or fishnet was verboten. As was terry-cloth, flannel, Pilgrim-like, and anything that had feet attached to the bottoms. After spending more time on her side of their closet than he'd ever spent on his, Shulman settled on a short silk Oriental robe (not dissimilar to the one Richard Chamberlain wore in *Shogun*), placed it next to the scented candle, and prayed that he'd guessed right.

Then waited. And waited. For Paula to get home. For the next two hours, Shulman divided his time between staring at a meaningless Mets-Astros game, checking the clock, reheating the cooling bathwater to the desired temperature, adding more bubble bath to revive the dissolving suds, and burning his fingers while scraping the melted wax from the scented candle off the vanity countertop.

At 11:23, at the exact moment a sportscaster was showing the highlights of that same meaningless Mets-Astros game, Shulman heard the key in the front door followed by Paula storming into their home, still very much a preoccupied citizen of whatever parallel universe she had just come from.

"I won't even begin to tell you what I've been through today . . ."

Okay.

". . . because you wouldn't believe it even if I told you."

Please don't begin to tell me.

Paula began to tell him.

You said you weren't going to begin to tell me.

"I made you a bath."

"Do you believe what I went through?"

"No."

"I told you."

"I made you a bath."

"Didn't I tell you?"

"Didn't you tell me what?"

"That you wouldn't believe the day I had?"

"That, you did."

I'll give it another shot.

"By the way, I made you a bath."

"Boy, what an ordeal. Unbelievable. And what did you do tonight?"

"I made you a bath."

"Do anything interesting?"

"I made you a bath."

"I am so tense. My neck, my shoulders, all full of knots. You know what I can really use?"

"A bath?"

"I'm going to go upstairs and take a bath."

Shulman had no idea what the record for the longest bath was. And though the one that Paula had been taking for an entire *Nightline* and the first fifteen minutes of Larry King, who, for some unfathomable reason, was discussing the anniversary of Fred "Herman Munster" Gwynne's death with a panel of experts, was no doubt shorter than whatever Guinness recognized, it felt like a lifetime to an anxious husband whose naked wife was sipping Merlot in a tub on the other side of the door. He'd given thought about going in there. About getting off the bed, gently tapping on the door, and whispering, "You okay?" through it. But then he remembered whom he was married to. And how she possessed an uncanny ability to say the tiny, three-letter word "yes" in such a way that it also meant "The last thing I want right now is to have company," so he didn't risk it and stayed put.

Let her come to me, he kept reminding himself. *Let her wonder why I'm not making an attempt to join her.* And why he had picked that stunningly asexual Oriental robe for her to wear. Such an uncharacteristic display of indifference. When he heard the gurgling sounds of draining bathwater, Shulman purposely started thinking about Maria. Conjured her image. Her expression upon first seeing him every Sunday morning. How she made him laugh during one of their training runs when they passed a rather tall, thin statue of the Virgin Mother that she referred to as Mary of Phallus. Those images helped his pose—enhancing the distant look he wanted Paula to see when she finally reentered their bedroom.

"Thanks for making the bath," she said.

"Huh?"

"The bath. It was great. Thank you."

"Oh. I'm glad you enjoyed it," he responded in the most distant way he could think of.

I wonder if she's buying this.

She looked great. Even with her wet hair combed back and wearing that silk Oriental robe that he suddenly remembered was a gift from her mother, who'd stolen it from a spa. She indicated the TV.

"What are you watching?"

"I'm sorry, Paula. What did you just ask?"

"I asked you what you're watching."

"Oh. I didn't even realize the television was on. That's Larry King, isn't it?"

If she's buying this, she's brain-damaged.

Paula stared at him for a beat and shook her head. But it wasn't the head shake of a person bemused that someone could be so distracted, as it was of a jaded woman looking at her husband and resignedly thinking, *So what else is new?*

There's a point when a changing situation ceases to be an act in progress and settles into a condition that becomes its new definition. Like when a person is no longer considered to be just putting on weight but is now described as fat. Or when a nice man who's been acting like an asshole disappoints people so many times until even his best friends start regarding him as one. Or when a marriage that's been having trouble for so long has deteriorated to the point where it's essentially over.

"Paula?"

"Yes."

"Could you kiss me?"

She was heading for the bedroom door and stopped. Shulman checked her expression in search of clues to her thoughts. It betrayed nothing, which quietly relieved him. A new beginning? A fair and balanced willingness to discard recently acquired baggage and return to a less cluttered time? Shulman sat up as Paula gingerly stepped toward the bed, bent over, and kissed him the same way his Aunt Henny used to kiss him whenever his parents would make him go over to her and say hello—except in that case Shulman was happy that both of her lips came nowhere in the vicinity of his. Okay, Shulman thought. A start. Hardly anything to raise a goose bump or give even the most microscopic drop of his blood reason to reconsider the current direction it was flowing in favor of offering its presence to anything that even looked like a boner. But right now Shulman's instincts were to give her the benefit of the doubt and assume that this was but a mere prelude to more involved activity. It had been a while since their respective flesh pur-

posely came in contact and perhaps this was a way of staking out
the terrain. She smelled good. Like someone who's just spent a
very long time soaking in bubbles representing the months of
June through September. He also smelled good. In fact, better
than good, thanks to a healthy splash of the Royal Copenhagen
cologne (her favorite) and the Tic-Tac he'd started sucking on
when she'd emerged from the bathroom, then quickly chewed,
dragged across his gums and palates with his tongue, and swal-
lowed lest any of its tiny white shards find their way into her
mouth once things did get hotter and heavier. To that end, Shulman looked into her eyes, held the gaze for a second, smiled,
ratcheted his head upward a few degrees, and sent his pursed lips
on a collision course with hers. Again, the result was something
less than what Shakespeare or either of the Brownings had written sonnets about, as Shulman couldn't help but notice that: a) his
head had traveled the entire distance between them while Paula's
hadn't budged an inch; b) of the four eyes that he and Paula possessed, his were the only two that even momentarily closed during
the kiss; c) of the four lips that he and Paula possessed, his were
the only two that had actually kissed during the kiss.

But he wasn't discouraged. Not at all. They were just getting
reacquainted and some people took longer to get back into certain
rhythms. If anything, he felt buoyed that Paula hadn't retreated.
That she remained frozen. In the same position with the same expression, and Shulman moved in for the kill. She was his wife,
goddamn it, and it was high time this nonsense came to a halt. He
was a man. No, he was more than a man. He was Glue. A hero
who had not only raised a reported $81,072 for AIDS research
but was receiving bags of fan mail and love letters addressed to
"Glue, Fort Lee, New Jersey," that the post office was holding
until he came forward and revealed himself to be the addressee.
He'd thought about that moment. When the great mystery would

be solved. Envisioning dozens of different scenarios in which he was either discovered or he and Coach Jeffrey determined it was prudent to come out of the shadows, and what Paula's reaction would be. She'd initially thought he was Glue but eventually accepted his denials and hadn't brought it up since. Just as well. It would only enhance the surprise when she discovered he was indeed Glue all along. And he was happy about how happy she was going to be and was actually getting excited thinking about her future excitement as he parted his lips and moved in for the kill.

"What are you doing?" asked Paula.

Those same words could have been delivered in a variety of ways that had a positive, even titillating connotation. For example:

"What are you doing?" in a breathy, rhetorical manner where the subtext is *Keep going, you naughty boy, you.*

Or "What are you doing?" in a tenor that, though slightly surprised and noncommittal, is still a turn-on in its duplicity.

Then there's the way that Paula said, "What are you doing?" which, to Shulman's great dismay, had a tone not dissimilar to the one homesteaders might have used right after they fired their rifles into the air and yelled, "Now get off my property or the next shot will take your fucking head off."

A shocked Shulman recoiled and looked into the face of his wife, who found it necessary to repeat herself.

"I asked what you're doing."

"You want to make out?"

This time her head shake was that of a woman who was thinking, *You just don't get it, do you?*

"I've got to make a call," is what she did say.

"A call?" asked Shulman. "Who are you calling at this hour?"

"Steven. Steven Snipper."

"It's almost twelve-thirty."

"I was at the Design Show with him when it started pouring outside and he just wanted me to call and let him know that I got home safely."

"He sounds like a gentleman," Shulman uttered without attitude.

He then lay back down on their bed as Paula exited to what they still called Jake's bedroom—even though he now slept there only a few nights a year—from where he heard her dial and then say into the phone, "Hi, it's me."

Mile 23

Shulman and Me

Though he was steadily falling further and further toward the back of the pack, the moment Shulman entered Central Park through the Engineer's Gate at Fifth Avenue and East 90th Street, it immediately dawned on him that he could very well finish this race. Everyone felt that way. The looks on the faces of the few dozen runners around him had magically relaxed now that they were within the same 843 expansive acres of the finish line. Even those who were hurting—fellow marathoners straining to will their way through the hurt they'd imposed upon helpless limbs and muscles that deserved kinder treatment—wore pained expressions of relief. And the tenor of the spectators cheering them on had changed from encouragement to tentative congratulations. Previous themes of "You can do it!" had since matured to ones that now proclaimed "Only three miles to go!"

Yes, it would've been insanity to quit at this point. Like dropping out of school a few weeks before graduation. Unheard of. But with the end of this undertaking now looming less than halfway around this very park, Shulman felt the weight of its imminence and the absence of clarity that lay beyond that finish line. This race had been mapped out. A charted route where sequentially numbered signposts dotted the path from a beginning to a conclusion. And while he wasn't so naïve to think that anyone's existence could ever be similarly structured, he did momentarily entertain the thought of asking the promoters of this fine event to plan the rest of his life for him. Or just allow him to spend it here in Central Park—the site of the entire course of the first New York City Marathon where, in 1970, the 127 entrants were asked to cover the distance by taking four laps around the park along the same roadway Shulman was now on.

Shulman had always loved this park. A lush respite from the chaos of all the cement and steel that surrounded it. Like spending the day in the country without having to leave the city. As a kid he visited its zoo. And as a young parent, he and Paula wheeled Jake in a stroller to the same zoo.

"That turtle looks familiar," he'd told Paula. "I wonder if it's the same one I saw when I came here on a field trip in third grade."

"I think it is," she had answered. "Look, he recognizes you."

From then on, all of the kids referred to it as "Daddy's Turtle," which made perfect sense considering that this was always Shulman's and Paula's park. This is where they'd played Frisbee on the Great Lawn. Fed the ducks in the Pond. Fell on their asses on the Wollman Skating Rink. Saw Simon and Garfunkel perform in the Sheep Meadow. And said good-bye to John Lennon in Strawberry Fields—along with Yoko and thousands of Beatles fans who were singing "Imagine" and "All You Need Is Love" as if in a vast outdoor cathedral, on a Sunday afternoon in December. He remembered how afterward, after they sang and cried with so many other grief-connected strangers, he and Paula didn't want to go home right away. That the lingering spirit of the ritual they'd just partaken of—where the melodies and lyrics were their own religion—made the cold, wintry park a warmer place to be than their apartment. So they held each other and walked. Aimlessly. Within the perimeter of their park, which was still filled with John Lennon. They walked in circles. From one extremity of their park to the other and back. Making sure that they kept their distance from those cement buildings. John had gotten killed near those cement buildings. Some sick son of a bitch had lurked in the shadows of one of those cement buildings, then proceeded to shoot the man who'd written "We Can Work It Out" when he was going into one of those cement buildings, and right now their park was the safest place on the planet. And as night fell and it got colder they held each other tighter and they stopped and they kissed. A lot. Two scared kids whose childhoods had ended a few days earlier reminding themselves that they had chosen to go through this life together and, in the end, despite any inevitable bumps presented along the way, would always be there for each other.

And now today he was in that same park. Without Paula. Thinking about another kiss.

The kiss that was destined for Maria. To be delivered in a suburban mall. Where he didn't recognize her at first because he had never seen her in anything but running clothes prior to today—so when she showed up at the outdoor fountain a few minutes after he'd gotten there, his eye was drawn to the attractive woman

wearing the cream-colored pants and navy blue sleeveless shirt before realizing that she was Maria.

"I've never seen you in real clothes before," she said, smiling.
For some reason, even her teeth looked different than they did on
Sunday mornings. Brighter. Whiter. For some reason her navy
blue shirt made her teeth look whiter.

*Now? Should I just grab her and kiss her now and get it out of
the way like Woody Allen did when he kissed Diane Keaton for
the first time in* Annie Hall?

"Any idea which store we should go to?" he asked as he
opened the door to the mall and let her enter first.

Nice ass.

"Yes," she answered. "I know one that carries some fun
things."

Real nice ass.

Willowbrook Mall was crowded. A Thursday evening in late
September. The colors of the fake leaves in store windows were
shades of autumn reds and golds, sweaters and corduroys dressed
the mannequins, and Halloween had already begun to replace
"Back to School" as the seasonal theme in card and novelty
shops. Shulman walked along with Maria—close enough to engage in conversation, but with enough distance between them to
make it look as if he were talking to himself like a deranged street
person if he was seen by anyone he knew.

"This is the one," Maria said, indicating a store called Things
Remembered. It was one of those eclectic gift shops that carried a
wide variety of items ranging from key chains to clocks to jewelry
boxes that could all be personalized because the store engraved
everything right there on the premises.

Shulman picked up a silver-plated back scratcher and asked,
"How about this?"

"You think so?"

"Sure, we can engrave each letter of your name on each one of the little fingers on this little hand so he can feel like it's actually you that's scratching his back."

"But what about *your* name? Don't you want to scratch Coach Jeffrey's back with me?" she asked.

"That's okay," Shulman begged off with mock gallantry. "I can sit this one out."

She laughed.

Now? Seize the moment? She wants to scratch Coach Jeffrey's back with me. God, those are the whitest teeth I've ever seen.

"Well, we *could* give him a back scratcher," she continued. "But if we really want him to know it's from the two of us, I was thinking of something more along *these* lines."

"A picture frame?"

"A *talking* picture frame."

"A what?"

She picked up the eight-by-ten frame and pointed.

What a beautiful, beautiful index finger.

"It's got a tiny microphone here at the top. So I thought we could go get our picture taken, put it in this frame, and then record something from the two of us that he can hear anytime he wants by pushing this button."

"You're kidding."

"No, watch."

Maria held the frame up to her mouth, pushed the button labeled REC, and spoke into it.

"Happy birthday, Coach Jeffrey."

Shulman then heard Maria's voice saying it once again when she pushed the PLAY button.

"That's great," said Shulman.

And so are you.

"Should we get it for him?" she asked.

"Absolutely."

He followed her to the counter, where a rather hefty, white-haired, triple-chinned woman who bore a striking resemblance to Senator Ted Kennedy (D-Mass.) looked up from the television she was watching, put down the submarine sandwich she was devouring as if it were her last meal before going to the electric chair, and pulled out a sales slip.

" 'Happy birthday, Coach Jeffrey'?" Maria asked Shulman about the engraving. There was a glass-partitioned section at the back of the store behind which an elderly man sat hunched over a jeweler's bench—doing his best to make good on the posted promise that all inscriptions would be done in an hour.

"That sounds good," Shulman answered. "It makes its point without going on and on. I hate inscriptions you can't read in one sitting."

"Me too," said Maria. "We're only on the planet for a short amount of time and I'd rather not fritter it away with excessive inscription reading."

She smiled. He smiled. A private moment in a crowded store. *Now?*

It was an especially *charged* private moment, unexpectedly enhanced by the interjection of the Ted Kennedy look-alike behind the counter.

"Names?" the saleswoman asked.

One word. Names. One syllable. Names. But when delivered in a New England dialect and inflection identical to that of the bloated senior senator it provided more than enough reason to induce uncontrollable laughter from a beautiful young woman with a toothpaste-commercial smile and the owner of a floundering stationery store who was hell-bent on kissing her.

"Is it *possible* that's Ted Kennedy in drag?" he asked under his breath.

"I sure hope not," Maria whispered back. "I mean, hasn't that family been through enough?"

Now?

"Names?" the saleswoman repeated with more than a hint of annoyance. The small television behind her was running the closing credits to the show whose ending she'd just missed.

"I'm sorry," Maria said to her. "But I'm not sure what you're asking us."

"I'm asking if you'd also like to have your names engraved on this frame."

Maria shrugged and then looked to Shulman for his opinion.

I can't remember the last time a woman asked me for my opinion.

"Sure," he said before offering a suggestion. " 'Happy Birthday, Coach Jeffrey. Love, Maria and Shulman'?"

"No. Your name should be first."

"You're the woman."

"True, but you're older."

"Oh, age before beauty, huh?"

"Something like that," she said, smiling again.

"Fine," Shulman conceded. "So it should read, 'Happy Birthday, Coach Jeffrey. Love, Shulman and Maria'?"

Maria nodded. Thought about it for a second. Then made a slight revision.

" 'Love, Shulman and Me.' "

Shulman and Me?

"Shulman and Me?"

"Yes," she said more affirmatively this time. "Shulman and Me."

But I thought you were my *'Me.'*

"I always sign my notes and letters 'Me.' "

"You do?"

"Sure. Haven't you noticed that on my e-mails?"

"Yeah, but . . ."

Then how special am I if you are lots of people's 'Me'?

"*ME* are my initials. Maria Ellenbogen. I've been doing that since third grade."

"That's very cute."

Third grade. I misunderstood something she's been doing since she was eight years old. I'm a blithering moron.

"No, I take that back," she said. "Since second grade."

"Even cuter."

Which means I'm an even bigger blithering moron.

For some reason, the Ted Kennedy woman now found this to be a good time to leap into the conversation.

"I sign all of *my* letters 'Me.' "

"You too?" asked Maria.

"Hell, it's a lot easier than writing out Melanie all the time."

"My friend Merrill does the same thing," another customer chimed in.

" 'Me' is also the abbreviation for Maine," said still another.

"It's probably the one for Mesopotamia too," shouted the elderly man hunched over the jeweler's bench behind the glass partition.

"Those are different," the saleswoman trumpeted. "Maine and Mesopotamia don't write letters and sign them 'Me.' They're written on the envelopes by people to other people who live there."

While this discussion proliferated and took on an unnecessary life of its own, Shulman looked over at Maria, who had turned her attention to a chart that showed about a dozen different fonts to choose the typeface for Coach Jeffrey's inscription, and wondered about the current status of his kiss. Should he still go through with it? Or did this "Me" business change things? What if he'd misread this entire situation? Maria might very well get offended. Being kissed by a man, an overweight married man, whom she liked but not *that* way. Then again, what's the worst that could happen if he had been wrong but kissed her anyway? Would she smack him across the face and they'd no longer be friends? Probably not. More than likely she'd pull away, say that it was inappropriate, he'd apologize, and they'd move on. Then again, what if she didn't accept his apology and they didn't move on? Then again . . .

Then again, who gives a shit?

So he kissed her. Right there in the store, amid those customers who were now berating another customer for positing that *ME* also stood for muscular dystrophy, Shulman put his hands on Maria's shoulders, spun her around, pulled her toward him, and kissed her. On her lips. Then inside her lips. And she kissed back. Matching both his enthusiasm and his desire to not stop anytime soon. She kissed differently than Paula did. Or was it just the unfamiliarity that made it feel so different? Its newness felt great. The uncertain ground. And its exploration was exciting. Without baggage. Marked only by the desire to get closer to another person.

So they kissed. In a store called Things Remembered. Where the customers eventually stopped bickering and turned their heads in Shulman's and Maria's direction ("Aren't they adorable," said one. "Aren't they disgusting," said another.). And where the saleswoman who looked like Senator Ted Kennedy stared at them, then turned her attention back to the television behind the counter, then saw something on the screen that prompted her to turn her attention back to Shulman.

"Hey, Romeo. This guy looks like you."

Shulman stopped kissing Maria and shifted focus. To a local newscaster. Who had a picture of the Other Shulman on the screen behind him. With a graphic underneath the picture that said, WE GOT HIM!

"Except you're chunkier than he is," the saleswoman found it important to add.

But the remark didn't bother Shulman. Not at all. Why should it? Because even without the volume on, he knew the only reason that the Other Shulman could possibly be newsworthy had to be related to the letter he had sent to the *Fort Lee Record*. That they'd received it, investigated the claim, discovered the facts to indeed be accurate, and were now exposing the man for what he was—a polluting money-grubber emblematic of all that's cold and impersonal in today's business world. Shulman's pulse revved up with anticipation of what was to follow. The red-faced apologies. The lame explanations. The possible fines. The ill-will engendered by the spate of negative publicity.

Good job! Shulman wanted to shout. *Great going,* Fort Lee Record*! You are a credit to responsible journalism everywhere!*

But he had to contain himself. Be mindful that he couldn't emote. Simply assume the role of just another local resident, another customer in a crowded store who was looking at a television only because he was told he sort of resembled the man whom the news story was about. A news story that he had no foreknowledge of, so whatever information being reported he'd be hearing for the first time along with Maria and all these other people.

Which is exactly how it played out. After the Ted Kennedy saleswoman turned up the volume loud enough for everyone to hear the newscaster make the announcement that the Other Shulman and Glue were one and the same person.

Shulman Unglued

Like anyone else who's ever fainted, Shulman had no idea he'd passed out until he came to. Until he was revived by the startling noxiousness of a broken capsule being waved under his nostrils by an off-duty paramedic who happened to be in the store picking up a set of engraved pacifiers for his twin nephews.

"You okay?" he asked Shulman, who could only nod in response. And then found it difficult to stop nodding.

Still nodding, he tried to orient himself by squinting around from his current position on the floor, where he'd been propped up to lean against the sales counter. He saw people. Squatting people. Kneeling people. And a saleswoman who, from her perch on the stool she'd dragged over to get a more comfortable view of her fallen customer, now looked more like an inflated Mr. Rogers than she did Senator Ted Kennedy (although the argument could certainly have been made that in recent years Senator Ted Kennedy looked like an inflated Senator Ted Kennedy).

And there was Maria. Seated on the floor next to him. Maria. The last woman, if he were to die anytime soon, that he'd ever kiss. As he watched her face crystallize into focus, he saw her expression of concern slowly ease into a smile. He felt himself smile back.

"We kissed," he whispered to her.

"I remember," she whispered back.

"We should talk about it."

"We will."

He felt himself smile again.

"What's that noise?" he then asked.

"It's the sound of your head banging against the counter," she said. "For some reason you're still nodding."

The off-duty paramedic helped him to his feet; Maria offered a supportive arm and led Shulman from the store. Small steps slowly growing into more confident, bigger ones. The fresh air felt good. But while it did wonders to restore lucidity to his no longer nodding head, those cobwebs were quickly replaced by the same rage that had induced this condition in the first place.

That motherfucker!

"Are you sure you're all right?" asked Maria. "Your whole body just stiffened."

That slimy motherfucker!

Maria tightened her grip as Shulman tried to wriggle free.

"Why don't we sit down," she said.

I'm going to kill that slimy motherfucker!

"Shulman, can I ask you a question?"

Kill him! You hear me! I'm going to kill that slimy mother-fucker!

"Shulman . . . ?"

"What?"

"Who's the slimy motherfucker?"

"Slimy motherfucker?"

How does she know about the slimy motherfucker?

"What slimy motherfucker?" he asked.

"The slimy motherfucker you want to kill."

How does she know I want to kill a slimy motherfucker?

"What makes you think I want to kill a slimy motherfucker?"

"Because," Maria told him, "when we were in the store you yelled, 'I'm going to kill that slimy motherfucker,' right before you fainted."

"Oh. That's just a figure of speech."

He looked into her face and saw that she was not accepting this. If anything, her feelings were hurt. She cared for him. And had just kissed him passionately in a crowded engraving store. What did he owe her? he wondered. What exactly were his obligations to this other human being at this very moment? Every leaning he had right now was to get into his car, drive over to the offices of the *Fort Lee Record,* break a few windows, then get back into his car, find the Other Shulman, and break his neck. A killing spree. Or did you have to kill more than one person for it to be considered a spree?

"Please talk to me," she pleaded.

Should he? There was so much to explain. Should he try? If he'd kissed Maria because of his situation with Paula, should he now start confiding in her for the same reason?

Although his breathing was still hurried with anger, he allowed his body to relax. Sensing this, Maria loosened her hold and let

Shulman take her arm as he led her to a nearby bench where they both took a seat. He hesitated for a beat. Just looked at her while deciding how to word what he was about to say. A thousand different thoughts competing for the opportunity to be expressed. In the end, though, he opted for simplicity.

"I'm Glue," he whispered.

"You're who?"

"Maria, I'm the one who raised all that money for AIDS research. That guy they showed on the news is an imposter."

Shulman looked at her looking at him and tried to gauge the depth of the connection. The answer came shortly. When he felt perversely relieved to see a wetness begin to well up in her left eye, gather as a tear at the bottom of the lid, and sort of hold there, as if awaiting the go-ahead to start the descent that would officially make her a person who was crying.

"I feel so badly for you," she finally said.

Boy, she looks beautiful. And so vulnerable.

"Well, I appreciate that, Maria. I really do. But this is *my* problem and I don't want you to be affected by it."

I wonder if I should hold her.

"But I can't help being affected by it. I like you," she said.

"I like you too. . . ."

"And I feel so badly that you have the need to make up a story like this."

Huh?

"Excuse me?"

"Why are you doing this, Shulman? To what end?"

"I'm not making this up, Maria. There's this guy out there who's been making my life miserable."

"The guy you're talking about is a hero. And you know why? Because he kept his mouth shut. He didn't do anything special other than to be in the right place at a time that a picture of his ass could be taken. Other people did the rest. The newspaper and the town. And he could've called attention to himself but he chose not to and it kept the whole thing alive."

"Yeah," Shulman interjected. "That was my strategy all along. . . ."

She shut him down with her silence. The impatient kind that lets the other person know she's not interested. That she's at a point so beyond whatever you are about to tell her that it's more prudent to let her have her say at the expense of imparting the truth as you know it to be.

"I lost a brother to AIDS, Shulman. That's why I'm running this marathon and that's why you and I met in the first place. I'm angry at whoever outed this guy, *whoever* this guy is. Because I'm concerned about people's interest in our charity after his fifteen minutes are up."

He'd lost her. At least for now. Their passionate kiss in front of a small crowd in Things Remembered might as well have not happened because this conversation was going to be the event that would headline the day. It was what they were both thinking when he walked her out to her car and didn't even hug each other before she got in and pulled away.

The simple explanation was this: An anonymous letter had come to the offices of the *Fort Lee Record* accusing Stationery Land of having environmentally hazardous vans that would soon be roaming their streets. So when two reporters were dispatched to check the validity of this claim, they were met by the Fort Lee store's proprietor, a T. O. Shulman, who greeted them by saying, "Nice way to treat the man who put your little publication on the map." Then he smiled, extended his hand, and said, "Hi, I'm Glue."

To verify this pronouncement, the *Record* took a picture, compared, and determined that he was indeed the man in the blurry picture that they'd run a few weeks back. Problem was that it never crossed anyone's mind that this actually proved nothing unless they first verified that the man in the blurry picture was indeed Glue. Which he wasn't. Nevertheless, the paper got excited, the anonymous letter was disregarded, and the Other Shulman had himself the best advertisement for his new establishment, as Stationery Land's new jingle virtually wrote itself:

> Stationery Land's your store,
> Stationery Land's my store,
> For office products,
> But there is much more,
> 'Cause our owner's,
> A man admired by me and you,
> Come in and say hello to Glue.

Shulman understood that vindication, if there was to be any, would have to come at the instigation of someone else. But who? To the best of his knowledge, the only other person who knew the truth about Glue's identity was Coach Jeffrey. Which only served to confound Shulman more. Sure, he could go whining to him about this infuriating turn of events. Get Coach Jeffrey equally outraged. But that would be wrong. Maria's words had landed heavily. In the long run, what difference did it really make who the accidental star of this homespun myth was? Especially to a man battling the very disease for which all of that money had been raised. To the man who had become Shulman's personal inspiration for wanting to help this particular cause. So Shulman resisted the urge. He knew the moment Coach Jeffrey learned about what had happened he would contact him to rail about the injustice. And offer to help by making a call. Or by writing a letter to an editor. To which Shulman already suspected he would thank Coach Jeffrey—yet gallantly tell him not to bother. Because the most important thing, the *only* important thing, was the overall good that this particular chapter had done. And, at the conclusion of their conversation, Shulman would appreciatively say good-bye, try his best not to say, "I'll see you at your surprise birthday party," hang up, and then schedule a maintenance crew to come over and clean up the body shrapnel that would adorn his floors, walls, and furniture after he exploded due to all his pent-up anger about this situation that had not been aired.

Shulman was livid. And the fact that sheer decency dictated that he personally take a backseat to the net effect of his good deed only made him angrier, given that there was no doubt in his mind that the Other Shulman had knowingly orchestrated things with this moral dilemma in mind. In addition to being a brutally sadistic son of a bitch, the guy was obviously calculating, to the extent that no move was taken without forethought as to the mul-titude of implications down the line. Like playing chess with a grandmaster. Even worse. Like playing chess with a grandmaster who not only wants to win the game but who would also like to hack you to death with the chessboard afterward.

He had to fight back. He wondered if there was another per-son out there who could help him. Not for his ego. To hell with his ego. This had nothing to do with ego. Maria was right. At its core, Glue was a bogus distinction. However, if someone did come forward, he would be helping Shulman by hurting the Other Shulman, which would ultimately help Shulman. That is, by ex-posing the Other Shulman as a fraud—of being the kind of lowlife who'd lie about such a thing for his own aggrandize-ment—his reputation in the community would suffer. And maybe they wouldn't want to patronize the stationery store of such an in-dividual. At the same time, perhaps the portrayal of Shulman as the sympathetic victim of identity theft who was honorable enough to remain quiet (who also didn't have an armada of air-polluting vehicles with the name of his store on their sides) would paint him in a way that decent folks would prefer to shop at his store instead. Was it possible that Glue could save him?

This is what Shulman was thinking about while he was driving to the Fort Lee High School athletic field. The place where Glue had made his first appearance. And the advance work was done by none other than Austin, to whom Shulman had given specific instructions.

"Now, the name of that soccer team was the Mustangs," he'd told Austin, who was poised at the store computer.

"Okay."

Shulman knew that the Mustangs were a summer league team that had drawn players from many nearby towns. So his initial thought was for Austin to access the team's roster from the Northern New Jersey Youth Soccer Organization (NNJYSO) website.

"NNJYSO," Austin said, pronouncing it as if it were, in fact, a word.

Shulman then asked him to please cross-check it against the posted rosters of any girls soccer teams on the Unified Fort Lee School District (UFLSD) website—hoping that perhaps some of the Mustang players (who were the only ones to have actually seen and climbed upon the real Glue) were now playing soccer for their school team.

"UFLSD," Austin said, almost throwing out his back trying to pronounce it as if it too were, in fact, a word.

"You do realize that those are abbreviations," Shulman told him. "They're not meant to be said aloud."

"How about NATO?" he asked.

"That would be an acronym," Shulman answered.

"And UNICEF?"

"Another acronym," Shulman said, while trying his darndest to mask his diminishing patience. "See the difference? Both of those examples are pronounceable."

"You mean like WASP, or NAFTA, or SWAT?"

This was just a fraction of what Shulman found so fascinating about Austin—how the kid exhibited such unbridled enthusiasm each and every time he acquired knowledge that, by all rights, he should have acquired a very long time ago.

"Way to go, Austin. I think you've nailed it. Now can you do me a favor and see if there are any girls from the Mustangs who are playing for their school?"

Austin tapped a key and the computer came up with a name, Lindsay Gilbert, that Shulman recognized as the girl who was quoted in the *Fort Lee Record*'s article about Glue when the story first broke. ("We just figured that if a chubby guy like that could have a dream, so could we. I just wish we knew his name so we could thank him properly.") Well, maybe she still can, Shulman thought to himself. Apparently Lindsay was now a member of the Fort Lee Middle School team, which played on the same high school field where she'd seen him just a few short weeks ago. Perfect.

In an attempt to get twelve-year-old Lindsay Gilbert's attention, Shulman, a grown man, deftly tucked enough of his GO BLUE shorts between his southernmost set of cheeks so they would read GLUE, and started running. The girls team was practicing on the field inside the track. Hence, the problem. By facing forward while he ran, Shulman could only be seen in profile by whoever was standing on the soccer field. And while his comparatively slimmed-down body offered a somewhat more attractive profile than it had when he'd started his training, the key to this particular mission was people's (specifically twelve-year-old Lindsay Gilbert's) ability to see the word GLUE on his butt before shouting out, "That's him!" A virtually impossible thing to do unless Shulman turned his body sideways, with his butt facing the field, shuffled his way around the inside of the track, and, for emphasis, thrust it outward every time he passed the goal where Lindsay Gilbert's team was working on their penalty shots. Which he did. For six laps. Which meant that for no fewer than a half dozen times did Shulman try to draw attention to his ass for the benefit of a squad of twelve-year-old girls. Until a parent walked onto the track and blocked his path.

"May I ask you what you're doing?"

The parent was of the father variety. Of the rather large, angry variety.

"I'm running," said Shulman. "Training for the New York Marathon, actually. It's in two weeks."

The rather large, angry father was less than impressed.

"I'm going to ask you again what you're doing. And I expect an answer."

"And I'm not sure I understand the question," answered Shulman.

"You were running around pointing to your big fat ass in front of a bunch of young girls. Is that how you get your jollies, you fucking pervert?"

The rather large, angry father got angrier as he spoke and took a step closer to Shulman as he did so.

"Whoa, whoa, wait a second," said Shulman. "It's nothing like that at all. Nothing. Are you kidding? I was just trying to get someone's attention."

"And who would that be?"

"Lindsay Gilbert."

"Oh, is that a fact?" the father asked in a way that was clearly more threatening than it was inquiring.

"Yes. Now can you please show me who she is? This will only take a second."

"What's going on?" asked a second father, running toward them.

"Queerboy over here wants to talk to one of our girls," answered the first father.

"Queerboy?" asked Shulman.

"Oh, Christ, it's you?" said the second father upon seeing Shulman.

Oh, Christ, it's him? thought Shulman upon seeing that the second father was none other than Sergeant Leonard January.

"Then again, maybe you're not you. Maybe you're not here," January said sarcastically. "Like the time in that doctor's office when you said that wasn't you on the surveillance tape."

"That *wasn't* me," Shulman insisted.

"You know this guy, Len?" asked the first father.

"Yeah. A real nut job."

This was followed by a moment of tense silence where three pairs of eyes provided the action. Where Shulman's were darting back and forth between those of the fathers'. Raw, icy stares registering mounting disdain. Impervious to reason or explanation. Daring him to make a move. Which Shulman did. By taking off. Turning and fleeing. A reflexive instinct sprung from that primal human desire to keep one's body from being torn from limb to limb by enraged soccer dads.

Did they chase him? Not really. Yes, they did run after him but without the full effort needed to actually catch him. More like the attempt homeowners make to scare a stray dog off their property. A look of scorn followed by a handful of committed steps. Just enough to make the point. That you are not wanted here. So don't come back. Because next time there'll be consequences. In effect, a warning shot.

Again, a lonely return to an empty house. Movement only in the form of a flashing red light on an answering machine. One message. Probably for Paula. Probably Steven Snipper. He called a lot. Furniture talk.

Shulman wasn't in the mood to speak to anyone. Emotionally, he couldn't even imagine feeling lower than he did at this particular moment. What a terrible day. Having been accused of lewd behavior in front of a girls soccer team by a cop who already had it in for him because he thought that he had spray-painted the walls of his family doctor and all.

But then Shulman reminded himself that he didn't have to return the call if he didn't want to. That was the inherent beauty of answering machines. That the ball was now in his court as to when the next attempt at connecting would take place. Besides, whoever's voice was on the machine was the closest he could get to having company right now. And who knows, maybe it would offer an unexpected surprise.

It did.

"Shulman, it's Maria. Could you please call me? It's important."

They'd never used telephones before. All of their previous communications were conveyed with the detached intimacy that develops when eye contact is supplanted by a screen and a keyboard. But this was startlingly different. Because here was Maria's actual voice. Right here in his house. Not that he wasn't happy to hear from her. Because he was. But along with this satisfaction came a particular brand of guilt he hadn't experienced before. That the voice of a woman he'd passionately kissed while buying a talking picture frame was in his home on a tape that could be replayed. Which he did.

"Shulman, it's Maria. Could you please call me? It's important."

The first time he'd heard it, the shock of who the caller was overwhelmed everything else. But on this airing, the combination of words and tone came through. She was upset. About them? The kiss? The way they'd left each other in the Willowbrook Mall parking lot?

Again.

"Shulman, it's Maria. Could you please call me? It's important."

He felt badly too. And he needed to talk to her too. It *was* important. So he got his roster of AIDS marathoners, found Maria's number, and dialed. Maria picked up before the end of the first ring.

"Hello."

Her voice was barely recognizable. Unsteady. Weak.

"Maria? It's me. Shulman."

"Hi."

Only a slight, only a very slight, hint of relief upon hearing that it was him.

"Maria, are you okay?"

"Shulman—"

"Look, Maria. I'm really sorry about our conversation yesterday. It was incredibly insensitive of me and—"

"Shulman . . ."

"Yes?"

"Coach Jeffrey died."

Coach Jeffrey (1971–2005)

Shock. The kind that numbs the entire body into a daze. Where voluntary movements become efforts. And pangs like hunger often go ignored.

Shulman knew that Coach Jeffrey was sick but had expected his death to take a much wider turn. But according to Maria, pneumonia could be as virulent as any cancer when it runs unopposed by an immune system.

"My brother died the same way," she said. "One night we were at a Yankees game, four days later he was in a coma."

Their plan was to meet at the chapel. Justin A. Campbell & Sons Funeral Home in New City—a small, rural community up in Rockland County. Whoever got there first would save a seat for the other. Shulman thought about suggesting they drive there together. That he'd pick her up and they'd spend as much time in each other's company as possible—which seemed appropriate given their relationship to Coach Jeffrey. But he decided against it given their relationship with each other. One that was still groping for definition and the rules of behavior associated with it. Mostly, he was curious about the ride home afterward. The denouement of what undoubtedly would be an emotionally wracked afternoon where they may not want to deal with their respective grief in the same manner. Where one would desire the other's company but the other would rather be alone, setting the scene for potential awkwardness when he dropped her off at her house. So he didn't bring it up, figuring that if they ultimately decided they wanted to console each other they'd arrange to take two cars to the same place.

On the other hand, there was no question that he didn't want Paula to be with him and wouldn't have asked her to be even if she hadn't been out of town at still another design show. No. This was going to be the kind of day where Shulman would rather not have to explain how he was feeling or impose introductions upon anyone who was feeling the same way he was.

The Justin A. Campbell & Sons Funeral Home was crowded. Packed with people who, at least for the next hour or so, were related. Upon entering, Shulman scanned the chapel and saw that the runners from the "Fred Mertz" pace group were sitting together and others whom Shulman recognized from Sunday mornings were seated with their groups as well; situated very much the same way as on those Sunday mornings, with the fastest group in the front and Shulman's three rows from the back wall.

Despite his advanced age, Shulman had never been to a non-Jewish funeral before. Not that he didn't know any Christian people. It's just that the ones he knew were still breathing. But, despite his unfamiliarity with the service that was about to begin, when two young men who looked exactly alike and who were dressed in the same blue suits with red roses in their lapels approached him with synchronized steps, Shulman had a feeling that this duo would be considered out of the ordinary at any funeral of any denomination.

"We are so sorry about your loss," said the young man on the left.

"So very sorry," said his equally young counterpart on the right.

"Thank you," Shulman responded, like a man who hadn't ruled out the possibility that he was suddenly seeing double.

"Family?" asked the one on the left.

"Friend?" asked the one on the right.

"Friend," answered Shulman.

As if their heads were connected by an invisible line of monofilament being tugged by either a fisherman or a puppeteer crouching between the pews, the two young men nodded in unison before closing their eyes and mournfully shaking their heads this way, that way, then this way again.

"We're so, so sorry," they both said.

Shulman found himself praying for a lifeboat when he saw Maria's hand shoot up and wave for him to join her.

"I see you met & Sons," Maria said as Shulman took his seat.

"Who?"

"The twins you were just talking to. They're Justin A. Campbell's & Sons. They greeted everyone the same way."

"Oh." Shulman reacted with mock disappointment. "And here I thought I was so special."

There's something unsettling about attending the funeral of someone you really don't know. It feels a little wrong. Intrusive. That

you might know a person only one way, because of a single dimension of his existence, and then fit the pieces of the rest of the
life he no longer has together by hearing things about him that
you didn't know spoken by people that you weren't aware of. For
example, first learning that a classical pianist was also an ardent
fan of Bob Dylan when members of his old string section played
"I Shall Be Released." Figuring out that his parents must be the
two older people in the front row. And not knowing that you'd be
allowed to laugh today until the anecdotes were being told. By the
close friends and cohorts who came up, one by one, to share the
man they knew as Jeffrey with everyone who was nodding and
laughing and dabbing the corners of their eyes because what they
were hearing was so typical of the person they already missed.
Stories about his Tabasco sauce collection. And about dressing up
as Millard Fillmore every year during the Presidents' Day pag-
eants he produced at his old elementary school. A cellist told of
the time that Jeffrey had finished running the Munich Marathon a
little slower than he'd anticipated so they had to hold the start of
the German Philharmonic twenty minutes that evening so he
could shower and change into his tuxedo. A young nephew told
about how last Memorial Day his Uncle Jeffrey barbecued far too
many spareribs for his guests—so he set up wooden police barri-
cades at both ends of his street and served the dozens of untouched
ones at an impromptu block party for the entire neighborhood. An
old classmate told about the day Jeffrey pulled up alongside a
man driving a Porsche and challenged him to a drag race in his
aged Datsun and, of course, the Porsche beat him soundly. Then
how, about a month later, Jeffrey had happened to pass a house
and saw the same Porsche in its driveway. So he got out of his
Datsun, walked up to the house, knocked, and when the man answered the front door Jeffrey said, "Two out of three."

But what resonated most were the words of a large, doughy

man with a sweet smile who spoke last. His name was Bryan. And he spoke from the heart about the man he'd been living with for the past six years. Stories. Some of them humorous. But it was the love he had for Jeffrey that moved everyone. A feeling relatable to anyone who'd ever felt this way about another human being. It wasn't sad—Bryan made a point of saying that Jeffrey had threatened to come back and rearrange their furniture if he was sad. This made people laugh. Shulman looked at Jeffrey's parents. They too were laughing. Their son was being eulogized by someone who adored him in a way that they never could and their appreciation was evident. Was this always the case? Or was there a long period of uneasiness and adjustment after they first learned their son was gay? Had Jeffrey been hesitant to tell them? Shulman, the father of three, used to wonder how he would react if any of his children came to him with similar news. He'd always hoped that they wouldn't be afraid to tell him and that he would be immediately accepting. That his love for his child would easily trump any personal discomfort he had about a lifestyle he didn't understand. Still, despite this resolve, he was relieved not to have been put to that test. As for Jeffrey's parents, whom Shulman estimated to be in their early seventies—well, no matter what road they'd taken to get here, they were not only laughing but further showed their love for Jeffrey in the way they hugged Bryan when he approached them after he stepped down from the pulpit.

During the course of the service, Shulman had his arm around Maria. Many in their running group were doing the same, or holding hands, as people often do when consoling each other at a time of common loss. Even the intermittent squeezes he gave her arm and Maria's occasionally putting her head on his shoulder could be regarded as nothing more than reflexive gestures tied to the emotionality of any given moment. And when they made eye contact it was pretty much the same. Sympathetic vigilance being paid to a friend who no doubt was reliving scenes she had experienced once before when her brother had died.

But then it was over and they were outside. On the top step of the funeral home that & Sons owned with their dad, Justin A., and Shulman's arm was still around Maria. And hers around him. People were hugging. Kissing cheeks. Some saying their good-byes. The rest forming a line with their cars for the drive to a cemetery where they would say their final good-byes to Coach Jeffrey. It wouldn't have been appropriate for Shulman and Maria to attend the burial—a private interment for the family and his closest friends—which made this particular moment even more awkward for them. Standing there. Shifting feet. Unsure of the next move. Like a couple at a doorstep after a date.

"What should we do now?" Maria asked.

It was starting to get dark. People were leaving. Pretty soon they would be alone.

"Well," he said. Maria's teeth were starting to look white, incredibly white, again. "We could—"

"Excuse me, but are you Shulman?"

It was Bryan. Coach Jeffrey's Bryan. Shulman had looked for him after the service to extend condolences but couldn't find him.

"Yes, I'm Shulman. I'm sorry about your loss."

They shook hands.

"This is Maria," Shulman said.

They exchanged nods, and then Bryan leaned in and whispered to Shulman, "Can I see you for a second?"

"Sure," answered a surprised Shulman. "I'll be right back," he told Maria and then let Bryan lead him a few steps away.

"Jeffrey spoke of you often," Bryan said.

"He did?"

Shulman noticed that Bryan's eyes were red and puffy. Like

he'd been crying. Understandable given the circumstances. But in direct violation of Coach Jeffrey's wish that no one be sad.

"Yes," said Bryan. "He referred to you as his 'special project.' And he wanted me to give you this."

He reached inside his jacket and pulled out an envelope that he handed to Shulman.

"What's this?" he asked Bryan.

"A letter that he wrote to you. Actually, it's a letter he dictated to me that I wrote to you. He got very weak toward the end."

Shulman took the letter, written on yellow pages from a Gold Fibre legal pad, out of the envelope and immediately recognized Bryan's handwriting, with a left-handed bias, to be the same as that in the "Your Coach Jeffrey" caption under the fourth picture on the birthday invitation. He then angled his body to take advantage of the light that just came on in through the window behind him and started reading.

Shulman—

I was thinking about you when I heard about that jerk taking credit for being you but I purposely didn't call because, well, because I was in the middle of dying so please excuse me for being preoccupied with other matters. But I was proud of you for not feeling the need to call me and crying "foul." And even if you felt like calling, thanks for not doing so because it would've been embarrassing for the both of us given that I was dying and all. (By the way, if any of this sounds incoherent or tends to wander, please blame it on these painkillers they're dripping into my veins and not on Bryan, whom I've instructed to not change a word because this is who I am right now and, let's face it, what good would it do me to impress you or anyone else with proper grammar at this point?)

Shulman looked up and made eye contact with Bryan, who, sensing exactly where Shulman was in his reading, smiled and nodded sheepishly.

"I understand." Shulman's smile returned in kind before he turned his attention back to the letter.

I'm glad I met you, Shulman. And if you have any plans whatsoever to feel badly because I won't be around to bug you, don't—because you will have missed my point. When we're born we're given these bodies to live in during the course of our lives and I had fun with my body. It carried me around a world that would've been hard to experience otherwise, it allowed me to enjoy the music that comes from some place else as it played through me, and it gave me the ability to communicate my deep affections to the people I have loved. Do I wish that my body would have stayed healthier longer? Of course. There are other things I never got around to doing and some other things that I would've enjoyed doing a few more times—although I must say that standing on a long line while my body waits its turn to buy a ticket to a movie that I often end up hating is not something I'll be pining for. But all in all, I'm pleased. Are you, Shulman? I sense not. Why do I say this? Well, because I also sense that you are searching outside the scope of that pudgy body you've been given for total integration. It's foolhardy, Shulman, to think that any form of life beyond the physical space you occupy can help balance what's lacking within. In the music world, it would be the same as assuming that a shitty song will stir an audience if it's played in Carnegie Hall. And in the world of 26.2-mile marathons, it's comparable to the illogic that someone can complete the damn thing just because the course runs through his old neighborhoods while he's listening to old songs.

Extended worlds provide nourishment, Shulman, but they can't sustain you. Only you can sustain you — just like only you can beat you. Don't lose to yourself, Shulman. No matter how scary it is, find the guts to confront your demons, whatever they may be, in whatever forms they may present themselves, meet them head on, put them to permanent rest, and commit yourself to whoever it is you really want to be. And once you do that, you'll be shocked how quickly everything else will fall into place.

I have to go now, Shulman. There's still much for me to do before I won't be able to do anything anymore. Take good care of yourself, my friend. Have fun during your marathon and remember what I said about what happens to your relationship with those things you can't control once you square things within yourself. "At the moment of commitment, the universe conspires to assist you." Ever hear that saying? I believe it's a quote by the German philosopher/playwright Goethe, although in my current loopy state if you told me that it was actually said by former N.Y. Yankees catcher/manager Yogi Berra I'd probably believe you.

Your Coach Jeffrey

P.S. Almost forgot — I never told you how to run downhill. Well, I'm glad I remembered now because it is, in its own way, the most deceptive and treacherous part of any race. It seems easy for obvious reasons. But the instinct that all runners have — to lean back in an effort to counterbalance the pull of gravity — is the worst thing you can do as it puts a dangerous amount of stress on your knees and heels. Especially toward the end of the race when your body's fatigued and welcomes the free speed. The trick, then, is to tilt forward. That's right, Shulman. Tilt from that economy-sized pelvis of yours in the direction of the

*downward slope and take advantage of the free speed. You've
earned it. So enjoy it. Until the next upwards gradient, that is. At
which point you'll go back to leaning in the opposite direction so
you can embrace the hill. Not a bad cycle, huh? Enjoying and
embracing. I told you this running thing could be fun.*

Shulman stared at the page for another beat. At the top of the
now deserted steps of a funeral home named after a man and his
twin sons. Wanting to linger in the world of the words dictated by
a man who, according to doctors like Marty Gordon, didn't exist
anymore.

He finally looked up. Just in time to see Bryan getting into the
front seat of the lead car of a procession about to take the love of
his life to a cemetery. Shulman held his gaze, hoping Bryan would
somehow feel it and turn his way. Somehow Bryan didn't feel it.
Still, Shulman stood frozen. For as long as it took twelve cars to
pull away and disappear around a corner. The next words he
heard were Maria's.

"Are you okay?" she asked.

She took hold of his arm. Then pulled herself toward him.

"Uh-huh," he answered, nodding. "You?"

"I'm all right," she said in the same unconvincing tone. "Listen, I don't know if you have anything planned, but if you'd like
to come over . . ."

Maria's voice trailed off the way people's do after they've made
their point but then lose confidence immediately after their point's
been made. Shulman understood this and tried to time his response
with the proper consideration. Quickly enough so Maria wouldn't
feel foolish by the silence, but not so quick as to give the impression he had a ready answer for her highly attractive invitation.

"I'd love to," he said. "But there are a few things I have to do. Can I call you later?"

Despite her smile, Shulman couldn't determine whether she felt badly or relieved.

"Sure."

Then they hugged. The way they used to.

Mile 26

On the Bus to Staten Island

During this particular mile of the New York City Marathon, the runners exit Central Park at 59th Street. Turning right, they cover the width of the park along surface streets—where they pass a number of fancy hotels and restaurants—and then reenter the park at Columbus Circle. It was at that point in 1994 that a Mexican marathoner named German Silva took a wrong turn into the park and subsequently left the course. He ran about twenty-five meters before noticing the looks of horror on spectators' faces. Realizing his mistake, he turned around, summoned up all of his speed, caught and passed his friend and training partner Benjamin Paredes at the twenty-six-mile mark before continuing on to win.

German Silva was one of thirteen children. He grew up on an orange farm with no electricity and legend had it that he did his marathon training at twelve thousand feet on the side of a volcano. These were but a few of the myriad dissimilarities between Shulman and this man. (In addition to the fact that, when Silva won his race, all the other runners were behind him while Shulman, at this point, couldn't help but notice that all the other runners were in front of him.)

There was one thing they did have in common, however. They both had great affection for their hometowns. Upon winning the marathon, Silva used his fame, wealth, and newfound influence to help secure electricity and medical aid for his rural village of Tecomate. As for Shulman, his love for the community of Fort Lee, New Jersey, was equally profound. Still. Despite the fact that its customers had abandoned him, its newspaper screwed him, and its police department was after him. It didn't matter.

The comfort derived from the familiar is a triumph of the irrational. Oftentimes, little more than emotional retardation posing as romance. But Shulman had undergone some woefully belated upheavals that lent substance to this resolve. Call them the lessons of Coach Jeffrey. Or was it Goethe? Or Yogi Berra? That change is an internal process. A function of the voluntary system. Subject to our control and manipulations. And once that commitment is made, well, then the hope would be that the universe does indeed conspire to assist you. Or, in the very least, New York's tristate area.

So Shulman dug in. And made the conscious decision to work with the God he'd been at odds with his whole life. Different than the deal Abraham had with his Almighty. No, Abraham did little in that relationship except believe. And brought virtually nothing to the table other than devotion without question. (Once again, what was going on with Isaac? By all accounts, the boy simply allowed himself to be tied to a stake so his father could kill him. Didn't he ever ask, "Dad, why are you doing this?" And even if his father answered, "Because God told me to," wouldn't Isaac, if he had half a brain, have said, "Give me a fucking break," resist his father's maniacal actions, and fight for his life? And after God stopped Abraham and told him to spare his son? How awkward was *that* ride home?)

In addition, Shulman's new deal with God also differed from the pact he had tried to strike so many years ago when his daughter Erin was so sick. That one was more of a proposal regarding the division of labor—of the "I'll take care of this, and you'll take care of that" category. This time around, however, there would be none of that. No implied deals, no expectations, no setting himself up for disappointments brought about by the nondelivery of others. Shulman would be responsible for all aspects of himself. Those priorities most dear to him. In effect, commit to being the Shulman *he* wanted to be. Embrace a revised identity with a particular emphasis placed on adaptability to a world forever in flux. And if survival accompanied by a calmer resting state resulted, it would be ideal. And if, at that point, God saw fit to have his universe conspire to assist him, even better.

So the week before the marathon was a hectic one for Shulman. According to the literature, he was finished with the hard part of the training. The body, if anything, needed rest to prepare. A couple of light runs to keep the blood flowing and the muscles loose. A stockpiling of carbs in the form of pastas and salads. And plenty of rest. This one was harder to accommodate due to the activity elsewhere. The attention being paid to the nonrunning portion of his life with the fervent hope that once this race was over, that is, once *he* finished, Shulman would be adequately prepared for whatever the rest of the universe had in mind.

———

At the store. Arranging furniture with Austin.

"Let's put it over here," said Shulman.

He was referring to the couch. The one from his basement that was originally in his parents' basement. The one he almost lost his virginity on. That night, sophomore year, with Nancy Graber. Who'd been lying upon that very couch. And when the severely inexperienced Shulman displayed his remarkable unfamiliarity with the female anatomy as an attempt at entry fell short of its intended mark and he placed "himself" between two cushions and was unaware of his error until after his mission was completed and an astonished Nancy Graber informed him that the *Eagle* had not, indeed, landed. So, technically speaking, it was the couch that Shulman had lost his virginity to.

"I'm getting this couch reupholstered," Shulman said, as if Austin knew its sordid history and needed assurance that it was free of any incriminating DNA.

"And what about these pictures? Want me to hang them?"

"Sure."

Black-and-white photos of Manhattan. New York sports heroes. And some vintage magazine covers. Shulman had bought them a few years back at a yard sale on a car trip he and Paula had taken to New England. They never made it onto a wall, though. Or even into frames. For a short while they sat on different coffee and end tables in scattered groups of threes and fours, serving as nostalgic conversation pieces, before relocating to a dusty pile in a corner of the attic.

"Who's the old dude?" asked Austin about a man pictured on a *Life* magazine. "Your grandfather?"

"It's Franklin D. Roosevelt," Shulman told him.

No hint of recognition.

"He was a president of the United States," Shulman elaborated.

No hint of brain activity.

"Of America," Shulman threw in for good measure.

Austin had turned into a statue of a dumbfounded human being.

"On second thought, *I'll* hang the pictures," Shulman said.

They provided an interesting spectacle. A near-broke, stationery-store owner and his trusty young assistant who had never heard of FDR pulling things from a rented van that one usually associated with fraternity houses or Salvation Army donations. Couches, comfortable chairs, coffeemakers, coffee mugs, a desk, lamps, an aquarium, two computers that his kids had left behind, a multi-colored throw rug, a television, and a handful of books that were considered classics despite the fact that they'd been sitting in a box next to his lawn mower for the past ten years.

They spent the next number of hours trying to make the place feel homey. It was Saturday. The next day was the New York City Marathon.

"What do you think?" asked Shulman.

"About what?" Austin asked back.

"This lounge. Does it feel like a place you'd want to come and hang out in?"

"I'm not sure if I'm the best person to ask," said Austin. "I mean, I hung out here before you made this lounge. So it's hard for me to tell the difference. But if you're asking if this lounge would make me want to quit so I wouldn't have to see it anymore, then no. I like my job. So I'm going to hang out here no matter what. Understand what I mean?"

A dilemma for Shulman. If he told Austin that he didn't understand, he ran the risk of Austin feeling the need to reexplain, although Shulman would've preferred sitting bare-assed on a cheese grater to hearing this drivel again. Yet, by saying that he did understand he could very well be endorsing a kind of syntax that did no one in any English-speaking country even an ounce of good. Shulman opted for hoping that the phone would ring. Miraculously, it did. It was Paula. She said he'd gotten a call at the house. Someone named Maria. Reminding him that today was the last day he could pick up his marathon packet.

In the city. At the Jacob Javits Center. Although there were literally thousands of marathoners in the huge convention hall, Shulman was afraid that he'd run into Maria. He'd returned her call, was relieved when he got her machine, and headed straight to Manhattan. They hadn't spoken since Coach Jeffrey's funeral. He wasn't avoiding her. He just needed time to himself. To think about Paula. His ultimate commitment. Back when two very young people had vowed "till death do us part." When two very young, very optimistic people had said they wanted to spend the rest of their time together. And now? Forget about what we were. Deal with what we've become, he kept reminding himself as he slowly worked his way to the front of the line, where it was now his turn to claim his race materials: an official marathon shirt, the microchip that would help record his individual running time, a pack of Aleve to combat the muscle aches that could occur during the event, a map showing the route through the five boroughs, numerous coupons for discount race-related products like canned pineapple chunks and sunscreen, as well as his runner ID number. On a bib that he was supposed to attach to his shirt with four safety pins that was also in the packet. The number was an estimation made by the race's organizers as to where an entrant would finish. Based on a runner's age, weight, body type, and previous running experience.

Most likely determined by computer. Still, despite the comparative good shape Shulman was in thanks to six months dedicated to a strict diet and a regimen of long-distance training, the computer was less than impressed. There were more than 32,000 entrants. Shulman was given the number 32,148. He would line up at the back of the pack. A perfect place for anyone desirous of having an excellent view of 32,147 people's asses.

"Will you be there tomorrow?" Shulman asked.

That night. In their bedroom. He was placing his clothes on the chair near his side of the bed. Layers. He would be leaving their house at 5 A.M. on a November morning. The temperature was sure to rise a great deal between then and the start of the race at ten-fifty. Hence, the many layers of clothing he'd be shedding on Staten Island while waiting for the race to begin.

"It would be fun seeing you along the way," he added. "Especially if you were wearing something really sexy like that black hat and veil you said you're going to wear to my funeral."

"I'm not sure what my schedule is yet," said Paula.

Her tone was casual. Noncommittal, but not so distant as to declare it an impossibility.

"I have a breakfast meeting in the morning," she added. "So maybe when we're finished, I'll try to figure out where you are and come watch you."

"A breakfast meeting on Sunday morning?" Shulman asked.

"With Steven Snipper. He's going out of town tomorrow and wants to talk to me before he leaves. I'm meeting him in the city."

"Really?"

"Yes. He didn't say what it was but he was very adamant about getting together."

"Sure."

— — —

Shulman didn't sleep well. The thought of what he would be doing in a few hours compromised all attempts to get some rest. On the face of it, there was really nothing to be nervous about. He had trained. There was an achievable approach to the undertaking if he just stuck to the (three minutes running/one minute walking) equation that had allowed him to complete every long distance they ran during their Sunday practice runs. And even if he fell below that pace? If he dropped to a slower speed or if he adjusted the run/walk ratio? If he ran for one minute and walked for three? Or even if he ended up walking the entire way? Like Coach Jeffrey said, "This may be a race but it's not a competition." And what was the worst that could happen? That for some reason, injury, fatigue, or being flattened under the wheels of the police cars reopening the streets for vehicular traffic, he didn't finish? Yes, that would be the absolute worst and he just couldn't let that happen. Shulman was now hell-bent on completing this marathon, this commitment. Nothing was ever more important— because to give up on it would be to give up on the surge of power a man feels when he is proud of himself.

This is what Shulman obsessed about. All night. So he was already awake when the alarm clock sounded at 4:45. He showered. And shaved. Curious things to do given the activity he was about to engage in. Comparable to shining your shoes prior to skipping through a cow pasture. Nerves. Habit. He dressed. Slowly. Deliberately. Like a soldier preparing for battle or a teenage girl on the night of the prom. He started with his feet. Two pairs of white socks. One thin, one thicker. The thought was to have one of each on each foot but after he accidentally dropped all four onto the floor, the chances that he would wind up with a pair of thin socks on one foot and a pair of thick ones on the other soared dramatically. He then worked his way upward to underwear. Jockey shorts for support—coupled with a generous application of a lubricant called Super Glide to minimize the possibility of chafing on his inner thighs. He also applied it to his nipples before turning his attention to the gold-colored T-shirt bearing the name of AIDS Project New Jersey that was issued to him and all the marathoners who would be running today. Shulman slipped it over his head, then spent the next ten minutes in front of the bathroom mirror attempting to pin the bib with his ID number, 32,148, onto the shirt in such a way that its angle wouldn't look as if a delirious drug addict had done it for him. Then, his New York Mets cap, which he put on with its insignia facing front, followed by his running shoes, the laces of which he tightened and double-knotted to reduce the possibility of dealing with well-meaning onlookers yelling, "Hey, your shoelaces are untied!" for 26.2 miles. And then, finally, his shorts. The ones from the University of Michigan that had GO BLUE written on the back of them.

This is what he was going to wear today. This was going to be his uniform. He looked at himself in the mirror. From every angle. So, technically speaking, he looked at himself four times in that mirror. He then turned forward one more time for one last look so, technically speaking, he looked at himself five times in that mirror before covering everything he was wearing with a sweatshirt, sweatpants, a stocking cap, and gloves because right now it was thirty-nine degrees outside. He then grabbed Austin's iPod before approaching Paula's side of the bed.

"Bye," he whispered to his sleeping wife. Paula opened an eye and didn't say anything while allowing it to focus.

"Good luck," she said.

"Thanks."

He stood there looking at her for a few beats. Even after her eye closed again.

Shulman had never taken a bus at this hour. A local New Jersey Transit Authority bus that he boarded on his side of the George Washington Bridge and rode across the river to Manhattan. He and the burly bus driver. The world was dark right now and they were the only two people awake and moving. They didn't speak. Just the hum of the engines scoring the quiet between them. *Now* he felt like sleeping. As the bus came off the bridge and swerved onto the West Side Highway, its rocking motion invited Shulman to drift off but he resisted the urge. Maybe if he were farther back he would've felt more comfortable doing so; but sitting in the first row across the aisle from the burly bus driver, who was doing his best either at the end of his long night or at the beginning of his long day to get Shulman safely to his destination, it would have been a breach. Of what, he wasn't exactly sure. But since the two of them were the only people in the world who were awake at this very moment, Shulman didn't think it would be right to bail on the guy. So Shulman just sat there keeping up his end of the silence and thinking about nothing in particular as the bus eventually left the highway and eddied its way inland and onto ramps that ended at the Port Authority building. Where the burly driver guided it into one of the parking stalls. The doors opened; Shulman stood, gathered his things, and started to exit.

"Bye," he said to the burly driver.

"Good luck."

"Thanks."

Shulman wasn't even out of the bus when it dawned on him that he had just had the same, exact conversation with this bus driver that he'd had with his wife.

Shulman entered the Port Authority Bus Terminal and somehow, when he exited its other side on Eighth Avenue, it was morning. Manhattan's sky was light and the street was filled with runners who, for the time being, were walking. In packs of three and four, drinking coffee from mugs and talking. Some in recognizable languages, others he'd never heard before. Colors. Some connoting nationality, others fashion choices. It was a three-block crosstown walk to the New York Public Library, where Shulman would be boarding his second bus of the day. This one would take him and everyone else to the starting line in Staten Island. New York City's "other" borough. The one that Brooklyn, Queens, Manhattan, and Bronx schoolchildren, if they were to forget the name of one of the boroughs on a pop quiz, would draw a blank on. Similarly, if Shulman himself had ever been there before, that sphere of his brain assigned to remembering the occasion hadn't seen fit to file it properly as he had no recollection of it at all. Still, during the course of the next few hours, Staten Island's population was going to increase by more than 32,000 people, including the mayor of New York and Maria.

"Shulman!"

She was waving her hand from the front of one of the seemingly endless lines waiting to board the chartered buses. Their plan had been to meet here, in the city, where she'd spent the night at a friend's. And whoever got to the bus line first would save a place for the other—a plan not exactly met with hardy approval by the hundreds of runners who'd been braving the cold for two hours when Maria let him cut ahead of her.

"Hey!"

"Are you kidding, mister!"

"Come on, give the guy a break. He's old!"

Shulman turned to Maria and said, "I'm not the oldest one here, am I?"

"No. Not *the* oldest," Maria said, laughing. Shulman couldn't help but notice that she looked great. And that her teeth were alarmingly white again.

They sat next to each other on the bus. Fourth row. Shulman on the aisle, Maria next to the window. When the bus pulled away from the curb and started downtown along Fifth Avenue, Shulman was aware that their legs were touching. And though he tried to write it off as an innocuous occurrence between commuters who share seats in virtually all modes of public transportation, he still wondered whether she was aware of this innocuous occurrence. *Focus, Shulman.* He looked over at her. *Don't look over at her. You're supposed to be focusing.* She was in profile. *Great profile.* Long brown hair. Small, inconsequential nose. The cute kind of nose that was probably excellent for purposes of breathing, though not any bigger than it absolutely had to be. The kind of small nose that when viewed in profile, a person could still see what's beyond it. Across the street. Through the window of a terrace restaurant. A couple having breakfast. The woman was also in profile. Also beautiful. Laughing. Obviously charmed by the man across the table from her.

Paula? Could that possibly be? She did say that she was going to have breakfast this morning. In the city. *With Steven Snipper.* Also in profile. Until he turned outward and, as if looking straight ahead at the passing bus, revealed himself to be the Other Shulman.

"Stop this bus!"

Shulman leapt to his feet, ran down the aisle, toward the back of the bus, and saw the Other Shulman smirking in his direction through each window when it was its turn to pass the restaurant.

"Stop this bus!"

Aggressive mimicry at its lurid best. Say your name is Snipper. Change your appearance to blend in. Lure your prey with behavior that's enticing. Make her feel comfortable. And safe. Then overtake her for your own advantage.

Shulman ran toward the front of the bus and yelled to the driver, "Stop the bus!"

"Can't," he responded.

"Why not?"

"Rules."

"Come on!" Shulman pleaded. "It's an emergency!"

But this bus driver, either unaware or unimpressed by the bond Shulman had forged with the man's burly colleague earlier this morning, held firm.

"Sorry."

And the passengers, no great fans of Shulman's—dating all the way back to when they were boarding—were more than happy to enter the fray.

"Sit down!"

"What's the matter?"

"Forget your walker, old man?"

The bus rounded a corner and continued to put more city blocks between Shulman and his wife. It was on its way to Staten Island for the start of the New York City Marathon, which Shulman had trained to run in and vowed to finish.

And that's what he kept focusing on. For the rest of this bus trip. As everyone was lining up to start the race at the Verrazano Bridge. When he was peeling off all those extra layers of clothing as if stripping down in preparation for a new beginning. And right now, as he was entering Central Park, he was just a very short distance from achieving his goal.

Mile 26.2

And Then Some . . .

Shulman was angry with Queen Alexandra. Not that it did him any good to feel this way but, truth be known, right now he had nothing but contempt for the woman who ruled England at the turn of the previous century. The reason was due to what had happened when London hosted the Olympic Games in 1908.

When the twenty-six-mile course was first measured, it began in front of Windsor Castle so that Queen Alexandra's and King Edward's grandsons had a good view of the start. As a result, the finish line ended up across the field from where the couple would be sitting in Olympic Stadium. But when Alexandra arrived at the stadium and saw this, the old broad insisted that the finish line be in front of the royal box, as it was with all other races. Hence, the official length of the race was extended to 26.2 miles for that, and all future, marathons. So, according to the way Shulman saw it, if that fucking queen had kept her big mouth shut (or had sprung for a pair of binoculars) his race would already be over. Instead, the finish line was still a fifth of a mile away. At that world-renowned restaurant called Tavern on the Green—originally built in 1870 as a sheepfold that housed the very animals which grazed across the street in Central Park's Sheep Meadow.

So he reentered the park, past the statue at Columbus Circle, and continued to run alone in the dark. Nighttime. No one else around. No runners. No spectators. Still, pleased with what he was about to accomplish.

"Hey, Shulman!"

Where he came from was a mystery. But there he was. Dressed like Shulman with the identical #32,148 on his bib and the words GO BLUE on his shorts. A few strides away but quickly closing the distance between them. And why was he there? Well, it was a safe bet it wasn't to cheer Shulman on.

"Hey, Shulman! Wait up! We have a lot to talk about!"

It was just the two of them. Shulman and the Other Shulman. Alone on a roadway in Central Park. Where the voice in Shulman's head was now Coach Jeffrey's.

In a marathon, finishing is winning.

So Shulman tried his best to stay within himself. To maintain focus on his breathing technique and on the ultimate goal—a red mat functioning as a finish line that might as well have been a thousand miles away right now.

"Hey, asshole!" the Other Shulman called out. "You've got a nice wife!"

In a marathon, other runners don't exist.

They didn't? Then what the hell did you call this guy? A guy who'd caught up and was now running alongside him.

"You hear me, Shulman! She deserves better than you!"

Shulman did hear him. He also noticed that the Other Shulman was starting to veer in his direction. Coming closer. And closer.

"And when this thing is over," he shouted, "that's exactly what she'll have!"

He then lowered his shoulder and rammed Shulman. Hard enough to startle him for a moment. But not squarely enough to prevent him from regaining his balance after a step or two.

"What the hell do you think you're doing?" Shulman yelled back. He knew the shove had been purposeful. As intentional as the one he'd given him that day on the running path.

"Hey, what do you know? He talks," said the Other Shulman. "The big zero actually talks."

His tone was more than taunting. It had a hint of challenge to it. One that dared Shulman to respond. The way a bully intimidates a weaker kid. Hoping he'll hit back so the bully can use it as an excuse to strike him again.

"But how about fighting for what's important to you? Huh? Or maybe it's not important enough?"

Shulman ignored the bait. Tried not to be goaded. Instead, he pulled away from the Other Shulman. Away from the center of the roadway, where he'd been running, as he was determined not to let anyone or anything distract him from his goal.

Finishing is *winning*.

"You know, she's loved you all along. My guess is she still does. She's just grown tired of waiting for you to get out of your own way. Paula wants you to take charge of yourself. To step up and be a man who doesn't hide from what he fears. Like me. You fear me, don't you, Shulman. Always have."

He said this as he was angling toward Shulman. Like a football player trying to push someone out of bounds to put a stop to a long run.

"What are you doing, hotshot? Trying to hide some more?"

Shulman tried to trick him by abruptly slowing down. Hoping that the Other Shulman's momentum would take him flying past him, so he could then circle behind him and continue with his own forward motion.

It didn't work. As if Shulman were a target locked in his crosshairs, the Other Shulman adjusted his own speed accordingly and hit him again. With his body. And again. With a closed fist.

"You can't trick me, Shulman! I know all your moves. At best they're predictable. That's what drives Paula nuts. She knows that change is uncomfortable but that life is about changing. But you never understood that."

Shulman, now running while attempting to rub the sting of the punch from his arm, looked up ahead. Tavern on the Green was still nowhere in sight. At the top of an incline and off to the left. So he literally couldn't make a run for it. He was exhausted. And breathing heavily. But even a short walk break was completely out of the question, as he'd just be a sitting duck for this lunatic.

"You really think that I'm going to let you beat me?" the Other Shulman shouted as he started to move in on him again. "After a lifetime of having my way with you?"

He drew closer. Drawing a bead on another shot.

And when you realize that finishing is winning, then you'll realize that you'll only be running against yourself . . .

"No way! When this is over, your *entire* life will be mine, Shulman!"

The Other Shulman clenched his fist and threw another punch. This one landed on the right side of Shulman's jaw, knocking his head sideways. This one hurt. A lot.

. . . Then it will be up to you, and only you, to do what it takes to win.

Shulman staggered for a few uncertain strides, regained his footing, looked over at the Other Shulman, and threw his fist into his face. It hurt Shulman's fist. A lot. But it felt great to hit back. So great that he did it again. And it hurt again. A lot.

The look on the Other Shulman's face could best be described as quizzical. One that conveyed *You're kidding?* as much as it did *Ouch!* A wry smile was soon added to this expression. Followed by a nod.

"This is going to be fun!" he shouted.

"Go for it, fuckhead!" Shulman shouted back.

Shulman was emboldened by the initiative he'd just displayed. An unfamiliar feeling of power enhanced by the combination of adrenaline and endorphins that was now offering him a ride he'd never taken before. Unbridled determination free from any temperance that results from forethought. There was no forethought. Only impulse. Hostility. Belligerence. Aggressive mimicry at its most illustrative. Behaving like the enemy in order to survive the enemy. Random thoughts strayed to that young boy watching *Ben-Hur* at the Avalon movie theater on Kings Highway. The chariot race. Where Judah finally overcame the demons embodied in the person of his nemesis Messalla (the Other Judah) by reluctantly employing the same tactics his tormentor had been using against him all along.

The Other Shulman struck a second time when he came toward Shulman and unleashed a flurry of punches that Shulman was somehow able to fend off. Once again frustrated by his inability to cause serious damage, the Other Shulman retreated back to the middle of the roadway.

"Where the hell did you learn how to fight?" the Other Shulman asked him.

Where the hell is Tavern on the Green? Shulman asked himself. Was it possible they'd moved the restaurant and the finish line along with it? A little joke that the faster runners played on the slower ones? That after they finished their marathon, they all squatted around the place, grabbed hold of it, and at the count of three lifted the building and deposited it a few blocks uptown? Probably not. *Probably* not? Boy, those endorphins were very, very special.

Up ahead some lights appeared and, just as quickly, disappeared behind the trees that lined the winding roadway. But they were there. Shulman saw them and he ran toward them. Forward motion. As opposed to the diagonal line along which the Other Shulman was approaching him for another go at it. Oddly enough, the prospect of this impending exchange invigorated Shulman, who actually welcomed what was about to happen. So he angled his body toward the Other Shulman and, palms upturned, beckoned him with both hands.

"Getting cocky, are we?" yelled the Other Shulman, who'd decided to change strategy and surprised Shulman by bending at the waist and coming in low. Body punches. The first of which landed and brought with it a sharp pain before Shulman made his own adjustment and hid behind an impromptu wall of raised forearms that downgraded the ensuing blows to glancing ones. Not unlike Muhammad Ali's patented "rope-a-dope" but without the rope.

Once again, the Other Shulman veered back toward the middle of the roadway but held his newest sneer as he watched Shulman grimace from the lone blow that had hit its mark. And watched Shulman's bewilderment when he looked at his hand after massaging his side and saw the blood. And watched the slow realization creep across Shulman's face when he looked over and noticed the blade the Other Shulman was holding in his hand.

An X-Acto knife. Shulman sold them at his store. Fourth row, top shelf. An excellent tool for lightweight precision cutting. Thick paper. Posterboards. And flesh. Which is why Shulman kept it on the top shelf; to make it harder for a young child to grab one while his mother's attention was elsewhere.

Shulman's flesh was now cut. His left love handle. The wound wasn't that deep. And even if it were that deep, it still wouldn't have been *that* deep given the surplus of flesh he had there. Nevertheless, the fact remained that the Other Shulman had a weapon and was poised to use it again.

"Did you think I wasn't serious, Shulman?"

It was a race toward those lights up ahead. The New York City Marathon now boiled down to a hundred-yard sprint as Shulman knew that if he could just get to those lights and whoever was near them before the Other Shulman got to him, all would be well. The pain in his side became a nagging footnote—trumped by the more pressing priority of avoiding further impalement. A straight line toward those lights. No serpentine attempts to trick or elude. No, he was banking on that geometric definition of the shortest distance between two points and prayed it was indeed true. Stride after stride. Each one stretched longer than its predecessor with every hope that the ground gained by its length would compensate for what it lacked in speed. Fighting for focus. Straining to get to those lights. Then hearing footsteps that weren't his and turning just as the Other Shulman's raised hand was coming toward him.

Instinct took charge as Shulman reached up, grabbed the wrist wielding the X-Acto knife, and yanked it in the direction he was running. Physics took over from there as the Other Shulman's momentum caused his body to pitch forward, lose its balance, and fall to the pavement. However, Shulman neglected to let go of the Other Shulman's wrist so he too fell to the pavement, where they both rolled over and over again before coming to a stop on the side of the roadway. The Other Shulman on his back. Shulman on top of him. And it was now that momentum gave way to rage as Shulman sat up, kept hold of the Other Shulman's wrist with one hand, and started punching him in his face with the other . . .

"And did you think that *I* wasn't serious, you sick son of a bitch!"

Again . . .

"Now you stay away from my wife!"

And again . . .

"From me!"

This was becoming fun. . . .

"And my store!"

And it was during this pummeling that he finally felt it. Paula had been right all along. Victims are self-made. Created by their private quests to feel comfortable and safe. No more! Never! Too bad it had to come to this. Years ago, when he and Paula were capable of spending comfortable and safe time with each other, they were in a furniture store. Standing on a multicolored rug with high piles. She looked down and noticed an ant that was making its way along the bottom of the rug.

"Interesting," she said as they watched the ant walking through one color after another. "That ant probably thinks he's been in four different rugs. But we know that he's only been in four different versions of the same rug."

Was she only talking about the ant or about him? About them? Paula was always smarter than him. More observant. Attendant to the realities Shulman had always chosen to either downplay or ignore completely. But that was then and, well, these punches were his ticket to a new rug. The first positive step since the shedding of all those layers that took place before this marathon started on Staten Island. With each succeeding punch he could feel himself regaining the strength that he'd granted to others, in particular, this guy, for so long. So much so that right now the only question he had was whether or not he should kill the Other Shulman. It would be so easy. He'd already wrested the X-Acto knife when the Other Shulman's limp hand became still another indication of the semiconscious state the rest of his body had fallen into. It was justifiable homicide. Who attacked whom? Who had been tormenting who all along? Yes. Shulman was merely defending himself from a demented assailant. And the poetry of committing such an act seemed to be so perfect. That a man, to fully expunge the evil that's been tormenting him, has to obliterate the vessel that contains it. Shulman's shrink, had he ever been able to afford one, would've had a field day with that scenario.

Once again, it was instinct that assumed control as Shulman, consumed by the heat of the moment, picked up the X-Acto knife, raised it above the Other Shulman's head, and tossed it down a nearby sewer before struggling to his feet and resuming his race. Slowly at first. Breathing that was labored for want of oxygen. But continuing forward. Toward those lights. Diverting focus only once when he turned around and saw the Other Shulman, now standing, hunched over, with hands on knees. His slight head-turn followed. A look in Shulman's direction. And then vanishing. As if dissolved by the night that surrounded him. Gone. It was over. So now it was time for Shulman to turn and continue. Forward. Running faster. And faster. Propelled not by the death of the Other Shulman as much as by the realization that he himself was the Only Shulman and better make the best of it.

Ahead, the finish line. And a handful of New York City Marathon volunteers who were dismantling it. Taking down the bastion that held the race clock. Lifting up the red mat covering the computer chips that would record his time. Unplugging the very lights he'd been running toward.

"No! Wait!" he shouted.

"What the hell . . ." said one of the volunteers.

"I thought everyone was finished," said another.

But here came Shulman and they rushed to prepare for his arrival. The clock got turned back on. The red mat was rolled back into place. And a volunteer started rummaging through a box.

"Hey, do we have any medals left?" she shouted.

She found one. Just in time to place it around Shulman's neck as he crossed the finish line (eight hours, twenty-two minutes, and seventeen seconds after he'd started) to their applause and scattered shouts.

"Good going, mister!"

"Congratulations!"

"You finished!"

"You can stop running now."

"Hey, where are you going?"

Excellent question considering that Shulman was still running like a man who had no intentions of stopping. Or slowing down.

Out of the park he ran. Across Central Park West and along 77th Street, where a number of other slow marathoners were having the marathon-issued microchips removed from their shoelaces while still others were being surrounded by family and friends, who had come to greet them after their great accomplishment.

It didn't surprise Shulman that no one was waiting for him. Such plans were never discussed. Just as well. He wouldn't have had time to socialize. Now that his marathon was complete, he just wanted to keep running.

So he kept running. West on 77th Street. For three minutes. Then walked for one minute. Then ran for three minutes again. Et cetera. No rush. No one was expecting him. Just a stamina-conserving homage to his Coach Jeffrey. Once he crossed Columbus Avenue, he realized that the one-way street was open to vehicular traffic. All the streets were at this hour. The city was coming back to the rhythms of its everyday life. No problem. He just moved to the sidewalk, where he drew the attention of a few kids playing, of all games, stoop ball. Kids who became curious when they saw a marathoner, *after* the race was over, running, then stop running, walk, then start running again.

"What's *he* up to?" asked one kid.

"Let's go see," said another.

And they did. So Shulman had three kids running behind him for the next three minutes, who then walked behind him for the next minute.

"Why are we walking?" asked one kid.

"Why are we starting to run again?" asked another.

"Maybe this guy's a little crazy," said one kid.

"Let's keep following him and see where he goes," said another.

"Boy, I wish we had something better to do," said another.

They followed Shulman as he crossed Amsterdam, then Broadway, West End Avenue, and Riverside Drive, where a few older kids caught sight of Shulman with the younger kids running closely behind him.

"Hey, why are you guys chasing Glue?" asked one of the older kids.

"We're not chasing him," said one of the younger kids.

"We're running *with* him," explained another one of the younger kids.

"Why are you calling him Glue"? asked another one of the older kids.

"Look at his shorts," answered the first older kid. "It says 'Glue' on his ass."

It was true. The GO BLUE shorts had done it again.

"Hey, let's run with Glue," shouted another one of the older kids.

And they did. Past Riverside Park and then, coming as a surprise to them all, onto the West Side Highway. Heading north. Shulman was now running along a major New York City artery and could not have been more oblivious to the flow of cars and trucks beginning to gather behind him and the kids. Cars and trucks that had to slow down. For three minutes. Then go slower for one minute. Then go slightly faster so they could be going slow again for the next three minutes.

When Shulman was a kid, he and his friends would play a practical joke by standing on a street corner, looking up in the sky, and pointing. Not a very original thing to do—but always effective as, like clockwork, within moments a growing crowd would have assembled. Looking up so they could get a glimpse—pointing and even jockeying for better position to get a better look at absolutely nothing. Few people even bothering to inquire about what everyone was looking at. And those who did bother to ask were answered with either a curt "Shh!" or by a fellow observer who'd point skyward with every hope that he himself would see what he was spending his precious time looking at. Crowd mentality. The desire to be a part of something (or even nothing) for the sake of not feeling left out. So it was in this case. Right now. As Shulman ran with those kids, the people in the cars moving slowly behind them wanted to know what they were running toward, and those in the passenger seats got out so they too could see what was going on. And when they started running again (for three minutes, then walked for one, etc.), the people in the cars backed up behind *those* people saw that they were leaving their cars and started to do the same. And not before too long, motorists traveling in the southbound lane of the West Side Highway were wondering what the commotion was all about on the north-bound lane and how it was possible they had missed whatever it was that everyone was running toward, as they'd just come from that direction and didn't recall seeing anything run-worthy. So they too slowed down, lost a few curious riders who hopped the divider and started making their way uptown, and were soon joined by other erstwhile southbound folks.

A handful quickly became dozens and eventually became hun-dreds. All following Shulman. All chanting, "GLUE, GLUE . . . GLUE, GLUE, GLUE" for reasons known only to the origi-nal group of kids, who could read the back of Shulman's shorts. The rest, well, they were just thrilled to be at the party, which soon drew the attention of the Eyewitness News traffic helicopter that had been heading southbound above the Hudson River. That made a U-turn upon seeing the festival taking place on the north-bound lane. That trained its bright lights and its camera on the leader and his growing multitude of joggers and exceptionally slow-moving vehicles.

"And they're all going at the same pace as Glue," said the traf-fic reporter into his microphone.

"The same pace as who?" the newscaster back at the studio could be heard asking through the traffic reporter's microphone.

"*G-l-u-e,*" spelled the traffic reporter. "We're going to try to move in to get a closer shot of the man's rear end but that's what all the people who are following him seem to be shouting."

And when the camera did zoom in for a closer look, the name/word GLUE was on television and could be seen by anyone who happened to be watching WABC-TV at that particular mo-ment, which included twelve-year-old soccer player Lindsay Gilbert and her parents.

"That's him!" she shouted, pointing to the man on their TV. "*That's* Glue!"

"No, it isn't," said her father.

"That's not the man whose picture was in the *Fort Lee Record*," her mother insisted.

"Well, I don't care whose picture was in that rag sheet. This is the man who raised all that money for charity that we jumped on in the mud that day."

Lindsay's dad leaned forward to take a closer look.

"Hey, that's the guy who came looking for you at soccer practice," he said.

"Glue came looking for me?" Lindsay asked with excitement. "When?"

"About a week ago."

"And you didn't tell me!"

"Lindsay, he was pointing to his butt."

"He has a right to point to anything he wants. The man's a legend!"

And after she ran to her room and slammed the door behind her, Lindsay's dad picked up the telephone, and dialed the number of the Fort Lee Police Department.

Paula, on the other hand, had no idea which Shulman she was watching. As she leaned in to get a closer look at the man running across her television screen, she had trouble recognizing him as the man she'd married because he looked so much like the man she wanted him to be. Confident. Assertive. In charge. The Shulman she always knew was within her husband but with whom she'd grown frustrated because she couldn't help him find those qualities within himself. Who was this man?

By the time Shulman reached the approach to the George Washington Bridge and the television coverage was now being carried by no fewer than four local stations, the only remaining question was whether he would take the bridge's upper or lower roadway. Historically referred to as "Martha," because she lay prone under "George," the lower level was probably the easier one to run along as it had a flatter gradient than the one above it. However, the pilots of the circling helicopters were happy when Shulman elected to traverse the Hudson via the upper roadway, as it provided the television cameras with a less obstructed shot of the parade that Glue was the grand marshal of. So now the synergy between media and the event was in full force, as the televising of this spectacle not only made more people aware that it was taking place, but also attracted more participants, which served to make it even more deserving of the coverage they were giving it. As a result, the throng behind Shulman continued to grow when people from Washington Heights left their apartments and joined the bridge-jogging retinue, as did a number of eastbound passengers, who left their cars to join Glue, who was now running westbound. Toward New Jersey. Fort Lee, New Jersey, to be exact.

"We've just gotten word that the person at the head of this immense pack is a gentleman who ran this marathon to raise money for AIDS research," said one local newscaster.

"A wonderful, wonderful cause," said a newscaster from another station.

"He sounds like a wonderful man," said a third newscaster.

"We understand he owns a stationery store," said still another.

Halfway across the bridge, at the exact point where New York meets New Jersey, the police were waiting. Three cars with flashing lights that said FORT LEE POLICE on their sides. And although the three cars were abreast, Shulman just assumed that the one in the middle was the lead car when its door opened and Sergeant Leonard January stepped out.

"Hey, Shulman!" he shouted.

"Are you here to arrest me, Sergeant?" asked Shulman, who, for the first time in recent memory, was actually running *toward* the cops.

"No. I'm here to say I'm sorry."

"Really?" asked Shulman.

"I still think you're weird, but follow us," said Sergeant Leonard January, who got back into his car and led the way. Three minutes. Then one minute. Then three minutes again. Three police pace cars escorting their very own Phidippides, who was returning after his long and arduous journey—hopefully without the collapsing-and-dropping-dead part.

When Shulman came off the bridge and stepped into the town of Fort Lee, the residents of the surrounding high-rise apartment buildings rushed to catch a firsthand glimpse of what they'd been watching on television. They too wanted to be a part of the celebration. There were those who took an elevator down to the street to join in the festivities. And those who opted to stay put did so at opened windows, out of which they added their voices to the chorus of "GLUE, GLUE . . . GLUE, GLUE, GLUE" that now filled their streets. Like a mighty wave that carried the throng into the heart of their humble village. Flat-surfaced roads. That led to a hill. Not a real steep one, yet with enough of an upward angle that an adjustment had to be made. Which Shulman did by sitting back and pretending he was in an easy chair just as Coach Jeffrey had instructed him. *Hills are your friends, Shulman.* And by taking shorter steps to maintain an even cadence. *Shulman, promise me you'll learn to love the hills.* And then everyone behind Shulman, who now numbered in the hundreds, leaned back and followed their leader. And they too embraced the hill. Which took them into the Rolling Fields strip mall. Past the Tower Records. And the pet salon, where pets had their hair and nails done. Past the women's salon, where women had their hair and nails done.

Past the big Blockbuster that used to be a much smaller Blockbuster, the ATM that used to be a bank, the Borders that was once
a clothing store, the Gap that was once a bookstore, the supermarket that used to be a grocery, the 1 Hr. Photo that used to be
a bakery. And up to the stationery store that was always a stationery store. The only place whose lights were still on despite the
late hour. Where Shulman stopped. And everyone behind him
stopped. And where Paula was waiting for him.

"I was hoping that you were you," she told him.

He smiled at her. And they hugged. The way they used to.

The front door to Shulman's opened and Austin peered out.

"Is it okay if I go home now, Mr. Shulman? A person can be
surrounded by pictures of dead presidents for only so long before
he feels like joining them on that wall."

"What a great place!" someone shouted, looking inside.

"A stationery store that has furniture and serves food!" exclaimed someone else.

"From what I can gather, Shulman's is a throwback," said one
local newscaster.

"A modern-day, all-purpose store with a homespun touch,"
said a newscaster from another station.

"The kind of place anyone would be happy to shop at," said a
third newscaster.

"I know I would," said still another.

And as the crowd, still growing, milled outside, Shulman
turned to Austin.

"Could you work a few extra hours tonight?"

"Well . . ."

"What if I gave you a raise and promised to return your iPod?"

"Sure," he answered.

"Good. Now do me a favor and put up a few hundred cups of
coffee. It looks like we may be here for a while."

Acknowledgments

To offset the solitude, writers tend to fill their lives with people they can turn to for support or suggestions, or to selfishly intrude upon when they really don't want to write that day. I want to thank the following people for falling into any or, in some unfortunate cases, all of these categories: Bruce Tracy, Suzanne Gluck, Peter Gethers, Carol Shafer, Bernie Brillstein, Greg Lipstone, Herb Sargent, Peter Hyams, Billy Crystal, Larry David, Megan Underwood, Amy Palmer, John Robertson, and the folks at AIDS Project Los Angeles, to whom a portion of this book's proceeds will be donated.

And my parents, who encouraged me; my wife, Robin, who inspires me; and our children, Adam, Lindsay, and Sari, who always make me laugh.

PHOTO: © ROBIN ZWEIBEL

An original *Saturday Night Live* writer, ALAN ZWEIBEL has won numerous Emmy and Writers Guild awards for his work in television, which also includes *It's Garry Shandling's Show* (which he co-created and produced), PBS's *Great Performances*, and *Curb Your Enthusiasm*. His many critically acclaimed theater credits include *Bunny Bunny: Gilda Radner—A Sort of Romantic Comedy,* which he adapted from his own book, as well as collaborating with Billy Crystal on his one-man Broadway show, *700 Sundays*. He recently published a children's book titled *Our Tree Named Steve,* and his fiction has appeared in such diverse publications as *Esquire, The Atlantic Monthly,* and *Mad* magazine.

Alan and his wife, Robin, live in Los Angeles and New Jersey and have three children, Adam, Lindsay, and Sari.